THE DETECTIVE'S
DAUGHTER

Also By Darcy Flynn

THE DETECTIVE'S DAUGHTER

SECRETS OF GRIFFIN GATE

DARCY FLYNN

ACKNOWLEDGMENTS

Years ago, when I was program director of Music City Romance Writers, I wrote a first page for the panel of editors and agents to review at one of our weekend retreats. Up until that time, I'd only written sweet romance novels, so I thought this would be a good chance to try my hand at romantic suspense. To my surprise, it was well received. Since that time, my critique partner has encouraged me to write the novel inspired by that first page.

Eight months ago, I began writing, *The Detectives Daughter, Secrets of Griffin Gate*. Thank you, Cindy Brannam, for encouraging me over the years to write this book.

Thank you Joy Allyson for your thoughtful critique. Your notes were well thought out and extremely helpful.

To my editor, Jeanne Hardt, thank you for your detailed and thorough edits of my manuscript, and for brainstorming possible options to include in this story. Thank you for loving my stories and for being an encouragement over the years.

And many thanks to my formatter, Jesse Gordon, and my cover designer, Karen Duvall.

And to all of my wonderful readers, thank you for sharing this adventure with me. You are the reason I do this.

Much love,

Darcy

DEDICATION

For Rhonda
Fifty-seven years of friendship is no small thing
In loving memory

CHAPTER 1

This wasn't the first time Lucy watched the video, longing for just one buried memory of her father. She sat in the over-stuffed, red-leather club chair and watched the handsome young man toss her high into the air; her four-year-old giggles making him throw back his head in laughter. He hugged her to his chest, placed a kiss on her head of short, dark curls, then turned and faced the camera.

Had he lived, he'd have been forty-four now. She tried to imagine how he would look today if he was still alive. Maybe he'd have a slight graying at his temples, giving him a distinguished appearance. Tall and broad-shouldered, with a smile that could still break a lady's heart. And eyes that held a deep twinkle in their depths—engaging and filled with humor.

She ran her hands up the length of her arms and wished she could relive what she'd surely felt twenty years ago. What would it have been like to be loved by such a man?

At that moment, her beautiful, young mother turned the camera on herself and made a silly face in the lens, then laughed and leveled the focus back on Lucy and her dad.

He lifted her small hand and coaxed a wave.

His smile suddenly faded as he glanced beyond her mother. He raised his hand, signaling her to stop, but instead, she turned with the camera toward what had caught his attention.

A black sedan pulled onto the gravel driveway. Just as the door opened, the camera lowered, skimming a pair of men's shoes. It recorded three seconds of grass at her mother's feet before going black.

Lucy had watched the video many times. As if another second—another clue to the owner of those shoes—would suddenly jump from the screen. But it was always the same —stopping before the truth could be told.

A familiar raw ache filled her heart; the acute loss almost overwhelming in that instant.

Frustrated, she hit rewind, then play, and watched the last few seconds again. Noting, for the hundredth time, the transformation on her father's face from joy to anger.

She lifted a finger to the scar embedded at her hairline. This recording captured the last time she'd seen her father, and she had no memory of it.

Lucy pushed through the entrance of Oak Haven Home and made her way to her mother's suite. She was met with her mom's warm smile as she entered the small living room.

"Hello, darling," her mom said.

Lucy kissed her mom on the cheek, then sat down on the floral, Queen Anne chair across from her. Lucy never liked the fact that her young mother—only in her mid-forties— had to be in a place like Oak Haven. Yet, the brain injury she'd incurred three years earlier put her there.

"I have good news," Lucy said. "Griffin Gate is on the market, and I've made an offer for it."

"For what?"

"I just told you, darling... For Griffin Gate, our family home."

"Oh, yes, that's right. You didn't haggle, did you?"

"No. Aunt Laura and I met his asking price with one contingency."

"Wonderful." Her mom beamed a smile.

"It won't be long before we're back in Diamond Creek," Lucy said.

"So how are your classes this semester?"

Lucy paused and took in her mother's expectant face. "I graduated last month in May, remember? I now have a Masters in Education."

Her mom cast a blank expression, then she smiled. "That's right." She shook her head. "Sometimes I wonder where my brain is. I forget things."

"That's okay. I forget things, too." Lucy pulled a floral notebook and a pen from her purse. "Mom, when you remember something, I want you to write it down in this notebook." She handed it to her. "Will you do that for me?"

Her mom took the blank book, opened it, then glanced at Lucy. "Sure, honey, I'll do that."

"Good. Keeping a record of what you remember may help you to recall more. And it'll be right here for you as you do that."

"Spurring on more memories," her mom said.

"Exactly." Lucy hadn't yet told her about finding the videotape and wondered if she should keep that to herself, at least for the moment. Before her mom's accident, she'd told Lucy very little about the day her father was killed, only that he had been shot and the bullet had grazed Lucy's head before hitting *her James.* Hopefully, Lucy would get more clues from what her mother remembered.

At the moment, her mom seemed happy and relaxed. *This might be a good time to question her.*

"Mom, what do you remember about the day Dad and I were shot?" Lucy held her breath. She never knew what would bring on the agitation and confusion, a hallmark of memory loss. Dr. Edwards had told Lucy to choose her words carefully when broaching the past.

Her mom stared across the room into the distance, and Lucy could see that her mind had gone someplace else.

"The black car— We couldn't see who it was."

"Why?"

"He was wearing a scary mask."

Scary?

Her mom gripped her hands tightly together, then looked directly at Lucy. "The bullet hit you first and I screamed, and you and James fell to the ground." Her eyes glazed over, and she began to shake. "So much blood."

Lucy jumped up and sat beside her, then gently turned her mom's face toward her. "It's all right. I'm here. You're safe, and I'm safe." This revelation had been the most detailed Lucy had ever heard about that day.

Lucy kept talking soothingly until the haunted look faded from her mother's eyes. In minutes, her shakes subsided, and she was breathing normally. Lucy had already known about the car from the video but not the fact that the man wore a mask—a scary one at that. Most likely, that detail was in the police report.

Lucy cleared her throat, hoping to lead her mom in another direction. "About the move. I thought I'd go on ahead and get settled and make any repairs to the house before you join me." She squeezed her mom's hand. "How does that sound?"

"Lovely, dear. You go and get everything ready."

Lucy glanced at her watch. "It's almost time for dinner. Shall I join you?"

"Yes. I'd love that. Today is meatloaf Monday, and I know how much you like meatloaf."

Actually, today was fish-fry Friday. Lucy slipped her arm through her mother's and walked with her toward the cafeteria. She just hoped her mom wouldn't notice her mistake.

CHAPTER 2

Saturday afternoon, Lucy and her aunt heard back from the real estate agent. The seller had accepted the offer contingent on Lucy seeing the property in person. The agent emailed the final document to Lucy's aunt, the trustee of the Carmichael Trust.

Secure in the fact the property would now be hers, Lucy stretched out on the sofa, opened the viewing screen on the small, hand-held video camera, and pressed play. Lately, she'd stopped the tape before it got to the very end. She didn't like seeing her father, jaw clenched and angry.

Had her dad not been all that he'd seemed? Or had an enemy arrived? At times, it worried her and frankly, led to more questions than answers. And the one person who could shed more light on all of this had long since faded from reality.

This time, when it got to the end, Lucy stopped the tape, closed her eyes, and played out in her mind what her mom had told her of the last moments of Detective James Ross.

She opened her eyes and could only imagine how distraught her mother must have been in that moment. Would she ever learn more than she had today? The latter being one of the main reasons for moving back to Diamond Creek, Arkansas. It was time for Lucy to do her own investigation into her father's murder—to get to the end of the mystery surrounding his death once and for all.

The next four days were filled with sorting and organizing her things, farewell lunches with friends, and shopping for any last-minute items. On Thursday, her Subaru jampacked, Lucy said goodbye to her mom and left Little Rock.

The drive to Diamond Creek took little over an hour. The first glimpse of the property came soon after she turned onto Maple Road. Even though the yard itself left a lot to be desired—with its spotty patches of grass and dirt—she remembered well how the house always drew attention. As the wheels crunched up the gravel driveway, the pink, Victorian home loomed up from the ground with whimsical elegance amongst the massive oaks like a picture post card.

Her sharp inhale at the sight came from pure pleasure. She was finally home. She parked her car, got out, and breathed in the fresh air.

A short, slender blonde, who looked to be around forty, stood waiting on the wrap-around front porch.

"You must be Lucy Carmichael." The woman greeted her with a welcoming smile.

"Yes, I am." The half lie didn't bother Lucy one bit. Not having any idea of what her investigation would lead to, it was imperative to keep her identity secret for as long as possible.

Lucy mounted the steps. "And you must be Jan Kelly, my real estate agent." Lucy reached out, and they shook hands.

"After dealing with your aunt, it's finally nice to meet you in person."

"Nice meeting you, too," Lucy said.

"Welcome to your new home... That is, if it meets with your approval. I thought it wise to add the contingency that you see the place before you decide. The house is unlocked. Shall we?" Jan pushed the door open and stepped across the threshold. Lucy followed her into the high-ceilinged, wide entrance.

Lucy gazed at the solid oak staircase that hugged the right side of the foyer wall. An image of her nine-year-old self, sliding down the banister, flashed in her mind's eye.

"Beautiful, isn't it?" Jan said. "It leads to a large attic room similar to what we might call a bonus room in the more modern houses. There are four dormers, two in the front and two at the back, giving the upstairs lots of natural light. It would make a cute extra bedroom or a nice office."

Lucy recalled the space, and even though it was mainly used for storage during her years there, she remembered hours of playing dress-up throughout the cooler months. She wondered if the old roll-top truck was still there.

"The living room is on the right and dining on the left," Jan continued.

They strolled through both rooms, while Jan pointed out the ornate scrollwork over the fireplace mantels, the conditions of the oak floors, and how beautiful they would look refinished.

They walked down the hallway, and Jan pointed out the updates that had taken place over the years—built-in closets being one of them. "The two bedrooms on the left are connected by one large bathroom. You'll find the master takes up most of the right side. When the house was renovated back in the sixties, the two bedrooms were combined to make the spacious master suite. It's quite nice even by to-day's standards."

When Lucy walked through, she had to agree. The room was very nice, but it still amazed her at how much smaller the house seemed than she'd remembered. As a child, every-thing appeared much bigger. A memory of having to reach up to grab the door handle flashed in her mind.

Until that moment, the house and all of her memories there had been seen through the eyes of a young child. Now, at twenty-four, it was all so different.

"I understand your mother will be joining you." Jan's pleasant voice broke into her musings.

"Yes. My mom and I have wanted a place like this for years. The size of the house is manageable and with enough land around it for peace and quiet. When I'd heard about it from a family friend, I decided to make the offer right away."

Another white lie—Lucy certainly hoped she'd not get too comfortable with telling them.

They spent the next several minutes doing the walk-through. A wide, center hallway connected the middle part of the house—the three bedrooms, and a large kitchen that led to a laundry/mud room.

The tour ended at the French doors that led to the back yard and patio. After looking over the plot drawing of the twenty-seven acres, Lucy opened the French doors and stepped outside onto the brick patio, followed by Jan.

She strolled along the patchy grass and scanned the prop-erty. The majestic oak trees were beautiful, and she recalled having played underneath them as a child.

A watering trough sat alongside a run-down paddock. "Did the previous owner have horses?" she asked.

"I think that was the intention of the Lambs when they rented the place." Jan shrugged. "But the condition of that fence now wouldn't keep anything penned in for long." Jan stepped up beside her. "It wouldn't take much to tear the whole thing down."

The yard had been neglected, too. It would take a lot of work to bring it back to life, but none of that mattered right now. The real purpose of her purchase was to track down her father's killer. Until that was accomplished, she wasn't certain whether or not she would make a permanent home there for her and her mom.

"Well, that's pretty much it," Jan said as they made their way back inside. "Except for the small basement that houses the heat and air units, the water heater, and the breaker boxes. Everything passed inspection, and I have that report for you."

"And the furniture stays with the house?"

"That's correct." Jan stepped in, closing the door behind her. "I think that's everything. Any questions?"

Lucy stood in the middle of the kitchen and slowly turned around. "The photos on your site and your helpful explanations of the house and property are just as you said." She stopped and focused on Jan. "I want it."

"Wonderful." Jan strode to the kitchen counter and removed a document from her satchel. "It just so happens, I've already removed the contingency and prepared another contract." Smiling, she handed it to Lucy. "Look it over at your convenience, then I'll email a copy to your trustee."

"How about right now? My aunt is at the ready."

"That works for me." Jan beamed.

Lucy read through the document. "This looks good. Go ahead and email it to my aunt. She's waiting to read, and then sign, once I okay the purchase."

"Talk about efficient," Jan said. "You sure do know what you want. After your aunt signs, I'll get this to Mr. Fisher for his signature. He wanted me to apologize for the condition of the place. Apparently, he was a friend of the woman he purchased the house from and told her he would keep whatever she left behind until she could make arrangements to come get it. That was three years ago, and for some reason, she chose to leave it, so everything here now belongs to you."

"And the reason he sold it *as is*."

"That leaves you with a mound of decluttering, I'm afraid."

"I really don't mind," Lucy added. "I'm just happy to have gotten the place. As for the boxes...it'll be like going on a treasure hunt. Who knows what I might find?"

"You're very understanding, and I'm sure he'll be pleased you've accepted. He was concerned it would take a long time to sell because of the assault I told you about." Jan handed Lucy two sets of keys. "Here you go."

"I can have these now?"

"Yes, Mr. Fisher wanted you to have them in case you chose to get an early start on any renovations you had in mind."

"I appreciate that." Lucy glanced at the keys in her hand. "Are these the original?"

"I believe so. They look like it anyway."

Jan glanced around the outdated kitchen. "This old house is full of charm and history. I hope you and your mother enjoy living here. Welcome to Diamond Creek."

"Thank you."

"Oh, by the way..." Jan pulled a glossy, silver-and-blue ticket from her handbag. "Here's an invite to the annual Police Officer's Ball. I can't go, and since you're new in town, I thought it might be a good way for you to meet some of the locals. This year's theme is a memorial for those officers who died in the line of duty. It's a fundraiser for the precinct, and it's a masked ball. Should be lots of fun. Just about everybody who's anybody attends."

"Masked? Where at this late hour would I get a mask?"

"A few of the town shops carry them for this event. Pickings may be slim right now, but since the ball's tomorrow night, that gives you plenty of time to find one."

Lucy nodded and took the ticket from Jan's fingers. She couldn't have picked a better segue into the community and through the Police Officer's Ball, no less. The police were exactly who she had come to investigate. Of course, if everyone wore a mask, then she'd be hard-pressed to identify anyone there, but then again, the mask would also protect her identity.

"Thank you, Jan. This," she held up the ticket, "is very much appreciated."

After Jan left, Lucy set about going through the house in more detail. She proceeded to open the cupboard doors in the kitchen and was pleased to see they held a set of dishes, pots and pans, and other paraphernalia she would need to set up house. The drawers held flatware, oven mitts, and other utensils for cooking and serving. Except for the dinner plates, none of it looked familiar.

Next was the living room, a large square room with ample seating. Several antique pieces pulled the space together rather nicely, and their warm patina gave the room a homey, lived-in feeling that Lucy found welcoming.

Even though it had been years since she and her mom had lived there, the living room still smelled like lemon furniture wax. She knew the man who'd bought the house from her mother and couldn't imagine him caring one whit for the furniture and assumed Jan had hired someone to get the place ready for her.

She recognized the sofa and sat down, surprised at the comfort and support for such an old piece. Two wingback chairs, upholstered in a small, blue check, sat stationed near the fireplace. They looked relatively new and not at all familiar, and even though the long coffee table in front of the sofa was a bit beat up, it would serve her purposes just fine.

There were even books on the shelves flanking the right of the decorative fireplace, mirroring the one in the dining room. She approached the white shelving and pulled a book from its slot. *Pride and Prejudice*—one of her favorites. Maybe, if time allowed, she would sit in that wingback chair and read the book again.

She walked down the hall and entered the first bedroom on the left. It looked like it had been used mainly for storage. Mr. Fisher had told her aunt that most of her sister's things had been boxed and stored in this room.

Lucy crossed the floor and peeked in the closet. A musty odor hit her. The boxes stacked in the far left corner looked like they'd been there for years. These had to have belonged to her family and Lucy couldn't wait to go through them. The thought that they might hold some significance to her past lifted her spirits.

Fourteen years ago, she and her mom had moved from the house into town when Lucy turned ten. She'd thought walking through the house would have brought forth more memories than it had. Maybe Jan's presence had blocked them. A bit disappointed, she continued on, savoring the bits and pieces that did surface.

As she moved through the house, she made mental notes

on what should be done first to upgrade the place—a thorough cleaning, for a start. In the dining room, she ran her hand along the wainscot. Surprisingly, the paint still looked good.

The furniture throughout was old and most likely had belonged to her parents. She felt lucky that it all had stayed with the house. Twelve years prior, when she and her mom left Diamond Creek, they'd rented the house pretty much with everything in it. Then, before her mom's accident, she'd decided to sell it, against Lucy's will.

Now, it was theirs again. Owning it meant the world to her. Within those walls—those very rooms—the story of her early years with two loving parents lingered. As she settled in, she hoped more memories of those days would resurface.

Lucy thought about her mother and tried to imagine her preparing a meal in the kitchen—reading by the fireplace—evenings in the living room—her life filled with joy, love, and laughter. Somebody in that town had taken that away from them. Tomorrow night, she would put on her finest, go to the Policeman's Ball, and begin her search for the truth.

CHAPTER 3

Friday night, Lucy stood at the entrance of the festive hall. She'd dressed in a soft, pink evening gown that she'd bought at a closeout sale at her favorite boutique in Little Rock. That morning, she'd found a lovely mask at one of the boutiques in town. The simple, but elegant, gold satin complemented her dress perfectly.

She took a deep breath, adjusted the cap sleeve on her right shoulder, and scanned the room. With one quick glance, she took in the dimly lit space, the cloth-covered tables, and thousands of twinkle lights adorning the Ficus trees that stood throughout the large space.

She'd been concerned as to how she'd be able to recognize anyone if they were masked, but it seemed providence smiled on her that evening. Half of the guests had already removed them, and lucky for her, it seemed to be mostly older people.

She walked forward and studied the faces of the middle-aged male officers—the focus of her search. One of the few times her mother had talked about the past, she'd alluded that someone on the police force had been responsible for Lucy's father's death. When she'd asked her mom how she'd known that, her mother shook her head, ending further discussion.

So, Lucy zeroed in on the men. Narrowing down the suspect list was crucial to finding out who murdered her father. The age of the officer would also be a factor. Even though some were still masked, she hoped they would remove them before the night ended.

Several of the male officers were in formal dress uniforms —striking in their short, navy jackets and pristine, white pants. Any medals they'd received were pinned under their left shoulder.

She eyed the officers in their mid-forties or older as she moved through the room. The number of men in uniform that fit the age bracket was six or eight at most. Since many of them had opted for a tuxedo, she'd have no way of knowing if they were police officers or civilians.

Low conversation and soft laughter grew louder as she crossed the room. So far, no one seemed to have noticed her —not surprising since she, too, wore a mask.

A small stage stood at one end, and a band played a slow, unfamiliar instrumental. Not too loud either, which made for good conversation amongst the guests. A few couples were already dancing in the open area in the center.

She slowly made her way to a long table laden with a variety of food. Having eaten before she came, she chose to ignore it. Tonight, her job was to keep her eyes and ears open for any clues that could help in her search.

But as she canvassed the room, something about the situation made the hope of finding clues there impossible. She sighed inwardly, the feeling of defeat weighing her down before she even got started. Who was she kidding? Did she really expect clues and suspects to simply fall into her lap? This would be a lot more difficult than she'd thought.

Lucy perused the crowd and realized that scrutinizing the guests, whether masked or unmasked, would lead her nowhere. At some point, she'd have to engage some of the people in conversation, while at the same time keeping her identity secret.

Her gaze fell onto the face of someone she *did* know. Bob Holland, who was now Chief of Police. *Uncle Bob.* She smiled at the memory of him and would recognize him anywhere. He'd been her father's friend and had stayed in her life for almost eight years after her dad's murder. He'd even taken her to her first father-daughter dance.

She hadn't seen him in twelve years and figured the woman next to him was his wife, Brenda. Lucy wondered if Uncle Bob would recognize her. She certainly hoped not. This early in the game, she was not prepared to give her identity away. She'd steer clear of him as long as she could, which shouldn't be too difficult if she kept an eye on his movements.

To her right, a beautiful array of flowers cascaded from an ornate, silver bowl in the center of a round table. She stepped over for a closer look and gently touched a pink petal of a rose.

At the base of the arrangement were stacks of brochures about that night's event. *Night of Blue Memorial Policeman's Ball.* She picked one up and searched for her father's name. She assumed he wouldn't be listed as one fallen in the line of duty, but she checked anyway. With a sinking heart, she tossed the pamphlet aside and continued her scrutiny of the guests.

* * *

Malcolm stood near the entrance of the ballroom, chatting with Officer's Chase and Kirby. All three of them were still masked and sipping on tall flutes of Lamarca Prosecco.

Malcolm tossed back the dregs and turned to deposit the glass on a nearby table. A woman standing tentatively just inside the entrance about fifteen feet from him caught his attention. Intrigued, he stepped away from the two officers, now deep in another discussion, leaned an elbow onto one of the tall tables, and watched her.

Dressed in a flowing, pink evening gown—her dark hair twisted up into what he assumed was the latest style—she was extraordinary—a combination of youthful elegance and mystery. As beautiful as she was, it was the latter that had caught and held his attention.

She stood still and ran her alert, wide-eyed gaze over the occupants of the room. Her eyes suddenly narrowed like a bird of prey. She was obviously looking for someone—not with anticipation but more like that of a predator.

She crossed the room toward the refreshment table. Being a detective, his cop instinct alerted. He moved from his position and slowly followed her, keeping a reasonable distance. She stopped, scanned the array of food, but instead of partaking, she approached the large floral arrangement. After a brief glance at one of the booklets, she tossed it aside, then turned away to continue her perusal of the guests.

* * *

As Lucy pondered just what to do next, she caught the eye of a tall, dark-haired, masked man dressed in a tuxedo.

He openly stared at her. If eyes could follow someone across a room, then his was an example of that.

With broad shoulders, a simple, black satin mask and short beard—he commanded the great hall. He was a good twenty feet away. Had he been watching her the whole time she'd been evaluating everyone else? A warning bell rang in her ears as he continued to examine her.

He held her with his gaze and moved forward. Her body stilled as he came closer—his approach—deliberate and noticeable. She licked her lips. Should she just ignore him? She searched her mind for any trace or connection to anyone from her past—a school or church friend, maybe? Another quick glance to the side told her she was on her own. So, she fixed her gaze on his, held herself still, and waited.

The man, taller than she'd first thought, stopped a few feet in front of her. Heart thudding against her ribs, she squared her shoulders and looked right at him.

An easy smile played at the corners of his mouth, causing a pleasant sensation in her midsection. The contrast of his gleaming, white teeth against his dark, well-trimmed beard was stunning.

His eyes held a warm twinkle that lit up with appreciation. She knew she was attractive, and she'd made a special effort to look older, more sophisticated, and a bit glamorous for this evening. It wasn't an effort to get noticed but merely a disguise—an attempt to camouflage the twelve-year-old child who'd moved away all those years ago.

"Hallo," he said. "I don't believe we've met?"

The man's rich, Scottish voice did something to her insides—a rather *nice* something. His deep, masculine accent had most definitely added to his sex appeal. Blatant curiosity filled the dark-blue eyes that held her gaze. Any other time she'd be interested, but not today.

She held out her hand, and he gently gripped it. "No, we haven't met," she said. "I just moved here."

He didn't say anything, just continued to stare at her with a slight appreciative gleam in his eye.

A whiff of his aftershave weakened her at the knees. She licked her suddenly dry lips. "My real estate agent actually gave me a ticket for tonight's ball, since she couldn't come, and told me it would be a nice way to meet some of the townspeople. Although, with half of them in masks, it's a bit intimidating."

"Don't tell me...Jan Kelly?"

"Yes."

"And you braved the masses by coming here alone. I'm impressed."

"Don't be." She smiled slightly. "I almost didn't come," she lied. Something about him made her want to keep up her guard. She was a friendly person by nature, but in this instance, she could not relax with anyone.

"Well, you looked a bit lonely over here, so I thought I'd introduce myself, as I'm relatively new, too. I'm Malcolm Knox."

"I detect a slight Scottish accent."

"You detect correctly." He gave her a smile that sent her pulse racing.

"It's not like that thick, dense accent one hears on TV and in the movies," she said, trying to still the erratic beating of her heart.

"It's because I'm from Ayr."

He smiled again and her heart flipped a summersault.

"It's a small town situated on the southwest coast, and we're much easier to understand," he added.

She gazed into his remarkable blue eyes. The man wreaked all sorts of havoc on her insides. Funny, how a mask caused one to focus solely on the eyes. She looked deeply into his, wondering what he must be thinking. *Are they the mirror of the soul?*

Then, there was his beard—also a mask of sorts, covering his lower face—making her focus on his mouth and his lips as he spoke—every curl and nuance. What would it be like to feel those lips on hers?

She swallowed and shoved such thoughts aside. "What brings you all the way from Scotland to this little Arkansas town?"

"Business."

"What kind of business?"

He pursed his lips as if thinking. "Research. I'm honing my observation skills. It's sort of a spectator role."

She thought about how, moments earlier, he'd watched her before he approached. "What are you observing?"

"The police department—but enough of that. I'd like you to dance with me." He took her hand and led her onto the open floor without asking or waiting for her reply.

"Are all Scots this forward?"

"I can't speak for all Scots, but I like to think of myself as confident."

"I'd call your actions authoritative," she said.

"I guess you could say it that way." His left arm encircled her waist.

He gazed down at her as the band started playing *Into the Mystic*. The man singing even sounded like Van Morrison, and the song was so very, sweetly, romantic.

Malcolm drew her close and moved across the floor. "So. When are you going to tell me?"

"Tell you what?" She gazed up into those blue, blue eyes, the bluest she'd ever seen—deep like the ocean on a stormy day.

"Your name?"

"It's... Lucy."

"She hesitates," he said. "And your last name?"

"Just Lucy."

"Cryptic, too." He paused slightly, then swung her left, sidestepping another couple. For the next minute, they simply slow-danced to the hypnotic rhythm of the piece. Fighting the urge to rest her head on his shoulder, she focused on the top button on his tux. She swallowed, and her heart fluttered.

Ever so gently, he cinched her closer. Completely aware of how his movement made her body yield to his, she willingly conformed. No longer a schoolgirl, she reveled in this moment of pure romance. Never in her life had she felt so drawn to a man. Strength and masculinity flowed from him —gentle and persuasive as he led her through each step.

She lifted her gaze to his as they danced, and she found him studying her with those dark-blue eyes that seemed to challenge—to question her in some way. Such focused attention sparked an interest she found hard to ignore. His very persona made her want to test him.

She wondered what he did for living and knew instinctively that his request for a dance went deeper then mere formality. She felt like a mouse to his cat and searched her mind for his motive.

Could he possibly know her identity? Surely not.

The song ended, and he lifted her hand to his lips. "Thank you. It's been a pleasure."

Lucy stood, stunned. "How did you ever learn to dance like that?"

"Six weeks of junior cotillion." He smiled. "But right now, I must excuse myself as I feel obligated to dance with several others here this evening. Until next time." He lifted two fingers to his forehead, then walked across the floor to another woman, a tall blonde, who'd been eyeing them during their dance.

Lucy's heart beat double-time. She left the floor and made her way to the refreshment table. She picked up a plate from one end, strolled along the outer edge, and selected several tasty-looking morsels. It would at least give her something to do while she scrutinized the other guests. Holding a plate and sitting quietly aside would hopefully deter any future requests to dance.

She sat in the chair along the wall near the center and picked up a seafood hors d'oeuvre. She nibbled the edge and studied the men in uniform. Several more had removed their masks, and except for Chief Holland, none of them were familiar to her. Yep, this was definitely going to be more difficult than she'd thought.

She sank her teeth into the crab appetizer, chewed, and thought about her next plan of action. Plate in hand, she stood and walked toward a woman who had sat down near her. It was Brenda Holland, her mask removed and hanging loosely around her neck. Mask or no mask, Lucy felt certain Mrs. Holland would not recognize her. Come to think of it, she thought it odd, as involved as her husband had been in her and her mother's life, Mrs. Holland had chosen not to be.

She took a seat near Brenda and smiled. Seeing her through the eyes of an adult, Mrs. Holland was much more striking than she'd remembered. Lucy figured she was close in age to her husband, but no one would ever know it from her creamy-white complexion and perfectly applied makeup.

"Such a lovely evening, isn't it?" Lucy said.

Mrs. Holland turned toward her. "It is." She sipped her wine and eyed Lucy, curiously. "I don't believe I've seen you before."

"Since I'm still in a mask, how would you know?"

"I've been here many years, and masked or not, I can identify everyone in this ballroom." Brenda's eyes held a twinkle in their depths.

Lucy smiled and nodded, then reached for another tidbit from her plate.

"So. Are you visiting?" Brenda asked.

"I'm actually in the process of moving here," Lucy said.

"Be careful what you buy," Brenda advised. "There's one on the market called Griffin Gate." She leaned left and tilted her head closer. "I'd stay away from that one. A murder happened there over twenty years ago." Mrs. Holland shuddered. "It sits at the edge of town and is an absolute eyesore. Has been neglected more years than I can count. In my opinion, the place should be torn down."

"Because of the murder?"

"Who would want to live in such a place?" Mrs. Holland pinched off a corner of her ham-and-cheese biscuit. "It sat there for years after the Lambs stopped using it, then it sold to a single man, and the place went further downhill." She popped the tidbit into her mouth, chewed, and swallowed. "You should have seen it. I swear the weeds were knee high."

So, the house had been *labeled* as a place of murder and mystery. As a real estate agent, Jan had told her as much, but Lucy cringed, hearing Brenda Holland say it in that *gossipy* way.

"It's nice to see young people moving into our little

town," Mrs. Holland continued before Lucy could say anything. "Growth is vitally important in keeping a community thriving. Having a young person like yourself choose our township means we must be doing something right."

"I agree," Lucy said.

"Since you just arrived, I expect you got your ticket for tonight's gala from Jan Kelly."

"Yes. I did. But how—"

A sparkling laugh fell from Mrs. Holland's lips. "She buys several each year to support everything from our children's charity, to this precinct, then gives them away. She never comes herself."

"I see." Lucy lifted the fruity punch to her lips. "Well, I'm glad she gave one to me. It's a nice opportunity to meet some of the town's esteemed residents."

"Her words, I take it?"

Lucy laughed. "Close." She gave Mrs. Holland a sideways glance. "Although, I did wonder since it was a masked ball. I had no idea if I'd get to know anyone here tonight."

"Oh, they eventually all come off. Look." Mrs. Holland lifted her hand. "There's several over there who are removing them now."

Lucy glanced in the direction Mrs. Holland had pointed. Lucy was fortunate most had removed their masks, although it hadn't been much help as she'd only recognized Chief Holland and the woman sitting next to her.

"Oh, please excuse me," Mrs. Holland said. "I see my husband motioning from the other side of the room. It was nice meeting you." She set her plate aside, stood, and wove her way through the dancers to her husband's side.

Lucy watched her leave, thinking it odd that neither one of them had exchanged names.

Malcolm, plate in hand, approached Lucy from the left and sat down. "I see you've met Brenda Holland?"

"Actually, she didn't introduce herself to me. We just chatted briefly before her husband motioned her over."

"She's Chief of Police Bob Holland's wife."

"So they're the big dogs in town."

"What?"

"You know... The leader of the pack... It's like saying... What's up big dog?"

Even masked she could see the confusion in his gaze.

She blew out a sigh. "It's the guy who makes everyone else fall in line."

Malcolm nodded. "I see."

"Don't they have that expression where you come from?"

"Yes, but it usually refers to a celebrity. Holland is a lot of things, but he's no celebrity. At least, that's the sentiment of some in the department."

"Including you?"

He looked horrified. "Forget I said that out loud, will you? If that gets around, they'll be packing me back off to Scotland." He smiled when he said it, but something about his tone told her it was the truth.

"I see you're still wearing your mask," Lucy said.

"Everyone knows it's me. The accent, slight as it is, still gives me away. I almost didn't wear the blasted thing." He popped a small, sausage cheese ball into his mouth, chewed, and swallowed. "I see yours is still in place."

"And that's where it's staying, too."

"Afraid someone may recognize you?"

She swung her head left. "Not at all." She toyed with a half-eaten spring roll. "It's obvious that I'm the only newcomer here tonight, and I'd rather not draw attention to myself. I just prefer to be incognito."

"Obvious?"

"That Mrs. Holland person told me she knew every masked person here, and since she didn't recognize me, I had to be a newcomer. So yes, obvious."

"And it's *obvious* to me you're here looking for someone. I suggest you stay until all the masks come off for the evening, then you may very well find him. It is a *he*, isn't it?" He stood, gave a slight tip of his head, then strode away.

Lucy watched Malcolm until he stopped on the far side of the room. Everything about him stirred something deep inside of her.

Animosity? Attraction? Fear?

Without having seen his entire face, she would still have been drawn to him. He possessed a magnetism that almost frightened her. Even masked, he was the most compelling man she'd ever met. Instinct told her he was not to be messed with, or lied to.

CHAPTER 4

Malcolm unlocked his apartment door, turned the handle, and walked in to his small flat above the drug store. Pickings had been slim in a town that size, and he was lucky to have found it.

He strode through the tiny living area to his bedroom, yanked off the bow tie, and tossed it on the dresser in his closet. His mask hung loosely around his neck and came off next. He slipped off his formal jacket, hung it on the rack provided, then continued to get undressed.

He padded to the bathroom, gripped the faucet handle, and turned right. After he splashed cold water on his face, he snatched up a white hand towel and mopped his face.

Ten minutes later, with hands tucked behind his head, he lay in the single bed, staring at ceiling.

A pair of secretive, emerald green eyes had stayed with him throughout the evening. From the moment he saw Just Lucy, he was determined to dance with her. Not since Becca had he been this mesmerized by a woman. Holding her in his arms had been sheer heaven. There was an open, forthright innocence about her he found totally appealing. But underneath that polished, guarded exterior, she held a secret. A secret that intrigued him immensely, and one which he determined to discover.

Her full name for one thing.

That shouldn't be too hard to figure out. In the morning, he would text Jan. As Diamond Creek's premier real estate agent, she would be happy to share that information—not only Lucy's full name, but also the property she'd purchased.

The following morning, he overslept. He rushed to get dressed and to the precinct, and it took every second of his time. Texting Jan fell into the category of *good intentions.*

Malcolm spent the bulk of the day investigating two property damage cases—one of which involved theft. After interviewing the irate shop owner, he arrived back at the precinct around 4:00 p.m. and except for one person at the front desk, the office was empty.

"Leslie, anything of importance come in while I was gone?"

"Mrs. Crowder called and said someone was in the old Victorian house out on Maple Road. The place has been empty for weeks, and she was concerned it may be a squatter."

"I'm leaving here in ten minutes. I'll check it out on my way home."

He made his way down the hall to the file room. Since his arrival, he'd wanted to check on a closed case his father had told him about. Years ago, his dad had served alongside an officer who had been murdered after his dad had moved overseas. The killer had never been found.

"If you ask me," his dad had said, "the precinct stopped working on the case much too quickly."

The more his father shared what details he knew, the more Malcolm felt convinced that something was indeed, amiss.

Malcolm had been approved for the foreign officer's exchange program, so he'd chosen the rural police department in Diamond Creek, Arkansas. The same town his father and his officer friend had served in as rookies. It afforded Malcolm the perfect opportunity to experience the variety of methods and ways policing was accomplished in the USA, and ample time to do his own investigation into the death of his father's friend.

Malcolm had access to past and current police files in the DCPD. Due to the precinct's size, and his ranking as detective, he was given free range to serve the department in that capacity.

Files from recent years were digital, but the older ones were still stuffed away in the precinct drawers. Malcolm flipped through the *cold case* files but found nothing. He then flipped through the folders in the *closed case* section, stopping when saw the name he'd been looking for. But why had it been closed?

You don't close a case, especially when it involves the unsolved death of one of your own.

He shook his head, pressed his fingers to the one marked, *Detective James Ross*, and pulled it out.

* * *

Saturday morning, Lucy dressed in sneakers, shorts, and T-shirt, quite a change from the pink gown she'd worn the previous night. Her mind drifted to the handsome Scot and how he'd held her with those remarkable blue eyes of his.

What would it be like to meet him again, unmasked this time? It would be impossible *not to* in such a small town.

Seven old, tired-looking boxes now stationed between the sofa and the fireplace brought her back to the present. Earlier, Lucy had spent an hour developing an action plan to declutter and search the contents of the house. There were at least twelve boxes in total, as well as drawers and closets to dig through. She'd start with a few, and over the coming days, build from there.

She'd flicked most of the dust off the tops with an old rag. While she stood contemplating the job before her, she tipped a cold bottle of water to her mouth and took a long drink.

She sat on the edge of the couch, leaned forward, and with both hands on the cardboard flaps, pulled outward. A puff of dust shot upward. She scrunched her nose and reared back.

Lucy blinked, waved away the dust, then reached in and pulled out what looked like a handmade quilt. Someone had taken the time to fold it neatly and with care. She held it up for a better look. The multi-colored, tiny floral-print fabric made it uniquely feminine.

To air out the musty odor, she gathered up the quilt and walked to the back of the house and went outside. A clothesline ran from the far corner of the house to a metal pole in the yard. She slung the quilt up and over the line and straightened it to hang evenly.

Back inside, she opened the next three boxes, separating the items in piles to keep and to give away. Needing a break from bending and sorting, she decided to clean the living room.

Earlier, she'd found a host of cleaning supplies in the

mudroom and had them at the ready. It took a few minutes to push the heaviest box away from the shelving. With her hair in a ponytail, she positioned a stepping stool at the base of the shelves, grabbed a duster, and got to work.

From top to bottom, she dusted the four upper corners, knocking down cobwebs and dust. Next, she tackled the mantel, working her way to each shelf.

When she'd toured the house with Jan, the lemony fragrance throughout had masked the degree of dust and grime, and Lucy realized a surface dusting would not be near enough. Starting with the top shelf, she removed everything on it, then proceeded to wipe off each item before putting it back in its place. She took care of the next two shelves in like manner, then broke for lunch.

With a plate of tuna fish salad, crackers, and a dill pickle in one hand and iced tea in the other, she pushed through the French doors onto the patio. She took a seat on the wooden bench and dove in.

As she munched on a tuna-laden cracker, she thought about all the things that needed to be done in the yard. Some sort of evergreen bushes should flank the back of the house, and maybe a few pots with flowers along the patio would be nice. She kept her mother in mind as she ran through her mental list of what she'd like to do.

By five o'clock that afternoon, she had managed to clean the rest of the shelves. Everything but the books had to be washed with soap before they would be in any condition to display. Once finished, she paused and pressed a hand to her lower back. The task had been more tiring than she thought it would be.

Finally finished, she took a much-needed break. She grabbed another cold water and plopped down on the sofa.

Someone knocked on the front door.

Ugh! With her head lolled back against the sofa, she was almost too tired to move. She sighed, pushed to her feet, and stood.

CHAPTER 5

Malcolm lifted a fist to knock a second time when the door opened. A pair of gold-flecked, emerald-green eyes stared up at him. The slow widening of her gaze did not go unnoticed. He'd recognized her, too.

Even with her dust-streaked cheeks and that disheveled, mass of dark hair hanging askew in a ponytail, he would know her anywhere.

"Well if it isn't Just Lucy. You look...different." He smothered a smile as a rosy pink crept up her smudged cheeks. "I searched for you last night. I'd planned to introduce you to a few people, but you slipped away like Cinderella."

Her gaze dropped to his waist. "I see you're wearing a badge."

"I am."

"You're a detective?"

"Yes. Does that surprise you?"

"It does actually. You could have told me that last night."

"And *you* could have told me your last name. Seems we're both keeping our cards close to our chest."

"How did you find me?" She clutched a water bottle to her midsection as if in protection.

"What makes you think I was looking for you?"

"I...well..." Her glorious gaze widened again, and her flush deepened even more.

"I'm here because we've had a report of a prowler at this location."

She craned her neck and peered beyond him. "From who?"

"A concerned neighbor."

She clutched her water bottle in one hand, folded her arms, and lifted her chin. "This house is mine... Well...it will be when the sale's finalized. You can ask Jan. The previous owner said it would be all right if I started moving in and making renovations... See? I have the keys." She snatched them up from the narrow table by the entrance.

"No need to fuss. I believe you."

He stood, staring down at her—chin raised—chest heaving—completely on the defensive and absolutely adorable. "May I come in?"

She blinked and stepped back. "Of course." She watched him warily as he crossed the threshold. "Would you like a cold bottle of water? That's all I have at the moment."

"No thanks." He stopped abruptly and glanced around the disheveled living room. "No wonder you look the way you do."

"What?" she shrieked and ran to the mirror hanging over the mantel. She squeezed her eyes tightly shut and shook her head. "Excuse me a minute. I'll be right back." She spun and left the room.

Malcolm took the opportunity to look around while Lucy was freshening up. Taking in the variety of packed and unpacked boxes, he crossed the room, then pulled the flaps open on the nearest one. The contents didn't look like much.

He spotted a stack of photographs lying on the coffee table and picked them up. As he flipped through them, Lucy returned.

He glanced up as she stepped across the worn-looking rug. "Now you look more like the woman I met last night—much younger but still her." He tossed the photographs back on the table.

"Your point being?" Her lovely eyebrows knit together.

"Last night, you were dressed to kill." He ran his gaze over her T-shirt, shorts, and sneakers. "Today, you look anything but... More like a teenager if you ask me."

She sucked in a breath. "What I wore last night was no different than what you wore. You wore a tuxedo—I wore an evening gown."

And you were on the hunt, hen.

"Today, you're in jeans and a button-down shirt with a badge clipped on your hip. I'm in shorts, sneakers, and a T-shirt because I'm cleaning this house."

"Play dumb if you want, but I'm no fool, Just Lucy." He took one step toward her and stopped. "I'll let the neighbor know that you're supposed to be here, so you shouldn't be disturbed by anyone else from the department."

He'd barely finished speaking when Lucy gave him a quick dismissive nod, bent over the cardboard box nearest her, and yanked the flaps. She yelped and sprang backward into his arms.

"What happened?" he asked.

"It's a mouse. I *hate* mice." She pressed her back deeper into his chest as if doing so would put more distance between her the tiny culprit. "Where is it?" she fearfully asked. "Do you see it?"

"Not yet," he said.

"Oh, my gosh! I can't stay here."

"Hold on a sec, will you?" He spotted the aggressor huddled in fright in the far corner of the room. "I think he's as scared of you as you are of him."

"I don't care how he feels. I have a real phobia of the creatures. Snakes, I can handle, but mice... No."

She gulped air and went rigid in his arms. Instinct had him tightening his grip.

Still pressed against him, she lifted her chin and glanced up—a hint of embarrassed pleading in her gaze.

He gave her a quick smile. "You okay?" he asked.

She swallowed and nodded.

He dropped his arms, and she stepped away. She ran her hands up and down her thighs. "Sorry about that."

"Would you like some help with him?" he asked.

"Yes, please."

Her wide-eyed gaze registered enormous relief, and he smiled. "It's amazing."

"What?" she asked.

"That the glamorous woman I met last night would be terrified of a little, gray field mouse."

"I know." She sighed. "It's ridiculous, but the fear is real."

"But snakes don't bother you?"

"Not at all."

"Do you have a mouse trap?"

"I saw a package of them in a drawer in the kitchen." She scooted off and was back with the package in thirty seconds.

He took the pack from her and began to open it. "I'm

going to need some bait. Do you have any peanut butter or cheese?"

She trotted back to the kitchen and returned a minute later with a piece of yellow cheese.

"Place that where I can't see it," she demanded.

"Yes, ma'am." Once he secured the bait, he set the trap and placed it along the floorboard on the opposite side of the room.

He stood and stepped back. "That should do it."

"Thank you so much."

"As you Americans like to say, I'm here to serve and protect."

"I'm sure dealing with that field mouse is not what the creators of that phrase had in mind."

He laughed, then eyed the other boxes. Would you like help with those before I leave? No telling what could be lurking inside."

She shivered and nodded. "You open each one, and I'll sit by and watch."

"Wouldn't you rather stand? That way if one springs out you can make a run for it."

"Don't tempt me." She smiled, and her green eyes sparkled like jewels. Yet, the night before, they held suspicion and stealth, like the eyes of a cat on the prowl. Had she found who she'd been looking for? Was that why she'd left so soon?

Malcolm refocused his attention, yanked open the rest of the boxes, and helped Lucy organize the contents on the floor and the coffee table. During the unpacking, he noticed the smallest box held letters and what could be important papers. "Do these things belong to the previous owners?"

"I don't really know," she said. "I'm going to go through

it all, and if any of it seems significant to the previous owner, I'll let Jan know."

In the process of unloading the last three boxes, she'd managed to get another smudge on her left cheek. After helping, he probably wore a bit of dust and dirt, too. He gazed at her untidy hairdo and her smudged face and grinned.

"Uh-oh," she said. "Do I need another wash?"

"Yes, and I imagine I do, too." He stood. "I'll have to leave you to it. Unfortunately, my workday isn't over. I have some paperwork that needs my attention."

A sharp snap echoed throughout the living room as he turned to go.

Lucy eyes widened. "Was that...?"

"It was. Bring me a small trash bag, and I'll take care of it."

In seconds, Lucy was back, handing him the small brown sack. She turned away while he took care of the trap.

"All done." He held the sack as he made his way to the door. "I'll get rid of this for you."

She placed her hands over her heart and mouthed, *thank you*, as he left.

He climbed into his department-issued vehicle, an unmarked, 2012 black Chevrolet Tahoe, and started the engine. Thoughts of how much she'd intrigued him emerged as he pulled out of her drive. She still hadn't told him her last name. In his position, it would have been easy to find out. He could text Jan, since he hadn't had time earlier in the day, but decided to leave it alone.

Frankly, he relished the mystery surrounding Just Lucy and would enjoy playing the game a little bit longer. The woman held a secret. And it wasn't just the fact that she'd withheld her last name. He'd play along until it suited him not to. A woman clothed in mystery was a challenge he'd look forward to solving.

* * *

Lucy made her way to the large attic. The oak stairs creaked as she mounted the steps to the top of the house. Like the first floor, the unfinished oak flooring there was also in excellent condition.

Dust motes floated in the light of the late afternoon sun streaming through the dormers. The natural light making, what would otherwise have been a dark and dreary place, a welcoming retreat. She could understand Jan's suggestion that the space would make a nice office or extra bedroom. It held a magical charm all of its own.

To her right, the head and footboard of an antique, iron bed leaned against the angled ceiling. An old pine chest of drawers stood to the left next to an ancient-looking sewing machine and a dressmaker's mannequin. A cherry wardrobe stood along the back wall, which held an assortment of outdated dresses and wool coats. And next to it sat the roll-top trunk. She wondered if in years past this room had been a bedroom for someone, as pretty much everything there pointed to that fact.

In a previous search, she'd seen an old corkboard propped against the wall, which would be perfect as a clue or suspect board. She stood, scanning the space, and spotted it along the wall to her left.

She gave it a good dusting, then carried it down to the living room and propped it up on the narrow side table along the wall near the sofa. The day before, she'd found a box of pushpins and placed them in a small dish to the right of the board, next to a notepad and some three-by-five note cards.

That done, she sorted through the box of paraphernalia at her feet, dividing the items from least important to important. Before long, she had that box filled and marked as throwaway.

The last, smaller box was filled with newspaper articles and other important-looking documents and letters. This was the box she'd looked forward to going through. With luck, she might find some clues lurking within.

She organized them on the coffee table in stacks to go through in the morning. Right now, she was starved and wanted something to eat. She hadn't done much grocery shopping and decided to get cleaned up and drive into town.

A clipping on the top of the pile caught her eye as she stood to go. She lifted the article and read about the black sedan that had been used in her father's murder. Chills pricked her skin. This box definitely belonged to her mother. Who else would keep this clipping?

The article turned out to be an interview of the owner of the car used in the shooting—Alex Crandall. This was a clue —her first clue.

The piece further stated the car was a collectible. What if Crandall still had it? She'd ask around and see if the family still lived in the area. She folded the article in half and tucked it into her purse.

It only took about five minutes before she hit the edge of town. As a child, she hadn't fully appreciated the charm and history of Diamond Creek. She'd been back less than a week, and already experienced the sense of community, the quaint and cozy atmosphere, and the simplicity that is often lost in a larger city.

Main Street, with its attractive old-fashioned buildings, stood graciously along the wide avenue. A quiet calm pervaded the faces of the people she saw strolling along the sidewalks. They seemed content—unhurried.

If things had been different, she may have grown up there—maybe even fallen in love there. But her life didn't mirror this picturesque little community. She'd been robbed of that life and someone in this town had taken it from her.

She blew out a frustrated breath. Once her mother arrived, Lucy hoped being back would awaken important memories that could lead to her father's killer. *Hope* being the operative word. One minute her mom seemed totally cognitive and alert, and the next, confusion crossed her lovely features.

Dr. Edwards assured Lucy that her mom would recover about ninety percent of her cognitive ability. Unless one knew her before the accident, one would never know she was lacking. It had been almost three years, and there had been some progress but not as much as Lucy had hoped.

She parked the car in front of a *meat and three* called Dottie's Home Cooking. Lucy pushed through the door to the smell of roast beef and baked biscuits. She inhaled deeply, savoring the aroma. It'd been quite some time before she'd had a home-cooked meal and was really looking forward to it.

"Sit anywhere you like!" the plump, middle-aged redhead from behind the counter yelled. "Be with you in a sec."

Lucy chose a table at the window and sat down. The menu wedged between the napkin holder and a large bottle of hot sauce. She pulled it free and opened it up. Today's special was, as the aroma conveyed, roast beef, creamed potatoes, fresh garden peas, and biscuits with gravy.

A minute later, the waitress stood at the edge of the table and beamed a smile. "Hi, I'm Dottie. You must be new. I haven't seen you before."

"Yes ma'am, I just moved here."

"Welcome to Diamond Creek." Dottie placed flatware, a glass of water, and a straw at Lucy's right hand. "We don't usually get young ones like you moving here. Nice for a change."

Lucy smiled up at the woman. "So I've heard."

"What'll it be?"

"I'll take today's special," Lucy said.

"Good choice. Would you like sweet tea with that, honey?"

"Yes, please." Lucy toyed with her watch as Dottie scribbled on the order pad. "May I ask you a question?

"Of course."

"Do you know if Alex Crandall or any of his family still live around here?"

"Why yes. They live on Lark Avenue. Been there for years. Patricia, Alex's wife, passed away several years ago. You a friend of the family?"

"No, but someone I know told me to look them up after I got settled, except I don't exactly know where they live. Do you recall their house number?"

"Three-twelve. Back in a jiffy with your meal."

Lucy watched Dottie walk away. She looked to be about her mom's age and from the conversation, she'd been there for years, if not for her whole life. She wondered if Dottie had known her mother. She gnawed her lower lip. Would it be safe to ask her? Would Dottie be friend or foe?

She fingered the saltshaker and glanced around the small restaurant. Considering it was Saturday night, she was surprised that it was only half full. Maybe there was another place in the area where the town's people preferred to go.

A teenage boy brought her tea to the table, set it before her, and left. She tore open her straw and plunged it into the glass. The bell on the door tinkled as she sipped her drink, and she glanced up.

Malcolm Knox entered the restaurant and strode to the counter. As he spoke to Dottie, she chuckled and handed him a to-go bag. When he turned to leave, he caught Lucy's eye. She lifted a hand and waved as he walked over.

"Hallo, Just Lucy."

There it was...that wisp of a Scottish accent. She could get used to hearing that.

"You give up on the boxes this soon?" He set his to-go bag on her table. "I imagined you toiling the night away going through all that stuff."

"I organized it, and then the hunger pangs hit me." She brushed her bangs aside. She'd been growing them out since graduation, and they had reached that pesky length of forever getting in her eyes. "Since I haven't been to the grocery store, I thought I'd clean up and brave the town—see what it had in the line of sustenance."

He glanced over at the counter, then back at her. "You picked a good spot. Nothing like a home-cooked meal, and Dottie's place is the best."

She eyed the to-go bag. "I'd ask you to join me, but it looks like you still have that paperwork waiting for you."

"Indeed, I do." A thoughtful smile curved his mouth.

He'd clipped his beard since she last saw him. Close like a second skin. Malcolm wasn't near as intimidating when he smiled. It brought the most divine twinkle to the depths of his eyes... as if he only had eyes for her. She blinked, swallowed, lifted the tea to her mouth, and sucked the straw.

"Plus, I'd hate for your meal to get cold," she added.

"You trying to get rid of me?"

"No!" The word burst from her lips as if she had no control over her reactions.

"I'm just teasing you." He laughed. "But you're right. I'd better go. Can't be microwaving Dottie's good cooking." He picked up his to-go sack. "Enjoy your meal."

In seconds, he strode out the restaurant and was gone. Lucy placed her elbows on the tabletop, rested her chin in her hands, and watched his tall figure pull open the Tahoe door and slide in.

He drove away, and she thought about his visit that afternoon. She'd been totally surprised to see him standing at her door, mask-less and completely gorgeous. As for her—what a sight she must've been—dirty-faced and mussed haired. She could still see the moment of shock that crossed his features when he realized who she was.

The boy returned with her food and set it in front of her. "Enjoy," he said.

She forked a morsel of roast beef, savoring the aroma as she placed it between her lips. Thoughts about the encounter with Malcolm returned. He hadn't seemed very shocked that the outcome of his inquiry turned out to be meeting her again. Or maybe he was just pleasantly surprised. He seemed to be in a bit of a hurry to leave... *Until the mouse episode, that is.* She smiled and broke off a morsel of biscuit. Maybe she should thank the mouse. Because of him, Malcolm had stayed another half hour.

Lucy finished her meal, and Dottie approached her table with a man at her side. "Lucy, since you're new in town, I wanted you to meet Rick Jacobs. He manages The Club. It's sort of an exclusive bar and restaurant for our local police officers."

"Hi." Rick smiled and stuck out his hand. "Nice to meet you."

"Same," Lucy said, clasping her hand in his.

"Here's your bill, sweetheart. Come back and see me." Dottie glanced between them. "I'll leave you two to get acquainted."

Lucy's mom had told her about the police officers special *club* and how they'd removed her dad's photos shortly after the rumors had started. Lucy had wanted an opportunity to check it out.

"I've heard nice things about that place." She smiled up at Rick. "You know, I could use some part-time work. You wouldn't have any openings right now, would you?"

He shook his head. "Sorry, no, but sometimes I need a backup when a waitress calls in sick. Have you any experience in that department?"

"I do, actually. Call me anytime. I'd love a chance to fill in."

"Will do, and nice meeting you," he said.

Talk about providential timing. All Lucy needed now was for some waitress to get sick. And if Rick Jacobs had been around during the time of her father's murder, he might even know something.

CHAPTER 6

The remnants of Dottie's cooking lay in a disheveled heap on the kitchen counter. Malcolm fixed a cup of coffee and headed to the living room. He set the coffee aside, grabbed the Ross file from where he'd set in on the side table and stretched out on the sofa. Time to get more familiar with the case.

Curious as to who wrote the initial report, he checked that first. Officer Charles Nichols—an unknown name to Malcolm. The officer must have either died, retired, or moved away.

The folder contained several photos of the crime scene taken from different angles. The body of Detective James Ross lay on the ground in a pool of his own blood. Malcolm was not unfamiliar with such photographs. Unfortunately, crime photos had become routine for him. One photo in the stack, however, created an acute ache in his heart.

According to the report, while the photographer documented the crime scene, Ross's four-year-old daughter escaped from inside the house and ran across the yard toward the body. The photo was taken just as the child—sobbing—held her little arms open wide and reached for her father's lifeless form.

The heartbreaking moment said it all. The right side of her forehead was matted with blood, and Malcolm assumed that had happened when they fell to the ground together.

He couldn't help but wonder about the child and where she was today. Maybe his next call to his dad would shed some light on what happen to the distraught little girl.

He scrubbed his hand across his mouth and continued to read. He found out Bob Holland had been Ross's partner during that time. According to his interview, Holland hadn't been aware of any wrongdoing by Ross. This was the first mention alluding to the possibility that Ross may have been involved in criminal activity. Malcolm found it interesting that Holland had been the one to bring that to the note-taker's attention.

Except for a few basic facts, there wasn't much to go on —*The black sedan, a masked man who'd jumped out and shot once, then got back into the car and drove away.* Apparently, Ross's wife had been too distressed to check the car tag. According to the report, she'd flung herself to the ground in aid of her husband and her young daughter.

It further stated the tire tracks were used to identify the black sedan, which had been stolen only hours before the shooting. The car had been found the next day on Highway 42. The only fingerprints found belonged to the owner, a local land developer, Alex Crandall, and his wife. Both had been questioned. They had been out of town and their alibi had checked out.

Ross's wife thought she saw a yellow-green Mustang drive by. Where was the follow-up on that? In a town that small, it was likely someone would know the owner. The unusual color would have been clue enough. But the report had no mention of one. Why hadn't anyone investigated that angle? And this case should still be cold, not closed. There remained too many questions for it to be closed.

According to the report, two weeks later, Detective Bob Holland added an amendment describing the evidence found in Ross's home after his death. Videotape from an outdoor camera in town had been found hidden in the back of a dresser drawer that revealed Ross accepting a bribe during a traffic stop.

How convenient.

Anyone visiting the family, including Holland, could have planted that before or after the funeral. That, along with a large amount of money found jammed underneath a mattress in Ross's home, had sealed it in the minds of the department.

As he sipped his coffee, he started a second, more thorough, read-through of the report. He'd developed this habit years ago at the suggestion of his father who had, on more than one occasion, missed something the first time around.

He flipped the page back over to the front of the document. His eyes registered the address. He sat perfectly still and stared. How could he have missed that? The address where the murder took place was the exact property *Just Lucy* had recently purchased. He leaned his head back against the upholstery and stared directly ahead.

"I wonder if she knows." He fingered his chin. "She has to know." Legally, Jan would've been obligated to disclose that information.

He closed the folder and clutched the report in his hands. Even after the second read-through, the report still read incomplete and vague and not at all thorough and what he would've expected for a fellow officer.

Could he reopen the case, or at least change its classification back to cold? Hopefully, he could convince Holland to reopen it, but if he didn't, Malcolm would still conduct his own investigation.

The fact that the property was now occupied might make investigating more difficult, but not impossible. His father had told him to trust no one. Malcolm assumed that included Chief of Police Holland who had been a contemporary of James Ross, and therefore, a suspect as far as Malcolm was concerned.

He realized in that moment, one of the few people he *might* be able to trust was Just Lucy. New to the community, she would have no connection to the murder. Not that he'd bring her into his confidence, but there was something about her he found utterly engaging. Yes, she was a beautiful woman, but it was more than that. For the first time in five years, he wanted to explore a relationship further—see where it might lead.

Maybe she'd be agreeable to letting him take a closer look at the house and property. It would be a long shot, but there were cases when evidence had been found even after many years.

Truthfully, he'd wanted another excuse to spend time with her and would use anything, even a secret investigation into the death of his father's old friend.

* * *

After dinner, Lucy made her way down the side street to her car. Earlier, she'd had to park a bit farther away due to the lack of available spaces at the time. Now, the street seemed deserted.

A noisy clang came from behind her. Heart thudding, she spun around. A man in an apron stooped to pick up a metal trash can, then walked back where he'd come from. Heart still pounding, Lucy blew out the breath and continued on.

Seconds later, the sound of steady footsteps clicked behind her. She glanced back. A man in a hoodie strode with purpose toward her. She quickened her pace, breathing in and out with each step.

A couple walked arm-in-arm from the opposite direction Lucy tensed, sucked in air, then slowly blew out the breath as they passed by.

She again glanced back. The hooded man still headed her way. The couple was still close by, so Lucy stopped and faced the man. He also stopped—right underneath a streetlight— placing him in full view. Her breath caught. He wore a mask similar to those worn at the Policeman's Ball, yet this one fully covered his face.

They stared at each other. Panic welled in her throat. Her hands trembled. Lucy reached inside her purse and clasped hold of her keys. She whipped around and broke into a run.

The street—the trees—everything blurred. Skidding to a stop at her car door, she shot another look over her shoulder. The man strode toward her, unhurried and with purpose, his strides even and methodical. Heart pounding, she unlocked the door and jumped inside.

The engine roared, she pulled from the curb and gunned it. She didn't look back and drove home as fast as she could.

Gravel spewed from her tires as she screeched to a halt outside her house. In seconds, she flew up the steps and stood at the door. She looked behind her. All was silent. Her hands shook as she inserted the key. She quickly unlocked the door and hurled herself inside.

She pressed herself against the wood panels and locked the door. She barked a shaky laugh as she secured the chain. *As if that will keep anyone out.* Hands trembling, she ran to the kitchen and yanked up a chair. She wedged it underneath the door handle.

Hands to her racing heart, she slumped in a heap against the wall just inside the door. The back of her eyes burned. She gulped air and waited for her shakes to subside.

She tried to logically think through the event as she leaned against the wall. No one knew her identity yet, so why would someone follow her? Was it possible she'd just overreacted to the man, the darkness and the empty street?

Sure Lucy, and he just happened to be wearing a mask.

That thought struck a memory. *And he was wearing a scary mask.* In her mind's eye she saw her mom, eyes glazed, saying those words. A masked man shot and killed her father and now, twenty years later, a masked man was stalking her. Was it simply a coincidence?

Not likely.

She covered her face with her hands. When she felt calmer, she pushed herself to her feet but left the chair in place. She walked through the house, turning on all the lights, then fixed a cup of herbal tea and got to work. She removed the article from her purse and pinned it on the corkboard.

It was nearly nine, still early, and plenty of time to tackle more of the piles on the coffee table. Maybe she would be lucky, and find another clue. She'd gone through about a third of the papers, having found nothing more of interest.

She stood and stretched her arms overhead. It was almost ten when she decided to call it a night. On her way to her bedroom, she carried the chair back to the kitchen. After a nice, long shower, she slipped into her pink-and-white-striped shorty PJs and brushed her teeth.

The house went dark.

She gasped and stood perfectly still. Her skin prickled, then crawled. She flipped the light switch. Nothing. Her mind flew to that evening's stalker. Heart pounding in over-drive, she tensed and stared into the dark. Everything stilled. Her breathing became so shallow; she thought she would faint. She ran her hand along the bathroom counter, found her phone, and pressed the light icon.

"Calm down, Lucy—it's probably nothing—just a fuse or faulty wiring." Hearing the sound of her own voice helped.

She left the bedroom and stepped slowly down the hall to the basement door. With her left hand on the railing, she descended the stairs. At the bottom of the steps, she panned light around the space, spotting the electrical panel on the back wall.

She hurried over, flipped open the cover, and checked inside the box. The switches were still in the *on* position. She panned the light left and found a large up-and-down switch in the *off* position. Goosebumps pricked her skin. She quickly pushed it to *on,* and the upstairs lit up.

This had been deliberate. Someone had pulled that main switch to the off position. Which meant someone could still be in the house.

Terror gripped her. Her heartbeat quickened. She froze in place and gathered her composure. With the help of her flashlight app, she tiptoed to the base of the stairwell steps and listened for any sound or movement from above. She glanced left, spotted a crowbar, picked it up and wedged it between her upper arm and her side. With shaking fingers, she dialed 911.

It took over five minutes for the police to arrive. The longest five minutes of her life. At one point, she'd come close to mounting the steps, crowbar in hand, but common sense won the day, and she waited for the authorities.

The wail of the siren brought immediate comfort. Seconds later, someone called her name. Not just any voice, but one with a Scottish accent.

"Malcolm!" she screeched. "I'm in the basement!"

A rush of footsteps, then Malcolm, tall, broad-shouldered and in the flesh, paused at the basement doorway. He wore jeans and a light-blue, collared shirt that he'd rolled up to his forearms. The light from the hallway reflected off the badge clipped to his waist.

He fixed her with his gaze—his face etched with concern. She dropped the metal bar, then ran upward. It took every ounce of self-restraint not to throw herself against that broad chest. Two officers were already searching the house when she got to the top of the stairs.

"Are you okay?" Malcolm grabbed hold of her upper arms. "You're as white a sheet." His eyes narrowed as he searched her face. "Are you hurt?"

"No. But I'm sure someone was in the house. When I was getting ready for bed, the main power switch to the house was shut off. I wasn't sure what to do."

"Show me."

She led him to the basement. Malcolm reached up to pull the string attached to the single light bulb hanging from the ceiling. They approached the electrical box.

"Are you telling me this main switch was in the *off* position when you got down here?"

"Yes. At first, I thought it was just a fuse, but all the switches were still in the *on* position when I checked the main box."

"Okay, I'll have one of the men dust it for fingerprints. It sounds like you're right about the intruder. He got into the house somehow."

"Thank you."

Back upstairs, Lucy excused herself and went to the living room while Malcolm gave several instructions to the officers. His voice matched the man in every way. Simply hearing that deep, masculine, accent allayed all her fears. Whether or not it would last after he and the other officer's left was another matter.

* * *

Lucy sat, huddled at one end of the sofa, bare feet tucked underneath her. Even though fear glistened in her wide eyes, she presented a sweet picture, dressed in the pink-and-white, candy-striped sleepwear. Malcolm fought back the urge to comfort her. If the other officers weren't present, he would take her in his arms right then and there.

He strode across the carpet and stood over her. "You were right to call us," he said. "I'd hate to think of you trying to fend off a prowler with that crowbar. It wouldn't take much for a man to wrestle it from your hands and use it on you."

"Right." She frowned and gave a quick nod.

"You're worried," he said. "Anyone would be after what you've experienced."

She ran her hands up and down her arms. The act obviously made her realize what she was wearing, and she folded her arms across her chest.

He smiled slightly. "Hold on a sec," he said and left the room. Down the hall to the right, he found what looked to be her bedroom. He noticed a pink, fuzzy thing lying over the back of a chair and snatched it up. A moment later, he held her chenille robe out to her.

"Thanks." She shoved one arm through, then the other, belting it at her waist. After she finished, she sat back down. As he took the chair opposite, he spotted what looked to be a suspect board propped against the wall. *What in the world—*

"There's something else I should tell you," she said.

He turned his attention back to her. "Go on."

"I had a scare after I left Dottie's tonight. I thought a man was following me. I hurried to my car and drove home. Do you think it could be related to this?"

"It's possible. Can you describe him?"

"Average height, small-framed, and he wore dark clothes like a jumpsuit one would wear at a service station."

"Hair color, facial hair?"

"It was dark, and he was in shadow." She licked her lips. "That is until he stepped into the light of the street lamp."

"So you saw his face."

She nodded. "Except he was wearing a full-faced mask."

That's not good... Malcolm leaned forward and took her hands in his, giving her his full attention. "I don't want to frighten you, but it's highly possible tonight's break-in is connected to the man who followed you."

"I confess. I'm not too keen on spending the night alone."

"That's already been taken care of. Two officers will be

posted outside until morning—Officers Chase and Simms. One will be parked at the front and one at the back."

"And tomorrow night?" Lucy's eyes gleamed with anxiety.

"Of course, if we feel it's necessary. But you're safe now, Lucy." To help her relax, he gave her a lazy smile. "We'll talk further tomorrow. It's late, and you should get some sleep." He hesitated as he looked down at her. "If you'd like… I can sleep on the sofa tonight."

"Oh. Thank you, but that's not necessary. I'll be fine, knowing the officers are close."

"One more thing." He glanced at the boxes of clutter. "Was anything taken?"

She shrugged, running her gaze around the room. "I don't know. I haven't really checked, but I don't think so."

"Until tomorrow, then. Sleep well, Just Lucy." He strode toward the door, then added, "Officer Chase will be right out front. All the doors and widows are locked. Lock the front door behind me."

CHAPTER 7

Sunday morning, Malcolm arrived at Lucy's house with hot coffee and sausage biscuits for the officers. After hearing their verbal report from the previous night, he sent them home. He mounted the porch steps, then knocked on the front door.

He could hear Lucy unhook the chain and turn the deadbolt. She cracked the door and peeked through the small gap.

"Good morning," she said, fully opening the door.

"Morning. Coffee?"

"I was just about to make a cup for me and the officers." She looked beyond him. "Have they already gone?"

"Yes, I brought them breakfast and told them to go get some rest."

He stepped across the threshold, and she closed the door behind him. "Let's go to the kitchen," she said.

He followed her robe-clad figure down the hallway. Even in PJs and a robe, her face free of makeup, she was lovely. As if she sensed his thoughts, she secured the robe tightly around her waist. "Would you like some eggs?"

"No thanks. I have breakfast for you, too. Unless you don't care for sausage biscuits."

"Oh no, that's fine. I love sausage...and biscuits."

They sat at the small pine, kitchen table and he opened the white sack. "I picked this up at Dottie's."

"Then I'm sure it'll be delicious." She accepted the biscuit, unwrapped it, and bit down. "Mmmm."

For a second, Malcolm simply watched her eat. She seemed to enjoy every morsel of her breakfast, but he found her quiet behavior odd. She hadn't looked at him since she started eating.

Experience told him something more was going on with her. She'd been in town for less than a week, and during that time, she'd been followed and had a break-in. She was definitely withholding something. There was more to her than she'd let on. He'd known it the first moment he'd laid eyes on her at the ball.

"Lucy."

She lifted her gaze to his and wiped her mouth on the paper napkin.

"Is there anything more you'd like to tell me?"

Her green eyes grew wide, then fluttered as she lowered them to her biscuit. She shook her head.

"How about you? Any leads?" she asked, taking another bite of biscuit.

"Still working on it."

Lucy continued to munch her sandwich, periodically pausing for a sip of coffee.

"How'd you sleep last night?" he asked.

"Great. I was out like a light. Amazing how safe one feels with the police on standby."

"Good." He stood. "I have to run, I'm afraid. I have a

full day." He lifted one of his cards from his breast pocket, scribbled something on it, and handed it to her. "That's my cell." He gave her another card. "Now give me yours."

She complied, then handed it back to him.

"I want you to call me if you think of anything else, or if you just need to talk. Okay?"

She nodded.

"Officer Chase will be here again tonight."

"Sure, if you really think it's necessary."

"Chase is looking into several other break-ins in the area, and hopefully, he'll have some good news for us before this evening. If not, I'd feel better if he stayed tonight."

Minutes later, Malcolm sat in his Chevrolet and stared at Lucy's house. He pulled the seatbelt over his chest and snapped it in place. *What are you involved in, Just Lucy? And who the hell is after you?*

* * *

Lucy got dressed for her Sunday morning visit with her mom, her mind on Malcolm. Part of her enjoyed his attention, but the thought he might be getting too close to her purpose for being there, concerned her. He didn't miss much, and frankly, made her a bit nervous.

With a final glance in the mirror, she snatched up her purse and left the house. The hour drive had flown by with the help of an audio book about self-defense. The voice had just described how to break free from masking tape tied around one's wrists, when Lucy arrived at Oak Haven.

Lucy always enjoyed her time with her mom, even heart-breaking as it could be at times. It troubled her to see her mother struggle with her memories.

She and her mom had just finished brunch when her mom presented Lucy with the notebook.

"You remembered," Lucy said.

"I did. There's not a lot in there yet. But I wrote down memories as I recalled them, like you asked." She lifted her hand and touched Lucy's scar on her hairline. "That's healed nicely."

As she lowered her hand, Lucy covered it with her own. "Yes, it has. It's hardly noticeable now."

Lucy turned her attention to the journal. There were just a few entries, and it only took a moment to read through them. Nothing of importance jumped out until the last entry.

She glanced up. "You say here that you were upset about the scar on my shoulder. That *he* hurt me. Can you tell me more about that? Who hurt me?"

"Yes. I remember. He hurt you."

"Who, Mom?"

"You fell and your father took you to the vet."

Bewildered, Lucy shook her head. "A former military person?"

"No, no. The veterinarian."

"Mom, I'm sorry, but I'm having trouble understanding." She gazed at the words on the page. "The vet hurt me? Or Dad?"

"The vet, of course. Your dad would never hurt you. You said to write what I remember. I remember that."

The scar on her shoulder was barely noticeable. It couldn't have been a serious injury. "Why take me to see anyone? Surely a small bandage would have been sufficient."

"James insisted on you seeing a vet—said it was important and that he would explain later." She placed her hand on Lucy's right shoulder. "You cried and cried."

"Did Dad ever explain?"

"No."

Obviously, Lucy hadn't needed a doctor, but why a vet?

"Was this veterinarian in Diamond Creek?"

"I think so, but I can't remember."

"What about the vet's name?"

Her mom shook her head. "I'm sorry."

"It's okay." Lucy held up the notebook. "This is good stuff. What you told me is a little confusing but helpful." Lucy smiled to temper her words. "Keep writing what you remember."

Maybe after more entries, Lucy would be able to get a clearer picture of past events.

With that information, she drove back to Diamond Creek, perplexed about the conversation with her mother. Why on earth would her father take her to a veterinarian for a small wound on her shoulder? That didn't make any sense. No doubt, she was missing something.

Lucy got home midafternoon. She grabbed a bottle of lemonade from the fridge, kicked off her shoes, and settled in at the kitchen table. She opened her laptop and did a search for veterinarians in Diamond Creek and the surrounding area. Fourteen were listed area wide, five of which were in Diamond Creek. She'd check out the local ones first, then go from there.

She grabbed a notebook and organized them by convenience to her house. She doubted the original vets were still in practice after all those years. If they'd already retired, hopefully, they were still living in the area and most importantly, alive.

She'd done all she could for now, and tomorrow she'd start calling the list. Currently, she wanted to continue with her search through the bits and pieces still laid out on the coffee table. There were several more letters to read. What she'd read so far were of little value to her search.

She wasn't sure when Officer Chase was to arrive, but her plan for that afternoon was to visit Mr. Crandall. If his car had been used in the murder, then maybe he might have some answers for her. She planned to visit him before it got too late.

She drove to Lark Avenue and cruised along until she spotted three-twelve on the mailbox. She pulled to a stop and shut off her Subaru. The home was very nice and what one would imagine belonging to a wealthy developer.

White columns and a wide porch ran across the front of the large, red-brick home. A lush, green lawn blanketed the yard, and well-maintained gardens skirted right along with the green hedges that bordered the house. A curved, stone walkway drew her to the front door.

Taking in the beautiful flowers, she ambled to the front door and knocked. No one answered. *Hmm...* She stepped right and peered into a front window. Except for some low lighting, all was dark inside.

She glanced around the area. Figuring the coast was clear, she walked around the right side of the house and looked into another window. It was fairly dark in there, too. Clearly, no one was home. In her haste to find the man, she'd forgotten to ask Dottie if Crandall had any children. Maybe he was visiting one of them.

Lucy pushed through a decorative iron gate and made her way to the back of the house. The place was eerily quiet. She walked up the stone patio steps and knocked on the back door. Under-counter lights glowed from the kitchen, other than that, the place looked empty.

A separate garage stood a short distance away. She crossed the well-trimmed lawn and tried the door handle. It was locked, too. She peered in the window to the door's right and sucked in air. It couldn't be? A classic, black car sat in the middle of the building. It was exactly like the one in the video. That had to be the same one used in her father's murder.

She considered breaking in at that moment, but the risk of discovery during daylight prevented her. The police would've checked the car out years ago, so it probably wouldn't lead to anything, anyway. But the temptation to break in—to inspect the car for herself was too tempting to ignore, and she might never get another chance like this. She decided to return after dark and break in then.

That night, as Lucy approached Crandall's backyard gate, a blinding light hit her square in the eyes. She quickly covered her face with her left hand against the piercing glare.

"You're under arrest for trespassing," an officer's voice boomed. "You have the right to remain silent. Anything you say may be held against you—"

"Please." Lucy stopped him. "I can explain." Her heart sank to her stomach.

A second later, the officer spun her around and put her in handcuffs. "That's what they all say, ma'am."

"You're making a mistake," she pleaded. "I was merely looking for someone."

"A neighbor reported a person casing the home and property for more than ten minutes." The officer pulled her along to his vehicle.

Lucy huffed out a breath. "Can't you just give me a warning this time?" she said as the officer put her into the back of the squad car.

Twenty minutes later, Lucy sat across a metal table from the arresting officer.

"I'm Officer Kirby," he said, "and I'll be asking you some questions. We have a witness who saw someone matching your description trying to enter the house on 312 Lark Avenue earlier today. The same property where we just picked you up."

Malcolm walked in and stopped midstride. *No, not him!* He gaped, fixed her with a stare and frowned. Heat burned her cheeks, as she locked her gaze with his. *Oh gosh.* She lowered her head and lifted her hand to the side of her face.

"What do we have here, Kirby?" Malcolm asked.

"This evening we arrested this woman trying to enter the house on 312 Lark Avenue. Say's her name's Lucy, but refuses to give us her last name."

"What about her driver's license?"

"Say's she's left it at home."

"I see." Malcolm folded his arms and leaned against the back wall, studying her.

She flicked her gaze to his, then quickly lowered it.

"Continue, Officer Kirby."

Groaning inwardly, Lucy sat, head down, clasping and unclasping her hands.

"Why were you trying to break in?" Kirby asked.

Still refusing to look up, Lucy gnawed her bottom lip and shifted uncomfortably in her seat.

Officer Kirby leaned forward. "Where were you between five and six?"

Lucy slowly lifted her gaze to Malcolm's. "Kindergarten."

Malcolm smothered a smile, and Officer Kirby, flustered, reared back, pressing his lips together.

Malcolm pushed away from the wall. "I'll take it from here," he said before Kirby managed to speak again.

"Yes, sir." Kirby seemed only too happy to relinquish her to Detective Knox.

Malcolm pinned Lucy with a meaningful look that said she had some explaining to do.

Lucy stared up at him and swallowed.

He took the chair the officer had just left. "I must say... this *is* a surprise. I did hope to see you again, but not here in my interrogation room." He placed his left hand on the edge of the table and leaned slightly back. "Let's dispense with the smart-mouth comments, shall we? I have a few more questions I'd like answered."

Lucy fidgeted in her seat.

"Who are you? No more games. Tell me, *now*."

"I've already told you, it's Just Lucy."

Malcolm leaned forward, placed his fingers on the report, and turned it toward her. "Says here you were trespassing. Is that true?"

Lucy clasped her fingers together and glanced right.

"Maybe a night in a cell will encourage you to a more co-operative state?"

She still refused to answer.

Malcolm stood, stepped over to the door, and opened it. "Officer Kirby, take Miss... Lucy to cell two."

Lucy lifted her gaze to his. "Okay, fine."

"That will be all, Kirby." Malcolm gently closed the door and sat back down.

She licked her lips and swallowed. "Would you repeat the question?"

"Were? You? Trespassing?"

"Maybe." She shrugged.

"Confessing so quickly?" He arched a dark brow and gave her a lazy look. "It's amazing how the threat of jail opens up communication."

"There's nothing to confess. I was...okay...fine." She rolled her eyes heavenward. "I was on someone else's property, but since when is it a crime to walk up to someone's door and knock?"

She tossed her hand toward the document on the table. "That's just the rantings from some ol' busy-body who should learn to mind her own business." She folded her arms across her chest with a thud.

He rested one arm on the back his chair. "Except, according to this..." He picked up the report with his right hand and tossed it over to her side of the table. "You did much more than that. Specifically, *jiggling door handles and trying the windows.*"

"I was...thorough."

"Were you looking for someone in particular?"

"I was looking for Alex Crandall. An old friend of mine told me to look him up."

"And just who is this friend?"

She dropped her gaze and ran her finger along the table edge. "Dottie. Dottie told me about him."

"Oh, your *old* friend of twelve hours, Dottie." He braced his forearms on the table. "What gives you the authority to search someone's property?"

She lifted her chin. "If you must know, I'm a private detective in training."

He raised both brows and sat back. "You're kidding, right?"

"Nope. It's true."

He stared at her in raw disbelief, then an amused twinkle

filled his eyes. "So, you have a master's degree in criminal justice?"

"No. I have a Masters in Education. And believe me, the eye-opening experience I just received working with high school boys may as well be classified as criminal justice education."

"So that's your criminal justice experience? Working with high school boys for what...a semester?"

She rubbed her wrist and gave him, look-for-look. "I'm studying a book if you must know."

"A book."

"Yes. *How to Become a Private Investigator*. It's a career guide of sorts."

"And you have a legal document proving this course is legitimate?"

"No, I don't. I'm in training."

He rubbed his finger across one eye. "Let me get this straight...you moved to this sleepy, little Southern town and started investigating an elderly man?"

"Maybe."

"I see." He tapped a finger on the table. "Why this Cran-dall fellow?"

"His name came up in my investigation. Alex Crandall is my first lead. Dottie told me where he lived. I knew the street, but I didn't know the house address."

"And just what are you investigating?"

"Sorry, that's private."

"You have a client?"

She sucked in a deep breath. "Yes. I have a client who wishes to remain anonymous."

"And you won't tell me who it is?"

"Nope. That's why it's called *private* investigator," she said.

For what seemed an eternity to Lucy, Malcolm sat and gnawed the inside of his lip. He leaned his elbow on the arm of his chair, pressed his fingers to his eyes, and then stood. "Come with me. Now."

"Are you locking me up?"

"I should be locking you up, but no, I'm taking you home. Do you realize Officer Chase is at your house right now, thinking he's protecting you, while you're across town, in the dark, playing some game pretending you're a private detective—and putting your life in more danger. Have you forgotten someone broke into your house last night after you were followed, no less?"

She stared at the floor, shuffling from one foot to the other. She lifted her gaze to his. "I'm sorry."

Malcolm bristled with what she could only call, *pent up anger*, at her stupidity. She had to admire his self-control and wondered if that was why he'd stopped his interrogation so abruptly.

"I should absolutely lock you up—for your protection, if nothing else." He spun and yanked open the door. "Let's go."

He waited for her to step around the table, then placed his hand firmly on her elbow and led her out of the room into the hallway. She hesitated at the door, peeking right, then left.

He followed her gaze. "Who are you trying to avoid?" He tilted his head sideways and eyed her.

She swallowed, licked her lips, and shook her head. "No one."

"Your actions say otherwise." He kept his eye on her as they walked down the hallway to the front entrance. They passed the photo wall of officers who'd died in the line of duty. She slowed her steps and gazed at the photographs. Malcolm also slowed, matching his steps to hers.

"Officers who died in the line of duty," he said.

"I know." Except one was missing. And no matter what it took, she'd see to it that her father's photo would end up hanging next to the others.

* * *

Malcolm led Lucy toward the exit. As he did so, Chief Holland pushed through the front door. In one lithe movement, Lucy jerked from his hold, spun behind him, then quickly stepped over to a rack of brochures.

"Detective, you're working late," Holland said.

From the corner of his eye, he noticed Lucy lift a brochure from the metal rack. "Just finished and on my way home, sir."

"Good. Enjoy your evening." Holland stepped around him and continued down the hall.

Lucy was back by Malcolm's side in a flash, casting an anxious glance behind her. "Can we go now?"

For a split second, he stared at her, then down the hall to where Holland had gone. It seemed when Lucy disappeared behind him, so had her bravado. Her panic-filled eyes said plenty. Was she afraid of Holland? Or was there someone else she was trying to avoid? Could it be the person she'd searched for at the ball?

He eyed her flushed face, grabbed hold of her arm, and didn't release her until they stood beside the passenger door of his Chevrolet. "Get in."

Without speaking, she did as she was told. For the first full minute, neither spoke as he drove her home.

"What was that about?" he asked.

"Sorry?" She scratched the side of her head. "You'll have to be more specific."

"Your sudden interest in the brochure rack."

"I don't know what you're talking about."

"I haven't known you long, but I recognize a lie when I hear one." He glanced at her profile. "Who were you trying to avoid back there?"

She shrugged and continued to stare out the side window.

He ran his hand over his bearded chin, deciding to try a different tactic. "As we walked through the foyer, I couldn't help but notice the intense way you examined the officers in the police station. Who are you looking for, or should I say, trying to avoid? Is it the chief? Because it's obvious you weren't the least bit interested in that brochure."

Lucy pressed her chin against her right hand—the tip of her pinky finger resting at the side of her mouth.

Malcolm tried another approach. "Does it have anything to do with who followed you and broke into your house?"

Silence.

He snorted and shook his head. "Why are you really here?"

She turned slightly and looked at him. "I could ask you the same question."

"And I'm certain my answer would be quite different from yours."

"I don't know about that. I'm observant, too. I've noticed things about you, as well." Her pretty lips formed into an adorable pout.

"Please, enlighten me." At the next block, he signaled, then turned right.

"The night of the Officer's Ball, you weren't forthcoming about your status in the community...or should I say... the police department."

"That's true, but then I'd noticed your secretive nature from the moment I laid eyes on you. My instincts told me to reveal very little."

He pulled to a stop in front of her house. "As much as I'd like to continue this discussion, we'll save it for another day. I'm tired, and I'm sure you are, too." He put the gear in park. "But rest assured, I *will* get answers to my questions."

The look on Officer Chase's face when he saw Malcolm pull up with Lucy would've been comical, except for the circumstances.

After they exited the vehicle, Malcolm took hold of Lucy's arm and walked her to the door.

"Officer Chase. Please note... I have brought *Miss* Lucy home and she is not to leave this house anymore tonight. I'm holding you responsible. Is that clear?"

"Yes, sir."

CHAPTER 8

Malcolm arrived home just before midnight. He tossed his keys on the entry table and strode to the living room. He picked up the James Ross file and flipped the page over. "Alex Crandall. I knew I'd read that name somewhere."

Who are you, Just Lucy. Why are you investigating this man, and why are you afraid of Holland?

She was no detective. So, she must be there on behalf of the Ross family. But why buy the house?

He texted Jan...

Please call me in the morning.

I have a question regarding the sale of the old Ross property on Maple Road.

His phone buzzed. He answered, pressed *audio,* and set the phone on the coffee table. "Jan."

"Hey Malcolm, what can I do for your at this ungodly hour?"

"You didn't need to call me this late." He sat on the sofa and braced his forearms on his knees. "Tomorrow would've been fine."

"No worries. I'm up. What do you want to know about the property?"

He grabbed a pen and paper. "Who bought the place?"

"It was purchased by Carmichael Family Trust."

He scribbled the name. "And the young lady's name who moved in?"

"Lucy Carmichael. Her aunt is the executor of the trust."

After he hung up, Malcolm poured himself a bit of Jack and sat back down. *Wasn't Carmichael Ross's wife's maiden name?* He'd have to ask his dad to be sure. Maybe Lucy was Ross's niece and came there to find some answers for the family.

Lucy had obviously figured out that Alex Crandall was the owner of the black sedan...but how? Without access to the report, she must have found something else. Another document, or a newspaper article from one of those boxes, or maybe she'd talked with Ross's widow.

The clippings in that one box had looked old. He could imagine James's wife keeping any and all articles and documents pertaining to her husband's murder. Malcolm sipped on Gentleman Jack, wondering what other leads might be in that house.

He tapped the top of the report with his index finger, then checked his watch. Six hours difference between there and Edinburgh. It was early overseas, but he texted his dad in case he was already up.

A message dinged on his phone thirty seconds later.

Fixing coffee. Will call in ten.

Ten minutes passed, and his father called him.

"Good morning, Dad."

After a few pleasantries, Malcolm got to the point. "I

wanted to update you on James Ross's murder. I have the file, and you were right to be concerned. After reading through the report, it's my opinion the case was definitely rushed and closed much too quickly—with way too many unanswered questions. I wanted to see if you could clear up a few things."

"I'll do my best, Son."

"Do you recall if James had a niece?"

"I don't think so. James had no siblings, and Cara, his wife, did have a sister, but as far as I know, she never married."

"According to the police report, James had a daughter."

"That's right," his dad said.

"There's a heartbreaking photo in the file of his little girl sobbing, reaching for his dead body."

"That's awful." Malcolm could hear the disgust in his dad's voice. "Why in blazes would they take such a picture?"

"The report said she ran from the house and practically dove across the body as the photo was snapped." He took a sip of whiskey. "I have no idea why they left it in the file, except it says a lot. Maybe that was the point."

"Their daughter was a cute little thing—with a head full of dark curls. They sent photos in their Christmas cards each year before James's death. Lucinda was her name."

Malcolm froze. "Do you recall her full name?"

"Yeah, it's Lucinda Carmichael Ross."

"Bloody hell."

"What? Son, are you okay?"

"She's here doing her own investigation."

"Is she a cop?"

"No, she's a bloody nuisance." *And completely and utterly adorable.*

His father laughed. "A wee scunner, is she?"

"Indeed, she is." He blew out a heavy sigh. "I need to get some rest. It's been a long day. Thanks for the call, Pop. You have a good one."

"Will do, Son."

So. Just Lucy was James Ross's daughter. Her stealthy actions and desire to remain incognito made sense. At this time, he'd keep that knowledge close to his chest, until he was ready to reveal to her that he knew. Then tomorrow, he'd pay a visit to Crandall—gather his own leads—ask to take a look inside his garage and see if the black sedan was still there.

Malcolm propped his feet onto the low coffee table and took another sip of liquid gold. He rested his head along the back of the sofa and rubbed the pulse at his temple. Even during his short time there, he'd heard the rumors that James Ross had most likely taken bribes during his time with the department and the phrase, *dirty cop*, more than once when referring to Detective Ross.

Malcolm's father had refused to believe that, and so apparently, had James's daughter. No doubt, she'd heard those rumors, too, and now, having grown up, had come to set the record straight.

The stalker and the intruder had to be linked to her investigation. She was in danger, and it had become clear to him that those first two incidents were merely to frighten her away. And if she didn't leave, they could get a lot worse.

In a day or two, he would confront Just Lucy with what he'd learned about her identity. At least, he now knew what had happened to the heartbroken, distraught little girl in the photo.

CHAPTER 9

Monday afternoon, Officer Chase tapped on Malcolm's doorframe.

Malcolm glanced up from perusing a file. "Come in."

"Hey, Detective," Chase said, "I wanted to let you know Malvern County Sheriff's Department caught the two guys responsible for the recent break-ins. Their investigation has video of both of them on Walnut Street in Hot Springs the same day and time of Lucy's break-in."

"Okay. Thanks."

Malcolm lifted a hand to his chin. *So. If it wasn't either of those two men, then who in blazes broke into Lucy's place?*

Malcolm took the rest of the afternoon to finish up some overdue paperwork, then left the precinct at five-thirty. He headed across town to Lark Street. He hoped to interview Crandall before stopping at Dottie's for a hot meal.

Malcolm arrived and parked on the street in front of Crandall's house. He got out of his car and made his way up the curved walkway. It appeared no one was home. He knocked on the front door, anyway. When no one answered, he walked around the back. After checking the premises, he made his way next-door to the neighbor, introduced himself, and asked if she knew if Crandall was out of town.

"Yes," Mrs. Beauchamp said. "He travels frequently with his business, and I always keep an eye on his place for him. He told me he'd be gone for a week, maybe two."

"And when did he leave?"

"Day before yesterday."

"Thank you, ma'am."

Since Malcolm wasn't supposed to be working this particular closed case, he'd give it another few days, then come back. He glanced at his watch. In the meantime, it was time to pay Lucy a visit.

On his way, he stopped by Dottie's, had dinner, and then drove over to Maple Road. As soon as he turned into her driveway, he could tell she wasn't home, either. Lucy's car was gone and her outdoor lights were on, a sure signal she wasn't home, not only to him, but also to whoever wanted to hurt her. He walked back to his car, making a mental note to speak to her about that.

Back in his car, he sat quietly and stared ahead. Where could she be? He tapped his index finger on the dashboard, and light slowly dawned. *She wouldn't*—he shook his head —*yeah, she would, too.*

If he'd learned anything as a detective, it was to trust his instincts. Instinct told him Lucy had gone back to Crandall's to break into his garage. He hadn't known her long, but long enough to know being hauled in for questioning would not deter her.

Twenty minutes later, he arrived outside of Crandall's residence. Lucy's car was nowhere in sight. *In sight*, being the key phrase. He drove down the block to see if she'd parked farther away and sure enough, she had.

He pulled up beside her powder-blue Subaru and spotted the UA Little Rock sticker on the back windshield. He'd noticed it before and assumed that was her alma mater. Satisfied it was hers, he parked in front of her car and walked back to Crandall's.

He carefully entered the property. The last thing he needed was Mrs. Beauchamp calling the police again. He did not want Lucy back in jail being questioned. *He* would deal with her.

A minute later, he spotted Lucy. She was dressed all in black and crouched before the garage door, trying to pick the lock. *At least this time she'd dressed for the part.*

Curious, he waited to see if she could do it. After a long thirty seconds, he decided to approach her. He stepped across the mowed lawn with the stealth of a leopard. He waited until he'd gotten about six feet away before he spoke.

"Just what do you think you're doing?"

Lucy gasped and jerked her head back. Her hand stilled, hovering over the door handle, the lock-picking device still in place. She didn't move but continued to gawk up at him.

He stepped closer. "You do realize I can arrest you for this?"

She placed her hand over her heart and stood. "How did you know I was here?"

He smiled and leaned against the garage wall, and in that moment, he made the decision not to reveal that he knew her identity. "In the short time I've known you, I've found you to be quite predictable."

"If you were going to arrest me, you would've done so already." She squared her shoulders. "I've gotten this far, and I'm going in. Arrest me, or come with me."

"I would need a warrant."

"By the book, I see. Where's your sense of adventure?" She flung out her hand. "Look around you. No one's here."

"And that makes breaking and entering legal in your eyes?"

Ignoring him, she squatted before the handle and continued picking the lock. He reached forward and grasped her wrist. The door cracked opened.

"Look, it's unlocked." She inhaled sharply and widened her eyes. "Oh, no. Did you hear that? Someone's in trouble." She didn't wait for his response, but pushed the door open and sauntered in.

Malcolm glanced around the dark yard, thankful for the moonless night. Against his better judgment, he followed her and carefully closed the door behind him.

Lucy was already putting up black plastic bags over the small, upper windows of the garage door. She was in the process of ripping strips of wide gray tape to keep the plastic in place.

"You could help me instead of just standing there," she said. "The sooner we get this up, the sooner we can turn on the lights and have a look at this car."

He moved forward and helped secure the plastic. "You learn this trick in your detective book?"

"Nope. It's pure common sense. Mrs. Nosy Neighbor is probably watching."

"Heaven forbid," he said.

Once done, he stepped back to the door and flipped the light switch. After the pitch darkness, they both blinked against the brightness.

The garage was clean, like a showroom with its black-and-white checkerboard flooring. Cool, vintage car posters hung on the walls—the perfect showcase for Crandall's classic vehicle.

Lucy moved toward the car. As she did so, she removed a folded piece of paper from her pocket, which looked like a newspaper article. "*The 1970 Cadillac Coupe DeVille, identified as the car used in the—*" She abruptly stopped reading and frowned at him.

"Go ahead and say it, *Miss Ross...* the James Ross murder."

Her eyes widened, and the color left her cheeks. "You—You know?"

He nodded.

She lowered the article. "For how long?"

"Since last night."

Her initial shock morphed back into her normal bravado. "Sure took you long enough." She shook her head, making her rich, dark hair gleam underneath the garage lights. "Some detective you are. I was beginning to doubt your investigative skills. I even contemplated loaning you my book."

The right corner of her mouth lifted in a half smile. "How did you find out?" she asked.

"This is a small town," he said, not ready to reveal his father's connection to hers, "and that's a very famous case. I wasn't here a week before some of the older officers told me about it."

"So, after all these years, there are *still* rumors," she said. "Seems the black mark on my father is alive and well in the Diamond Creek Police Department."

The dark pain in her voice spoke volumes. That news hurt her, and he could understand why. He thought about his detective father and the pain it would cause if the world believed Stuart Knox had been a dirty cop.

She licked her lips. "Where was I?" She looked back at the article. "*The car used in the James Ross murder was found twelve hours later on Highway 42.*"

Malcolm ran his gaze over the classic vehicle. According to the police report, this was exactly the car the shooter used that day. And it was in mint condition. He stepped to Lucy's side and slipped the article from her fingers, scanned it, then handed it back. "What are you thinking now?" he asked.

"The car's in excellent condition," she said. "Probably detailed recently. It smells citrusy, like lemon."

Malcolm nodded. "Crandall has obviously taken care of this classic vehicle. Scotland never had cars like this."

"I'd say this is the same car. What do you think?" She nodded at the black sedan.

"It's obviously the same car that's described. And what I think is that we need to leave. *Now.* We've pushed the limits as it is. It's time to go."

"One more minute, then we'll go."

"Fine." He huffed out a sigh. "So, what are you planning to do with this information?"

"At this point, I'm simply gathering clues."

When she finally glanced up, he smiled at her from across the top of the car, then glanced at his watch. "What does your detective-in-training book say you should be doing next?"

"Dust for fingerprints, which isn't necessary at this point. Although, the gorgeous detailing could suggest he's covering up something more recent."

"Why? According to your article, he's not the perpetrator. So what does he have to cover up? He could just be a man taking care of a beloved, classic car."

"Right." She pressed her fingers along her forehead at her hairline. "I guess the *next-next* thing would be to take pictures as I continue building my case." She slipped her cell phone from her back pocket of her jeans and began doing just that.

Malcolm folded his arms and observed her. The heartbreaking picture of the distraught four-year-old, and her small, bloodied face, formed in his mind's eye. The trauma she experienced in that moment must be what drove her. Unsatisfied with the results of the DCPD investigation, she was determined to find out for herself.

Lucy was meticulous as she shot the driver's side, taking photos of the front, close-ups of the left side as well as the left front wheel.

"And just what are you going to compare those pictures to? There's no photo here in the paper."

She looked down and to the right. "I'm not sure yet."

She's lying.

She snapped a few photos inside the driver's side, then opened the back door and took a few more. She moved methodically in and around the black sedan.

She entered the driver's side, sat down, then closed the door. She lowered her gaze from the windshield, placed her hands at 10:00 and 2:00 on the steering wheel, and glanced at her watch. She inhaled, opened the door, stepped out, and lifting her right hand, shot once with her thumb. Then she hopped back in the car and slammed the door, then looked again at her watch.

She'd timed it. He held his breath and eyed her. For a second she sat there, knuckles white, gripping the steering wheel. He could only imagine what went through her mind at that moment.

As he watched her, the photo of the toddler—distraught —crying—reaching for her father—filled his thoughts.

She'd just reenacted what she believed had happened on that traumatic day when her father had been murdered—exactly what had been described by her mother in the police report.

Her expression clouded, settling on her lovely features, to be replaced seconds later by one of resolve. She opened the door, got out, and looked right at him.

"Now we can go."

Where had Lucy been between all those years ago and now? Malcolm really wanted to know and not just as a detective.

He walked Lucy to her car parked behind his.

"So that's how you knew I was here." She pressed unlock on her key fob and turned toward him.

He stuffed his hands into his pockets and stared down at her. "I'm going to ask you a question I want you to answer honestly."

She licked her lips and gave him a tentative glance. "Okay."

"Have you come back to Diamond Creek to do your own investigation into your father's death?"

She lowered her gaze and slid the toe of her sneaker along the asphalt. "Yes."

"Listen to me. I want you to leave any investigation into his death with the police. For your protection, you need to stop investigating. Is that clear?"

"That's not fair." She lifted her chin and boldly met his gaze.

"I mean it. No more investigating."

"How can I not?" Her gaze shifted to one of appeal. "How can I move on with my life without knowing who killed him and why? How can I live in this town, suffer the dark looks, the pitying glances of those who think my father was a dirty cop? How can I ever—?"

He lifted a hand. "I can only imagine how you must feel—"

"Twenty years ago it was left with the police," she argued. "And you can see how well that turned out."

"I do understand, but tonight was a one-off. Whatever it is you're trying to accomplish, you must go about it legally. I catch you breaking and entering again, and I will arrest you. Is that understood?"

She drew in a deep breath and nodded. "Understood." She opened the car door, then turned back to him. "I'm going to miss having you call me, *Just Lucy*. I rather liked it."

"It or the anonymity?"

She shrugged. "Both, I guess."

There was something about the way she stood gazing up at him, with the warm light from the street lamp shining on her upturned face and her slightly parted lips. Her sparkling eyes revealed a combination of apprehension and anticipation. He wanted to kiss her. She didn't know it, but she'd always be *Just Lucy* to him.

* * *

Lucy was too excited to go to bed. After she'd gotten home, she uploaded the photos of the black sedan into her computer and printed them out on photo paper. She pinned one on the corkboard next to the article. She'd snuck in a shot of Malcolm while he had focused on the hood of the sedan. *That* photo, she set aside.

She retrieved the handheld video camera from the bureau drawer, flipped open the side viewing window, and pressed play. She fast-forwarded the tape, stopping it at the car.

She gnawed her bottom lip and pressed the forward arrow. She watched each frame of the tape click by—pausing it to compare the image on the screen with her photographs. It was definitely the same vehicle. Of course, the police had confirmed that years ago, but it was important she do so, as well.

At the remaining seconds of the tape, she hit pause on the killer's shoes. They were mostly black with a white, center strip. One of her college professors wore that exact shoe every day to class. His were solid brown, but they were the same shoe style.

She rewound the tape and stopped play right as the camera filmed the feet of the man just having stepped from the car.

She reached for her laptop and typed *men's lace-up shoes* in the search bar. Pages of men's footwear filled the screen. Way too broad. To narrow down the search, she typed in, *men's two-toned, leather lace-up shoes. Wingtip* popped up. She took a screen shot and saved it on her computer.

She watched the video again, stopping at the shoes, then compared those on the computer with the ones on the video. They were the same. *Wingtip*. According to her search, mostly worn by men and occasionally, by women. Maybe she should consider a woman as the shooter.

It was so hard to be certain. Twenty years was a long time, and the tape wasn't digital. Suddenly weary, Lucy fell back against the sofa and closed her eyes.

She thought about Malcolm. Why hadn't he arrested her that evening for breaking and entering? When he caught her, she thought she was done for. Instead, he'd teased her and actually entered into her little adventure.

At first, she'd thought it odd that he hadn't asked her what she had been looking for. It was as if he knew. But when he'd said her father's name, then she understood. He *did* know. It was unfortunate his information came from the ugly lies and rumors about her dad. What he'd heard from the department gossips was all one-sided, not the truth at all.

But that hadn't seemed to bother Malcolm—almost as if he was open to another scenario—like he'd been on her side in all of this. Without even knowing what her side was. Or was it simply his way of telling her she could trust him?

More than once, she'd been the recipient of Malcolm's intense, and at times, amused glances. Was this some sort of game to him? Diamond Creek *was* rather dull. Was she simply entertainment—a sideshow to escape the small-town monotony?

She sat up and grabbed the photo of Malcolm and attached it to her board. Not so much as a clue to the murder, but to something she had yet to figure out. How did he fit into this puzzle, this maze she'd entered? Would he help or hinder her?

More importantly, why was a detective, the caliber of Malcolm Knox, really there?

She looked again at her corkboard and all the empty space that was left for her to fill in. She didn't know how she would do it, but she would find more clues and fill up that board until it led to some answers.

CHAPTER 10

After spending Tuesday morning in court, Malcolm stopped by Dottie's and ordered one of her famous BLTs to go.

"You keep coming here like this, and you're gonna have to buy stock in this place," Dottie said.

Malcolm laughed. "And it would be an excellent investment, too."

Twenty minutes later, he sat at his desk and scarfed down his sandwich as he contemplated his next move.

The Ross case file seemed to mock him as it sat unopened on his desk. He'd pretty much exhausted all the clues inside. It was time to come at this from a different angle.

Whether Lucy knew what she was doing or not, she'd obviously stumbled on some information the report didn't contain.

Since her arrival, she'd been the target of some mischief. Was it the result of her snooping? If so, she'd gotten close to something, but what?

Alex Crandall was a developer. Maybe the connection was the property—Griffin Gate. Could there be something more to the place other than an old house and twenty-seven dusty acres?

He decided to email Jan and see if there was anyone in her office that had worked there twenty or more years ago. He let her know that he had a few questions that might help with a case he was working on.

While he waited for her response, he considered the issue. Alex Crandall had been a developer in Diamond Creek for many years. Crandall's car had been used by the shooter to kill Ross. Even with an alibi, was it likely Crandall could still be the connection?

The message bell dinged from his phone. It was from Jan.

Dave Franklin, the owner of the agency, would be happy to see you. How is tomorrow at 2:00 p.m.?

Perfect! Malcolm typed.

Malcolm arrived at Franklin Realty promptly at 2:00 p.m. on Wednesday. The rain predicted in that morning's forecast started to fall just as he stepped from his Tahoe. He made a mad dash from his car to the entrance, shaking off the wet as he stepped through the door.

A few minutes later, a tall man, somewhere in his late sixties, shook Malcolm's hand and invited him into his office.

"Have a seat," he said.

"Thanks." Malcolm briefly took in the caramel leather, polished brass, and dark wood as he chose a leather club chair.

"I'm just having my afternoon lift." Franklin held up a coffee mug. "Would you like a cup?"

"No, thank you." Malcolm crossed his legs and sat back. "I appreciate you seeing me today."

"Not a problem at all." Franklin sat down on the plush sofa opposite Malcolm. "What can I do for you? Jan said you had some questions?"

Malcolm nodded. "I'm looking into an old case regarding something that happened twenty years ago."

Franklin took a sip of coffee. Keen interest lit his eyes. "How intriguing. What kind of case is it?"

Malcolm hesitated. He didn't want to give more information than necessary, but since he came for information, he decided to be frank. "Homicide."

"Homicide? The only murder I can recall happening around that time was that of Detective James Ross." He shifted in his chair. "Is that who—"

"Yes."

Franklin lifted his eyebrows. "I can't imagine how I could be of any help."

Malcolm clasped his hands together and leaned forward. "During that time, do you recall if anyone tried to buy James Ross's property?"

"That's rather broad. Is there anyone specific you have in mind?"

"Alex Crandall."

"Ah yes, our esteemed developer. He's tried to buy a good many places in this town over the years. People around here like to keep their homesteads. As a result, Alex shifted his interests to several other surrounding towns in the area."

"But to your knowledge, he never tried to buy Griffin Gate?"

Franklin fixed Malcolm with a stare. "Alex Crandall is a very...influential member of our community and one which I prefer not to aggravate."

Malcolm sat back. "And you're afraid to rock his boat, is that it?"

"He's a powerful man around these parts, but I'm not afraid of him. Do you think he's behind the murder of Detective Ross?"

"I'm not at liberty to say any more than I already have," Malcolm said.

Franklin lifted his mug and brought it to his lips. Malcolm was good at reading people and their actions, and Franklin's said plenty.

"I understand your hesitation," Malcolm said. "Anything you say to me will be kept confidential."

Franklin lifted his eyes to his. "Twenty years ago, Alex Crandall approached me as a last resort to convince Ross to sell his property. Apparently, he'd been hounding Ross for months, and I guess Alex thought I'd be able to sway Ross to change his mind."

"But you didn't."

"That's correct. Crandall even went so far as to try and get the property through eminent domain. I'd heard for years that Crandall paid off his share of city officials to get what he wanted. Thankfully, two members of the city council voted against it."

"Did Crandall give you any reason why he wanted the property so badly?"

"I believe it had something to do with building a country club on the outskirts of town. I can't quite recall all the details, but Crandall had already bought up some of the surrounding land and needed one or two more pieces to have enough for the club."

Franklin stood and carried his coffee cup to his desk. "When it fell through, Crandall cut his losses and sold the other properties. He was quite angry about it, too. At the time, it seemed to me there was more to wanting that land than he'd let on."

"How so?"

"He'd gone after property before and never had that drastic of a reaction to losing one," Franklin continued. "In the end, he built a second home and his country club in the next county."

"Do you have that address?"

"I do." Franklin retrieved it from his phone and wrote it on the back of his business card. "There you go."

"Thanks." Malcolm held up the card. "How far of a drive would this be from his house here?"

"Thirty—forty minutes, at most."

"So why keep his house on Lark?"

"Probably because his offices are still here."

"I see." Malcolm stood and shook Franklin's hand. "Thank you for your help."

"Anytime."

* * *

Wednesday afternoon, Lucy stood at the entrance of Diamond Creek Police Department. She'd put off seeing Chief Holland long enough. She took her narrow escape the other night as a warning, and decided it was best to see him on her own terms—let him be the one surprised.

She mounted the steps of the large, stone-and-brick building and pushed through the heavy glass-and-oak door. The trim around the doors and baseboards were a dark oak, and Lucy figured it had looked just like this when her father worked there.

She took a deep breath and thought about that. She was seeing it the way he saw it—pushing through the same door—walking the same halls. She shoved those thoughts aside and passed the front desk, then entered the hall on the left. About halfway down, she spotted the words *Chief of Police,* on the door. She lifted her fist and lightly tapped the solid wood.

"Come in."

Lucy turned the handle and entered his office. Dark, oak paneling ran along the lower half of the walls and off-white stucco on the upper half. Bob Holland sat perusing some document on his desk. Even though she'd seen him at the ball, her fear of recognition had made her keep her distance. At the ball, she'd missed that dappling of gray at his temples. And he'd certainly put on weight since she and her mom left twelve years ago, but his face was still recognizable, as was his crew cut.

"May I help you?" he said.

Here goes... Lucy smiled. "Hello, Uncle Bob."

His eyes widened, and he stood to his feet. "Lucy?"

"It's me." She nodded. "In the flesh."

He stepped around the desk and put his hands out to hers. She grabbed hold, giving them a slight squeeze. He shook his head. "My, my, little Lucy Ross is all grown up."

She smiled a bit broader and again nodded. "*You* haven't changed much, though."

"Ha!" he laughed. "Thirty pounds heavier, I'm afraid."

"You wear it well."

"Flatterer. Please sit and tell me what you've been doing the past few years." Uncle Bob took the chair next to hers.

Lucy knew her mom had kept up with him until her accident. "Finishing my Masters in Education, doing my best for Mom, you know, just regular old, everyday kind of stuff."

"Hardly everyday." He grew more serious. "That's much more than most young people your age have to deal with."

"Thank you."

"How is your mother?"

Lucy sat up straighter. "The doctor says she's getting better, but truthfully, I haven't noticed much change in the past several months. She seems to have plateaued."

"I'm sorry to hear that." He leaned forward and patted her hand. "So. What brings you to town? Are you visiting?"

"Nope. I've actually moved back into Griffin Gate," she said, eyeing him to see how he'd react.

His eyes widened, and he sat perfectly still. Her words had stunned him. A brief moment of shock flicked across his features, then just as quickly, morphed into one of pleasant surprise. "And I'm just *now* finding out?"

"I know. I should've come sooner, but I've barely made a dent sorting through everything in the attic and basement. I've never seen so much stuff. That and with all the rain, I haven't done much except rummage through boxes, clean shelves, and try to make the house livable for Mom."

"You have been busy. And I know Cara loves that place. Diamond Creek was her home for many years. I'm sure she'll be happy to come back."

"It's all she talks about, really. And I'm hoping the familiar surroundings will help restore some of her memories."

"What about you? Wouldn't you rather live someplace more exciting?"

"Maybe...someday." She shrugged. "I have years, yet."

"In the meantime, do you need a job? I've some influence with the school board. There could be an opening at the high school, if you're interested?"

She shook her head. "Grandpa Carmichael left us well

provided for. I won't need to find a job for at least a year or so."

"Well, if you change your mind, I'd be happy to introduce you to the high school principal, Jeff McClure."

"I'd actually love that at some point." She shifted in her seat. "My first priority right now is Mom and her health and happiness."

"And do you have a second?" His eyes narrowed with shrewdness.

"Astute as ever, I see," she said.

He smiled with fatherly affection.

Lucy clasped her hands together in her lap. "I think it's time I know more about what happened to my father."

"I see." He nodded.

"Would you let me read his case file?"

Uncle Bob gave her a commiserating look. "I can't do that, Lucy."

"Then, I'll just have to look it up online."

"And you'll find it won't be there," he said.

"Why? I'm twenty-four years old and I'm ready for some answers. I *need* answers."

"Surely your mother has shared what she knows with you."

"Just the facts of what she witnessed, but she doesn't know what you've discovered in your investigation. That's what I'd like to know. What did you find out? What were your leads? Where did they take you?"

He lifted a hand, silencing her. "We did everything we could to solve the case—followed every lead and then some, until they led nowhere."

"Except to the false conclusion that James Ross was a dirty cop—that he abused his position and his authority."

Lucy's gut churned. Her heart pounded. This was all so wrong.

"Trust me when I say, it pained us all when our investigation led to that."

"Then you should've searched further."

Chief Holland fisted his hands and braced his forearms on the arms of the chair. "Lucy, we found a roll of five thousand dollars hidden underneath his mattress. We have a video of him accepting cash from a driver he pulled over. Your mother knows this, even though I tried to keep those facts from her as long as I could."

"I don't believe it." She stared at his resigned features. This crime was all in the past for him—all over and done with. She felt sick.

They sat in silence.

She sucked in a ragged breath. "And the murderer?"

"I know you want closure—"

"The man who shot and killed my father is still out there!"

"And we exhausted every lead until they went cold."

"I didn't know my father, but Mom did, and she told me he would never have abused his position. He was a good and honorable man."

"I agree with you."

"Then why accuse him of being a dirty cop?" She threw her hand toward the door. "There should be a photo of him out there on that wall! Honoring him. Showing everyone who enters this building that he died in the line of duty."

"I'm sorry Lucy, I really am. But the evidence and the facts told us otherwise."

She squeezed her hands tightly in her lap and hung her head. "Then you leave me no choice but to conduct my own investigation."

"And if you do, you may find yourself in a lot of trouble." He unclasped his hands and sat back. "My darling girl —leave it alone."

How strange to hear him use that endearment, and after so many years of silence. Even the tone in which he said it lacked genuineness, completely rubbing her the wrong way, especially in light of their current discussion. Malcolm had remarked that Bob Holland wasn't seen as a celebrity in the precinct, and maybe this was why. If he acted this way to everyone, why would anyone like the man?

"To dredge up the past now," he went on, "would only end up hurting you and your mother."

"Do you think looking into my father's death will somehow put me in danger?"

"Of course not. I'd just hate to see you get hurt, that's all." He spoke in a quiet voice, eyeing her with slow calculation as if gauging her response to what he'd just said.

The room suddenly became uncomfortably warm—a strange sensation, considering how much she'd loved this man during her childhood.

Lucy shot to her feet. "I mustn't keep you. I just wanted to let you know I was back and ask your help with my father's case."

"And I would, if I thought it would change the end result." He heaved himself from the chair as he spoke, then gave her a big hug as if the previous conversation hadn't happened—as if all were back to normal.

"Don't be a stranger, young lady."

She stepped back, putting distance between them, and nodded. "I guess I'll see you around. Give my best to Mrs. Holland."

"I sure will," he said.

When she got to the door, she turned and waved. He lifted a hand, then refocused on the paperwork at his desk.

Lucy closed the door behind her and released a breath. She rubbed the goose bumps along her arms and made her way to the exit.

She paused on the front steps as the wet drizzle slowed to a stop. The sun broke from behind a dark cloud, and she lifted her face to the rays streaming down from the sky. Just standing in the soft light after the weirdness of the past few minutes, calmed her. She stood, breathing, until the dappled sunlight and the smell of rain helped put the last few minutes in perspective.

She was simply reading something nonexistent into his words. *I just have the heebie-jeebies, that's all.* Who wouldn't after being followed and broken in to? Bob Holland was old-fashioned and by the book. He'd meant well and his refusal to allow her to see the case file was just an extension of his fatherly protection over the years.

She clipped down the steps and crossed the parking lot to her car.

She buckled up, started the ignition, and then pulled out of the lot. Next on her list was a visit to Franklin Realty and Jan Kelly. She had been meaning to bring Jan a gift since the closing.

She turned right on Main Street and crept along behind a John Deere tractor going about ten miles an hour. She took advantage of the slow-moving traffic to get a good look at the quaint downtown. The curbed walkways, old-fashioned streetlamps, and the well-preserved wood-slatted buildings with their gabled roofs still held the charm of the late 1800s.

Up ahead, as she approached the real estate company, a

black Tahoe was just leaving the premises. As it disappeared in the distance, she wondered if it was Malcolm. A minute later, she pulled into the designated customer parking spot for Franklin Realty costumers. After shutting off the ignition, she lifted the gift out of the ice chest on the passenger seat and got out.

Jan was sitting at her desk when Lucy walked in. After another few seconds typing on her computer, Jan lifted her head.

"I come bearing gifts," Lucy said.

Jan sat, eyeing the three-tiered chocolate cake Lucy placed in front of her. "Oh, my gosh, that looks amazing."

"It's nothing." Lucy shrugged. "Just a little thank you for all of your help."

Jan stood and placed her hands on her hips. "Do you know what this is like?"

Lucy grinned. "I'm not exactly sure what you're getting at so why don't you tell me."

"This is like bringing Jack Daniels to the home of an alcoholic. You do realize that a sugar addiction is far worse than that of alcohol?"

"Oh, dear." Lucy gave a look of mock horror. "What do you suggest?"

"I suggest, we hurry up and have a piece before I change my mind."

Jan procured the plates and forks from the kitchen, and Lucy cut two generous portions of cake. She served Jan first, then herself.

Jan closed her mouth around a large piece and sighed. "Heavenly." She forked another bite, and her face radiated utter pleasure. "What do you think of our Scottish detective? I'm assuming you've met him by now."

"I have." Lucy licked the end of her fork and nodded. "I met him at the Police Officer's Ball."

"You just missed him. He had a meeting with the owner."

So that was *his car.*

"What do you think of him?"

Lucy's mind went to the night in Crandall's garage and figured it was best to keep her answers generic. "He's very handsome...you know, in a rugged sort of way."

"I think it's the beard." Jan scraped up a small bit of icing with her fork. "I'm not much for beards, but I like his because he wears it short."

"I agree. On him it's perfect." Lucy sighed and forked another piece. "And his earthy, brogue accent is to die for."

"Yep. Not too much and not too little."

"Definitely swoon-worthy," Lucy added.

Fifteen minutes later, Jan placed her hand to her stomach. "That was *the* most delicious cake I've ever had."

"I'm glad you enjoyed it."

Jan took Lucy's plate and fork, stacked it with hers, then set them aside on the credenza. "So what's up? Surely you didn't drive all the way into town to bring me a cake."

"I did actually, but now that you mention it, I could use your help with something else."

"Shoot."

"My mom's in assisted living in Little Rock, and I'd love to get her closer if possible. She had a brain injury about three years ago and needs extra care right now. Since the cleanup on the house is taking longer, I was hoping to find a facility I could move her to until I can get the house ready. I've found two in the area, but I have no idea how reputable they are. Since you know a lot of people in town, I was hoping you could ask around for me?"

"Of course. Where are they?"

"One's in Pine Bluff, and the other is in Hot Springs."

"Hot Springs is less than thirty minutes from here. That sounds ideal—distance wise." Jan tore a square piece of paper from a pink floral writing pad and wrote down the towns mentioned. "I know three families that have loved ones in similar circumstances. Give me a few days to get back with you."

"Wonderful. Thank you so much, Jan. I'm planning to see her on Friday, and I didn't want to bring it up again with her doctor until I found something closer."

Lucy's spirits rose as she left. Having her mom a short distance away would be so much better than hauling back and forth to Little Rock several times a week. Her only concern was convincing Dr. Edwards.

Two days later, Lucy enjoyed tea and cake with her mom in Oak Haven's restaurant. Unfortunately, it was a short visit, but Lucy left her mom happily chatting with three other ladies sitting at their table.

Lucy hugged her mom goodbye, and made her way to Dr. Edwards' office for their appointment. After some pleasantries, she told Dr. Edwards her idea.

He leaned forward and clasped his hands on top of the desk. "I completely understand you wanting to have your mom closer. But you're only talking about a matter of weeks here. At this time, I feel it's more important to consider your mother's well-being. Before you make such a significant change, you need to consider a few things.

"Will she be comfortable in a new environment, with new staff, and a new doctor? She's settled in a routine here, and I'm making good progress in her sessions. Why disrupt that now? Take another month or so to get the house ready. It doesn't have to be perfect, in fact, why don't you think of some ways Cara could contribute? Having her help might be good for her."

Lucy left Oak Haven a bit disappointed but with the knowledge Dr. Edwards was right. What would another month hurt? And his idea that her mom took part in a few of the renovations made absolute sense.

As she left the home, Lucy began making a mental list of some of the ways her mom could contribute.

While in town, she planned to have the unusual stone she'd found examined. Having spent the last twelve years in Little Rock, she was somewhat familiar with Rose Hill Jewelers on Gable Avenue. A few minutes later, she parked in front of Rose Hill's charming storefront, then exited her car.

She stopped for a moment and gazed at the variety of jewelry displayed in the bay window. The milky-brown stone she carried in her purse looked nothing like the perfect jewels presented there. She pulled the brass handle at the entrance and stepped inside, breathing in a hint of lemon polish as she walked over to the counter.

A middle-aged woman glanced up at Lucy's approach and smiled. "How may I help you today?"

Lucy withdrew the stone from her purse and placed it on the black felt pad stationed at the counter. "I found this on the ground behind my house. I have no idea what kind of stone this is. From the looks of it, I can't imagine it has any real value, but it's pretty, and I thought I might have something made out of it—a pendant or even a ring."

The woman picked up the honey-brown stone and held it in front of her face. She then placed a magnifier to her eye for a closer inspection. "I'm not the expert, but it could be a golden beryl, or possibly a diamond. Our stone expert, Paul Keenan, is on vacation, but if you could leave it, he'd be able to make a positive identification when he comes back next week."

The woman placed the stone back onto the felt. "I agree with you, real value or not, this stone is rather pretty, and once it's cleaned, cut, and polished, it should make a lovely pendant."

Lucy filled out a form with her contact information and left the stone with the promise that Mr. Keenan would call her in a week or so. Her phone buzzed as she pulled her seatbelt in place. "Hello."

"Lucy, Rick Jacobs here."

"Hey, Rick."

"One of my waitresses called in sick. I know it's last minute, but I could use your help tonight at The Club. You still interested?"

"Yes."

"Great. Wear a black dress and heels. Doors open at seven, so get here at six. I'll have the rest of what you'll need...and thanks."

CHAPTER 11

Malcolm opened the passenger door to his Chevy and held out his hand to Evelyn Sanders. She placed her well-manicured hand in his, planted her black heels onto the asphalt, and stood. Without releasing her, Malcolm led her to the entrance.

Their relationship wasn't at all serious—which suited him perfectly. Especially since Evelyn had made it clear she felt the same. She was lovely company and the perfect nonserious date.

For years, The Club had been home to area police officers and only occasionally visited by local clientele if accompanied by an officer. After opening the door, he placed his hand to Evelyn's back and led her through.

The floor-to-ceiling, hand-carved ornate bar held court over the entire room. He'd learned the semi-dark interior, wall sconces, and dark oak paneling hadn't changed in seventy-five years and gave him the feeling of home. The warm, low lights of the interior reminded him of a Scottish gentlemen's club.

The place was already packed, just like every Friday night. The Club host greeted them, then led them to their table near the center of the room.

They'd just taken their seats when Malcolm spotted Lucy on the other side of the restaurant. *What the devil is she doing here?* After his initial shock, he realized she was one of the waitresses. He had no idea she'd gotten a job there. She may have been dressed to serve tables, but she was intently cruising the photos of police officers that lined the wall toward the bar. As he watched her, she made a furtive glance over her shoulder, then quickly removed a small photograph.

Malcolm turned to Evelyn. "Excuse me a moment."

"Of course." She picked up the menu and began studying it.

He threaded his way around each table and carefully approached Lucy from behind. When he got closer, he tapped her on the shoulder. She spun around and stared up at him with those remarkable green eyes of hers.

"I hope you're not doing what I think you're doing," he said.

She exhaled and placed a hand to her chest. "You startled me."

"You'd better have a good reason for being here."

She lifted her chin. "I'm working. Not that it's any of your business."

He glanced at the empty spot on the wall, then gave her a meaningful look.

"It's true," she persisted. "Rick Jacobs called earlier today. One of his waitresses got sick and he needed help." She lifted her right shoulder. "You can ask him."

"Don't worry, I plan to." He eyed the photos on the wall behind her. "Who are you looking for?"

"You actually, but I don't see you anywhere. Don't you rate a wall photo?"

"Nice try." Malcolm held out his hand, palm up, and continued eyeing her.

Several long seconds went by. Lucy reached into the apron pocket, pulled out the photograph, and placed it in his hand. He gazed at the three men in the photo and focused on the face of the man in the middle.

"Who are these men?" he asked.

"The one on the left is Chief of Police Holland. Of course, he's much younger there."

Malcolm gazed at the man's face and nodded. "And the man in the middle?"

She shrugged. "Haven't a clue."

"And the one on the right?"

She lifted accusatory eyes to his. "I'm sorry, is that a trick question?"

He crossed his arms and fixed her with a stare. "I never ask trick questions."

"You know exactly who it is. It's my father, James Ross."

"Then why take the photo? Surely you have others."

"I was just looking at it."

"In your pocket?"

She rolled her eyes. "Don't you have a date or something to get back to?"

He did actually. "This conversation is not over." He turned on his heel and snaked his way around the tables back to his seat. The sooner he questioned Jacobs, the better he'd feel. Lucy was still investigating, and he didn't like that one little bit.

"So." He smiled at Evelyn and picked up the menu. "What looks good tonight?"

* * *

Of course, Malcolm would be there. Why hadn't she realized that earlier? Lucy slipped her cell phone from her pocket, then quickly snapped a picture of the photo, now back on the wall.

Upon arrival, she'd taken some time to peruse the walls of memorabilia throughout the club. There wasn't one photo of her father except for the one she'd had in her pocket. Had they missed this one when they took his pictures down—thinking he was a dirty cop?

Before her mother's injury, she'd told Lucy that photographs of her father were all over The Club. Ever since Lucy had arrived in town, she'd wanted a reason to be there, an excuse to come.

Earlier, as she searched the walls, it became more and more clear that Detective James Ross had been erased. How could Uncle Bob have allowed that to happen? Even after her conversation with him, she wondered why he hadn't spoken up for her dad—quelled the rumors that he had been involved in something nefarious.

There had to be an explanation for the video and the wad of money—he had to have been set up. If anyone should have come to her dad's defense it should have been Bob Holland.

When Lucy turned fifteen, she'd asked her mom why they'd left Diamond Creek. "So you would never hear the awful rumors about your father," she'd said.

The fact that her father was not in one picture amongst the hundreds hanging in The Club told Lucy it was much more than rumors with these people. They actually believed them.

She'd come to this town to find out who'd killed her dad, but now she had another mission...clear his name.

"Lucy, would you clean up table five, then take the order for the couple at seven?" Rick said. "This place has suddenly gotten busy."

"Sure thing. I'll get right to it."

After Lucy deposited the used dishes from table five, she dried her hands, then made her way to number seven—Malcolm's table. And it looked like his date was the same blonde from the Policeman's Ball. She was quite beautiful, but were they an item? Even though the woman was seated, she looked tall, a nice complement to Malcolm's six-foot-*plus*-inch height. Her coco-brown dress was simple, but elegant, and her makeup, perfectly applied.

Lucy approached the table with a smile, her order pad in her left-hand, and a pen in her right. "Good evening, Malcolm. How lovely to see you." She thought it best to act as if they hadn't had that run-in along the memorabilia wall.

She turned to the blonde. "Welcome to The Club. Is this your first time visiting?"

"No." A warm smile lit up her face. "I've had the pleasure of being here several times."

"Lovely. I see you've already had your drinks taken care of." Lucy's glance included both. "Any questions about the menu or today's specials?"

"We're ready to order." Malcolm gestured to the menu. "The lady will have the salmon special with the sauce on the side, and I'll have the ribeye—medium rare—with a Caesar salad."

Lucy scribbled everything down. "Excellent choice." She noticed Malcolm had already finished his water. "I'll send someone with more water for you."

She stepped over to the table next to Malcolm's. "Can I get you gentleman anything else?"

"Nothing, thanks." The ruddy-faced man sat eyeing her with blatant regard. "What's your name, sweetheart?" Obviously, the man had had one too many.

"Lucy."

"Lucy what?" the man slurred.

She caught Malcolm's eye. "Just Lucy." She smiled. "If there's nothing else, I'll get your bill."

Near the end of the evening, Rick moved Lucy from the floor to behind the bar. She stacked a set of clean tumblers on the counter along the wall, then stepped over and stood beside him.

She leaned her forearms on the bar top and studied him as he poured a shot of whiskey for the man seated to his left. Rick looked to be about forty-five and had managed to keep in shape over the years. He was a friendly man, and Lucy found herself drawn to him. Had he lived, her father would've been just a few years older than Rick. She ran her finger along the countertop and glanced at Rick's profile.

"You've been here a long time, haven't you?"

"I sure have. Started here as a waiter in my early twenties. Today, I manage The Club and run the bar."

"I bet you've seen a lot of cops come and go." She shrugged. "I mean, being a small town and all, I wouldn't think there's much room for advancement."

"That's true, I guess." He grabbed a cloth and started wiping the top of the bar. "It all depends on what a body wants. Some guys prefer to be in a sleepy town, and others want the big city. It's preference, really."

"This town doesn't seem to be the kind of place that would have a lot of crime," Lucy said.

"Diamond Creek has had its share. Don't think it hasn't." He folded the towel in half and moved his hand in a circular motion along a different spot.

"That sounds intriguing." She picked up a wet tumbler and twirled a cloth in and around the glass, then picked up another one and did the same. "Got any stories to tell?"

Rick gazed straight ahead and brought his fist to his chin. "There was this one incident about twenty years ago. A cop was murdered—a detective. I'd barely gotten to know the man when he was killed." Rick shook his head. "It was a sad day around here. But it got worse when the rumors started."

"What kind of rumors?" Her heart thudded.

"I'm not a cop, so I'm not privy to the details, but apparently, this officer was up to no good—had gotten involved in some shady dealings."

At Rick's words, her throat tightened, and a sudden pain weighed heavily against her heart.

"They never found out with who, and the case was never solved," he added.

"What was his name?" She held her breath.

"I don't recall, but his photo is over there."

Her heart sank. Rick couldn't even remember her dad's name.

"Come... I'll show you."

She followed him to the photo she'd tried to steal.

"That's him." Rick tapped his index finger on her father's chest.

"Sounds like you liked him, though...at first."

"Everybody liked him. I guess that's what made it so shocking." He shook his head and stared at the photo. "Discovering that about him was a sucker punch for sure. He was the last man you'd think would go bad."

"If that's how everyone felt about him, then why is his picture still on the wall?"

"It was left as a reminder—if it could happen to him—it could happen to anyone."

CHAPTER 12

Saturday, it was all Lucy could do to crawl out of bed. After the previous night's discovery, sleep evaded her. Tired of staring at the ceiling, she'd gotten up at 2:00 a.m. and took way too much melatonin. She didn't wake up until noon and felt drugged from the large dose. Still groggy, she turned to her side and nestled into the pillow.

Until her talk with Rick, she hadn't realized the extent to which the police department had despised her father. Even though she had no memory of him, it grieved her just the same. And when it got out that his daughter was back in town—to stay—then what? Would she be run out of Diamond Creek? Shunned?

When she felt more rested, she sat up, threw her legs over the side of the bed, and stood. A few minutes later, she cradled a hot cup of coffee in her hands. She took a sip, then slipped out the back door onto the patio. After testing the seat cushion for dampness, she sat down and took another drink.

Not sure what to expect when she'd arrived at The Club,

she been delighted at the warm intimacy of the place. The officers and the other guests had treated her as a newcomer with kindness and support. They were salt-of-the-earth people who'd unfortunately tried to erase her father's history with the department by blackballing every photo of him from the memorabilia wall...except for one. And they left it only to remind the other officers to mind their p's and q's, to do the right thing, and to beware the dark side of dealing with criminals.

Lucy had actually enjoyed her time there until Malcolm arrived on the scene. And of course he would be the one to catch her pocketing the photo. He'd assumed she had more photos of him, and she did, but none in his uniform.

She'd been surprised at Malcolm's presence, for no other reason except he didn't seem to fit in with the rest of the officers. He was different, and it wasn't just his mesmerizing accent. He seemed to be more perceptive than the other officers she'd met, and even more astute than Chief of Police Holland. He had become slothful in his appearance. Maybe he'd taken his position for granted. He seemed to have very little interest in disturbing the status quo.

She brought the mug to her lips and gazed across the patchy, dirt-and-grass yard, her mind back on Malcolm. Maybe it was the old-world charm of The Club that he enjoyed. The aged wood and brass fittings probably resembled the bars and pubs back in Scotland. Did he miss his homeland? Could there be a special girl waiting for his return? It seemed unlikely, as his attendance to Evelyn was one of keen interest.

Lucy had covertly watched the couple throughout the evening. They'd chatted amiably and seemed to smile at the appropriate time throughout their conversation. She'd observed all of this from a distance, and there were moments she'd like to have heard what he'd said to her.

They looked to be about the same age and seemed like the perfect couple. At twenty-four, Lucy had yet to experience the attention of a man like him. Her dates had always been close to the same age as herself. College students.

She'd been attracted to Malcolm from the minute he'd asked her to dance at the Policeman's Ball. Considering his position, he was at least eight to ten years older than her. Having just finished her master's degree, some would say she hadn't really started living.

She took a sip of her coffee, now cold, tossed what was left on the ground at her feet, then went back into the house. The clock said it was lunchtime, but she fixed eggs anyway, along with bacon and wheat toast.

While she ate, she opened her laptop and continued her search for area veterinarians. There were several, and none looked any more promising than the others. She bookmarked three, closed the laptop, and decided to work in the yard the rest of the afternoon.

Lucy dropped to her haunches and began pulling weeds in the flowerbeds along the back patio. There were masses of them, but the soaked earth made pulling them easy. Her navy shorts, white blouse, and a baseball cap kept the afternoon sun at bay. Most of the zinnias had started to bloom, their large pink, orange, and red floral heads adding masses of color around the patio.

"Luucyy!"

The cry came from the front of the house.

"Around back!" she hollered.

Lucy waved as Jan rounded the corner of the building. Jan approached, dressed in a white, sleeveless dress and matching flat pumps with a neat little straw hat covering her head.

"You must be off to sell a house," Lucy said.

"I have a three to five open house."

"Love the hat," Lucy said.

"Thanks." Jan fingered the brim, giving it tweak. "What are you doing?"

Lucy sprinkled tiny granules along the base of the plants. "Trying to grow flowers, but the weeds are having none of it." She smiled. "Seems to be a losing battle."

"Can't you hire someone to do that?"

"I could, I guess. But I like working the ground and growing things."

"We're expecting more rain later today and lots of it, so that should help." Jan held up the blue willow plate. "I'm returning your cake holder."

"Just put it anywhere," Lucy said.

Jan set it on a patio chair, then joined Lucy by the flowerbed. "These zinnias are gorgeous."

"And the only flower that seems to flourish here." Lucy swiped her damp brow with the back of her glove.

"True. Zinnias can grow in anything. Perfect plant for those of us without a green thumb."

Lucy stood and peeled off her garden gloves. "I've tried other plants without success. I think the problem is the soil. It's the worst. Except for this...look." Lucy pulled one of the opaque nuggets from her pocket. "I keep finding these. I have about ten, so far. What do you think they are?"

Jan took it from Lucy's hand and held up the dark, honey-colored stone to the light. "I think it's a diamond, rough of course, but I'm pretty sure that's what it is."

"That's not the color of a diamond."

"Diamonds come in a variety of colors." Jan handed the stone back to Lucy.

"You said that rather nonchalantly."

Jan laughed. "It's not unheard of around here. I only know a bit about them because Diamond Creek is near Murfreesboro—the home of Crater of Diamonds."

"The what?"

"It's a state park. We went a lot during my childhood. Seems the making of diamonds has something to do with volcanic soil that's thousands of years old."

"You're kidding?" *I can't believe I don't know about this place.*

"Nope." Jan took a few steps around the yard, spreading her shoe back and forth along the damp earth. "This looks a lot like the soil in the park. Probably one of the reasons you're having trouble growing your flowers."

"Are you saying I'm sitting on a diamond mine?" Lucy glanced at the stone in her hand with renewed interest.

"It's possible, but don't let that excite you. The one in Murfreesboro was discovered in the early 1900s. After the initial excitement, they later learned it didn't produce much. Eventually, it closed, and now it's a state park and open to the public."

"Can people search for diamonds there?"

"For a fee, yes. And they can keep whatever they find. Lots of stones have been discovered over the years, some quite valuable. And who knows, you may find something special here, too."

"A couple of weeks ago, I found a beautiful stone about twenty feet from here." Lucy gestured to the right. "I took it to a jeweler in Little Rock. I want to have a pendant made for my mother. I haven't heard back from him yet, so I have no idea if it's valuable."

"Well, if it's anything like the one you showed me, I'm sure it'll be stunning."

About twenty minutes later, Jan waved goodbye, and Lucy went back to the weeds and flowers. It was close to five when Lucy called it a day. She headed inside for a well-deserved shower and to make a few phone calls before dinner.

After talking with each clinic, only one of the three agreed to see her the following week. The veterinarian, Dr. Ted Billings, had an afternoon opening on Wednesday and agreed to see her at 2:00 p.m.

Lucy fixed a big salad, adding prepackaged, baked chicken strips on top. She ate in the living room so she could study her suspect board. "I know. I still have lots of work to do and clues to figure out," she said to no one.

Lucy didn't mind her times alone. As an only child, she'd had to learn to like being by herself and had developed a habit of talking out loud. She smiled, thinking of the sweet little tabby cat she'd had during her childhood and teen years. Poor Button had endured loads of one-sided conversations with Lucy.

She sat on the sofa, propped her feet on the coffee table, forked a mass of fresh greens, and shoved them between her lips. An idea struck her as she munched her salad and perused the board. But it would have to wait until tomorrow afternoon after she visited her mom. Plus, she was beat. Between her previous short night's sleep and hours of yard work, she just wanted to go to bed.

* * *

Since Malcolm had arrived in Diamond Creek, he'd worked every other Sunday, and today was his Sunday off. A good day to devote some quality time to the Ross case.

He'd been meaning to check out Curbside Classics. Apparently, they'd been in the area for many years and might know something about the yellow-green Mustang. Of course, it had been years ago, but if they were as good as he'd heard, they might have a record of a sale. The color alone should be a clue as to the date and model of the car.

He pulled into the car lot to a barrage of colorful, helium-filled balloons dancing from ribbons tied to most of the cars on display. A one-story, red-brick building, with double-wide glass doors and a red-and-green striped awning sat in the midst of the classic vehicles.

Malcolm had barely set foot on the asphalt when an eager-faced man approached him.

"Hi, Ed Friendly, here." He stuck out his hand and Malcolm took it. "Looking for something special today?"

"We have Mustangs, Torino's, Chevrolet's," Ed continued before Malcolm could answer. "And if you don't find what you're looking for, then we'll find it for you."

Malcolm ran a hand over his chin. "Thank you, but I'm not—"

Lucy strolled from the dealership office beside a pleasant-looking young man. Her presence stopped Malcolm in mid-sentence. The man led Lucy in the opposite direction from Malcolm and Ed.

Malcolm lifted a finger. "Excuse me one moment."

Malcolm followed Lucy and the salesman across the lot to a white Mustang. As Malcolm got closer, he stopped beside a powder-blue Chevrolet and did his best to eavesdrop.

"Now this, Miss Carmichael, has your name written all

over it." The young man flashed her his boyish grin. Malcolm shook his head. *She's using you, man.*

"Sorry, Ralph, but this won't do, I'm afraid," Lucy said. "The white is nice, of course, but my heart is set a particular color—a pretty yellow-green. I believe that color was only on the 1970 Ford Mustang Coupe."

The young man shook his head.

"Twenty years ago, someone in Diamond Creek bought a car just like that one," she said. "You wouldn't have a record of such a purchase, would you?" She smiled sweetly.

"I don't know." Ralph scratched his head. "That's way beyond my time."

Malcolm slipped back to where he left Ed and flashed his badge. "Sorry, but I'm here looking for information. Let's go inside your office."

Ed's jaw dropped. "I-um-well. Of course, Officer." Once Ed recovered from shock, he led Malcolm inside the brick, single-story building. Malcolm rolled up his sleeves and followed Ed into his office.

He'd heard how hot the South could be in the summers there in the States and fully appreciated stepping into the crisp, cool air-conditioning.

"How can I help you?" Ed said.

"I'm looking for information about a 1970 Ford Mustang Coupe. It's a yellow-green color, and I understand that was the only year that color was used."

Ed had already started typing Malcolm's description into his computer. "I pulled up the car, but unfortunately, we never had one like that in all the years we've been open. Have you checked with the surrounding towns?"

"I haven't." Malcolm shook Ed's hand. "Thanks for your time."

Malcolm leaned against his Tahoe, feet crossed at his ankles. He stuffed his hands into the pockets of his jeans and
watched Lucy approach with Ralph. They were still too far
away for him to catch their conversation, but when Lucy
bubbled a laugh at something Ralph had said, the man actually blushed.

Dressed in soft lemon-yellow slacks and a white, silky-
looking, sleeveless blouse, Lucy appeared cool and collected.
Her low, strappy heels and her hair twisted up in some loose-
looking fashion, she presented a picture of wealth and so-
phistication. Malcolm marveled at how she always seemed to
dress for the part she was playing.

She spotted him against his car and froze. Her reaction to
his presence made him smile. He lifted a hand, waved, and
continued to watch her. She turned to Ralph and said something to him, making Ralph's goofy smile vanish. After one
single shake to his hand, she left him staring after her.

Lucy sauntered up to Malcolm and stopped a few feet in
front of him. "Good afternoon, Detective."

"Afternoon." He looked beyond her. "You interested in
that Mustang?"

She shrugged. "Maybe."

"You buying or trading in?"

She folded her slender arms across the front of her silky
blouse. "I'm thinking about it. And you? Aren't you tired of
driving everywhere in that police-issued Tahoe?"

"It suits me for the time being. It's unmarked, and as
long as I stay within my jurisdiction, I'm encouraged to use
it." He pushed off the car. "What's wrong with the white
Mustang? Color not to your liking?"

She tapped those pretty strappy shoes on the asphalt.
"Are you following me?"

"No. I'm as surprised to see you here as you are to see me."

She reached up and hitched her purse strap over her shoulder.

"So." Malcolm quirked his eyebrow. "What'd you find out from Romeo Ralph? He doesn't look at all pleased to having lost a sale."

"Nothing, but I'm sure you flashed your big, bad, badge and found out plenty."

He gazed at her stubborn features and decided to let her keep guessing. Maybe if she thought he'd discovered something, she'd leave things alone.

"Well?" She planted her fists to her hips. "Did you?"

He folded his arms and gave her his best, 'I'm the detective and you're not,' look. When that didn't move her, he lifted his had to his mouth, pretended to lock his lips, and then threw away the key.

She rolled her eyes and stomped off in the direction of her Subaru.

CHAPTER 13

Wednesday arrived, and Lucy was anxious to finally meet Dr. Billings. She knew going in, she shouldn't get her hopes up. It was unlikely he'd have answers for her, and it would frankly be a miracle if he did.

It was a thirty-minute drive to Hot Springs, and Dr. Billings' clinic was about an hour or so from Little Rock. That would give her plenty of time to make her appointment with Dr. Edwards at noon, then grab a bite of lunch on her way to Hot Springs.

She chugged down a protein shake at 11:45, then headed to Oak Haven for her appointment with Dr. Edwards. Traffic was light on the way into town, and she arrived with plenty of time to check in on her mom.

Wednesday was her mom's bridge day. Lucy checked the card room first and found her mom dealing. Lucy never cared for cards, but her mom loved it. After a brief hug and a quick introduction to the other three players, Lucy waved goodbye and headed to Dr. Edwards' office.

"How did you find your mother?" Dr. Edwards asked.

"Happily playing bridge."

He laughed and nodded. "That's right, today is her bridge group."

"So. How is she doing? Interacting with her earlier, no one would know she'd suffered memory loss."

"Cara's progress is very good, and I have hopes for a most, if not a complete, recovery."

"That's great news." Lucy folded her hands in her lap and smiled.

"And what about you?" he asked. "Since you've been back, has anything about the house or Diamond Creek jogged your memory about those early years with your father?"

She shook her head. "Nothing yet."

"It may only take one thing, one object, to open up a locked memory. It's important to be patient. You haven't been back long. These things take time."

"I understand."

"You're not worrying about it, are you?"

"I don't think so."

"Good.

"But this is something kind of neat." She pulled several of the sparkly stones from her purse and held them palm up.

"Very pretty." He reached across the desk, selected one, then held it to the light. "This reminds me of the stones you can find at Crater of Diamonds in Murfreesboro."

"That's twice in a matter of days. A friend of mine just told me about that place."

"I've taken my twin boys there several times," he said. "Where did you find these?"

"On my property."

"Seriously?"

She nodded. "I found a lovely one right after I bought the house. I left it with Rose Hill Jewelers. They're making a pendant out of it for Mom."

He placed the stone back in her palm. "Lucy, one or more of these could be valuable. You should have them examined."

"I plan to stop at the jeweler in Diamond Creek when I get home today."

"That's a good idea." Dr. Edwards stood. "I'll walk you out. And please, keep me posted on your progress." He led her to the door.

"Will do," she said, taking his hand.

She popped in one more time to say goodbye to her mom, apologizing for her short visit since she had to make the two o'clock appointment in Hot Springs.

On her way out of town, she pulled through a sandwich shop and ordered a chicken sandwich, fries, and lemonade. Nibbling on a fry, she wound through town and got on US-70 West toward Hot Springs. The drive took less than an hour, and Lucy arrived at the clinic in plenty of time for her appointment.

The small, clapboard one-story building of Billings Animal Hospital sat nestled amongst tall oak trees on the corner of Park Avenue and Third Street. The dirt drive to the building seemed appropriate for his furry, four-legged patients. Lucy got out and stepped over the cobblestone walkway to the entrance.

She pushed open the door to the smell of canine, fur, and disinfectant.

"Can I help you?" The receptionist behind the desk greeted her with a smile.

"Yes. I'm here to see Dr. Billings. We have an appointment at two."

"You must be Lucy Ross. We talked on the phone."

Lucy nodded.

"Please take a seat, and he'll be with you in just a moment."

A few minutes later, a rosy-cheeked young man stepped toward her. "Lucy?"

Lucy hesitated. "Yes." The man was too young to have been the vet in question. She stood and clasped his hand.

"Come this way, please. Would you like coffee or water?"

"No thanks." Lucy followed him to his office and took the chair opposite his desk. "Thank you for seeing me. But I think there's been a mistake. I'm afraid you're much too young to have been the vet I'm looking for." She shifted in her seat. "I'm trying to find the veterinarian who knew my father twenty years ago."

He sat forward and clasped his hands on the top of his desk. "The misunderstanding may have been between me and my receptionist. I was in surgery at the time and would have agreed to see anyone at that point during the operation." His smile was apologetic. "I'm not sure how I can help you. It's my father you should be talking to."

"I thought I *would* be talking to your father." She sighed. "I'd assumed he was still working here."

"He retired last year." He lifted a finger and stood. "You said the man's name is James Ross."

"Yes."

"Let me see if I can reach my dad."

Dr. Billings returned within a few minutes. "Good news." He retook his chair. "I just talked with my father. He didn't know anyone by that name but told me his old veterinary technician might have. Apparently, he worked a short time for a vet in Diamond Creek before coming to work for my father. His name is Peter Saylor, and according to my dad, Saylor now has his own practice in Pine Bluff." He scribbled something on a piece of paper, then handed it to her. "That's the name of his practice and his number."

Bluff Veterinary Clinic 555-374-9821

She stood and tucked the note into her purse. "Thank you."

He walked her out, and Lucy caught a glimpse of a technician scanning the shoulder of a golden retriever.

She paused and turned to Dr. Billings. "What's she doing?"

"Microchipping. Carol has placed an implant into Scout's shoulder. The chip is embedded with contact information in case Scout gets lost or stolen."

Lucy ran a finger along her right shoulder. "Like the owner's phone number and address?"

"Yes. And right now, she's testing the area to see if the information comes up properly onto the chip reader."

"Has that ever been done on humans?"

"Yes. In recent years, Sweden implemented a program. People can have everything from medical information to credit card and bank info on their chip." He opened the door to reception and held it as she passed through. "You can find more online. It's quite interesting."

They stopped in the reception area and shook hands. "I hope you get the answers you're looking for," he said.

Lucy sat in her car and dialed Saylor's number in Pine Bluff. "Bluff Veterinary Clinic," a woman answered, seconds later, "may I help you?"

"Yes, I'd like to speak to Peter Saylor on a private matter," Lucy said.

"I'll connect you to his voicemail. It's his personal number here at the clinic, and he's the only person who checks that line."

"Thank you." It only took a few seconds for the sound of the beep.

"Dr. Saylor. This is going to sound strange. My name is Lucy Ross. I'm Detective James Ross's daughter. I'm trying to track down the veterinarian who may have put a microchip into my right shoulder twenty years ago. If this is you, would you please give me a call on my cell? Thank you."

It was almost dark when she arrived home, her stop at Hamilton Jewelers having taken a bit more time than she'd thought. The initial exam of the stones shocked her. Out of the ten stones, seven were diamonds, which the appraiser believed were quite valuable.

She parked in front of her house, contemplating what her next steps should be in regard to the property. What if she and her mom turned out to be wealthy women? Wouldn't that be something? But at that moment, she didn't really care. What loomed most was solving her father's murder and clearing his name. The stones could wait.

* * *

It was near quitting time when Malcolm placed a single tap on Chief Holland's door. "Do you have a second?"

Holland looked up. "Of course. You just caught me. I was about to leave for the day. What's up?"

Malcolm briefly hesitated, then handed Holland the Ross file. He took particular note on the chief's expression as he read the name on the tag.

"James Ross. Now there's a name I haven't heard in more years than I can count...until recently, that is."

"Sir?"

"Ross's daughter moved back to town and is hell bent on doing her own investigation."

Malcolm decided to play dumb. "Really?"

"Yes, really." He scowled and tossed the file on his desk. "What's *your* interest?"

Malcolm stuffed his hands into his pockets and glanced at the file. "An old friend of Ross's asked me to take a look at it."

"And who is this old friend?"

"My father."

Holland widened his eyes, and his mouth fell open. Malcolm knew Chief Holland would be surprised, but the stunned expression threw him. The man acted more shocked than anything else. "Knox—of course. You're Stuart Knox's son."

"Did you know my father?"

"Only briefly. Not long after he moved to Scotland, I took his place as Ross's partner. I certainly understand your father's interest in the Ross case. It was a tragedy. We all mourned him." He picked up the file and stood. "But this case is closed."

"Right. That's what I wanted to ask you about. Shouldn't it be a cold case, sir?"

"Everything that could be done was done years ago—every lead followed. Dredging up the past will only cause more harm than good."

For whom?

"I'd like to keep investigating if that's all right. On my own time, of course."

"I'll tell you what I told Lucy—leave it alone."

"But, sir."

"Is that clear?"

Malcolm hesitated. "Yes, sir."

"And another thing," Holland added. "As a detective, it's one thing for you know the contents of that report, but Lucy is not to. She threatened to look it up online, so I had Officer Simms remove it."

"I understand, and I agree. The photos alone are disturbing."

"Good. I'll return this." Holland held up the file. "You won't be needing it anymore."

Malcolm pulled the chief's door closed and made his way to the evidence room. He had a hunch that if he didn't check the physical evidence now, he'd never get the chance. Malcolm slid his key card in the reader and walked into the room of solid-block construction.

It took a few minutes to navigate through the rows of shelving. He found the correct evidence box on the second row, reached up, and removed it. He set the box on the table in the center of the narrow room and lifted the lid. He pulled out the inventory sheet, read through it, then began examining each piece of evidence.

He lifted the clear plastic bag, which held the bullet taken out of Ross. Another bag held one spent casing. He studied the photo of the money found at the Ross home, then placed it back inside the box. The last items were the high-resolution photographs of the tire tracks and one of both a right and left shoe print—a size ten.

There was no handgun, which didn't surprise him, as the report stated it had never been found. His visit with the chief fresh on his mind, Malcolm positioned his phone and took photographs of each item. He wouldn't put it past Holland to have the physical evidence, along with the written report, removed.

Last was the video-cassette tape. He opened the case and slid it in the machine provided. Only seconds long, it showed Ross taking a package from a man in the car he'd pulled over. As Malcolm watched the video, he had to admit, the image looked bad for Ross. According to the inventory sheet, the man in the car had never been identified.

Malcolm left the precinct about ten minutes later and headed for Dottie's. While driving through town, he turned down Main Street and spotted Lucy leaving Hamilton Jewelers.

Dinner could wait. Malcolm found a space across the street and parked. Curious to see what she'd been up to, he got out of the car and headed to the store.

He strode to the counter and flashed his badge. The jeweler was only too happy to give Malcolm the information he wanted.

The man unwrapped a soft cloth displaying about ten stones. "This is what she brought in," he said. "Says she found them on her property."

Malcolm ran his finger through the colorful stones, then selected one. "What kind of value are we talking about here?"

"I can't give you an exact figure without further appraisal of each one. But from my initial examination, I can tell you most of these are valuable, and will be more so, once they're cut and polished."

He thanked the man for his time, left the store, and made his way back to his car. Would Lucy, having just discovered this news for herself, put a photo of the stones on her clue board?

Thieves broke into people's homes for a lot less. And if those stones were as valuable as he'd been told, and the fact there could be hundreds—if not *thousands* more—would be reason enough for the break-in and motivation for the perpetrator's attempts to frighten her away.

He headed toward Dottie's with his mind still spinning. Had Crandall been aware of the stones and their value? The Ross estate would be worth a great deal to someone who knew that information. If that were the case, Crandall's anger at losing the property made perfect sense. A man with his reputation would not take that lightly.

Malcolm pulled in front of Dottie's, beating the rain by seconds. Lightening lit up the sky as he pushed through the front door. He sat at the counter and ordered the blue-plate special: fried chicken, creamed potatoes, and collard greens.

He took a sip of iced tea and slid out his notepad from his back pocket.

How on earth could it be a problem to allow him to investigate this case? Smiling to himself, he shook his head. He was starting to sound like Lucy.

Since Holland told Malcolm to drop it, his plan to interview Crandall was now out of the question. Malcolm understood Holland's refusal to allow Lucy to see the file, but what harm could there be in him taking another look? After all, he hadn't been there when the murder happened, and Malcolm would've thought having a fresh perspective on the unsolved case would be a good thing... unless that was exactly the reason behind Holland's refusal for Malcolm to do so.

Twenty years was a long time, and Malcolm knew from experience that time didn't always cover up evidence. Sometimes it revealed it. There were things in that report he felt had not been followed up. Was it merely sloppy reporting, or deliberate? His father had known it twenty years ago, and after reviewing the facts, Malcolm agreed.

He'd suspected some level of reaction to his request but not like the one Holland made that afternoon. Good thing he made a photocopy of the entire report. That was not usual procedure, but nothing about this case was typical.

While he waited to be served, he glanced over his notes from the Ross file. The only new lead from examining the physical evidence was the shoe size. A ten could be a man or a woman. He tapped his finger along the edge of the counter top.

He had no doubt Lucy was still investigating and was surprised at the clues she'd acquired without having read the report. So where had they come from? She was onto something, but what? Sure, her mother had seen the Mustang and felt certain that was how Lucy knew about it. The fact the crime had never been solved told him she could be in dangerous territory.

CHAPTER 14

For dinner, Lucy fixed one of those prepackaged meals with all the ingredients included in the box. This one was salmon and asparagus. She didn't care too much for cooking and started using the boxed meals the previous year while working on her master's.

All through dinner, she wondered if she'd actually been mircrochipped. The more she thought about it, the more she rejected the idea.

But after she ate, she found herself standing in front of her bathroom mirror and examining the small scar on her right shoulder. After so many years, it was barely visible—just a slight, raised ridge on her flesh. The only reason she could still make it out was the fact that she'd grown up with it.

Was it really possible her father had put pertinent information onto a chip and had it embedded into her shoulder? When she was growing up, her mom told her the scar had been the result of a fall into a metal-and-glass table, but since her confession the other day, she couldn't be certain which story was the truth.

She lowered her sleeve and left the bathroom. Before leaving her bedroom, she stopped at the window and watched the deluge. Thunder rolled in along with the downpour as she made her way to the living room. A moment later, she sat on the sofa, opened her laptop, and typed *microchipping humans* into the search bar.

Dr. Billings had been correct. More than 4,000 Swedes had replaced most methods of payment for chip implants. Everything from credit card information to emergency contact details could be stored on the tiny device.

She clicked on another link and read, *Microchipping pets started in the late eighties.* More than fifteen years before she was born. She took a screen shot of the chip and reader device, then hit print.

By the time she reached the printer, the page had slid out of the machine. She retrieved it, and a sudden desire for munchies hit her. A few minutes later, she stood in the kitchen while the fragrance of butter and corn wafted from the microwave. She poured the hot snack into a ceramic bowl and went back to the living room.

After setting the bowl aside, she stood at the suspect board and pinned what she hoped was her latest clue onto the cork. She gathered a handful of popcorn and lifted the warm buttery morsels to her mouth just as lightening cracked overhead. She cringed, scrunching up her face.

That was close.

Her gaze fell on the black sedan as she reopened her eyes. It's image as dark as the menacing clouds overhead. The current weather seemed fitting at that moment.

She re-read the article mentioning the owner of the sedan, Alex Crandall. Nothing new there. She studied the wingtip shoes similar to those worn by the shooter. She dropped her gaze to the second row and to the photo of a yellow-green Mustang like the one her mom saw driving by at the time of the shooting.

Her gaze rested on the picture of Malcolm. Maybe she should remove it. He had a habit of showing up, and the last thing she needed was for him to see his picture on her suspect board.

She turned her focus to a photo she'd found in one of the boxes of her as a child with her mom and dad. The three of them looked so happy. She sighed and moved her attention to the copy of the photo with the three officers on The Club wall.

She still didn't know the identity of the man in the middle, not that it mattered, but he must have known her father. And if the nameless man was still alive... Perhaps one of the boxes she'd gone through held a picture of him. There were several photos that had no meaning for her on the first go-around. Maybe she'd find the man if she looked again.

She made her way to the unused bedroom that held the last of the boxes and other clutter. She stopped midstride at the sound of breaking glass and gasped. The noise came from somewhere near the front of the house.

Heart in her throat, she ran back to the living room.

She skidded to a halt and stared at the shards of glass on the floor underneath the center window. A brick sat in the midst of the broken pieces with a note wrapped around it.

She pressed her hand to her mouth and stared out the window into the dark. Lightening suddenly lit up the sky. A man dressed in solid black and wearing a mask stood staring at her.

She screamed, and the man fled. She ran to the door and

yanked it open. Rain stung her face as she stood there, but the man had gone.

She shut the door and locked it, marveling at her own stupidity. What if he'd been standing there? He could have forced his way in. What would she have done then?

Her legs shook as she crossed the floor to pick up the brick. Mouth dry, she could hardly swallow. She slid the rubber band off the brick and unwrapped the damp, but readable, note.

How is your mother? I understand the amenities at Oak Haven are quite nice.

Her body went limp. Lucy sank down and with shaking hands, snatched up her phone. She released the brick and the note to her lap and pressed 911.

* * *

The rain had stopped by the time Malcolm arrived at Lucy's. He stood in the doorway and scanned the room before entering. He took in the shattered glass, the array of boxes, and the anxiety on Lucy's face as Officer Kirby questioned her.

"Here's the note." She handed it to Kirby.

"Can you describe the mask?"

Malcolm crossed the room. "I'll take over, Kirby. Check the rest of the premises, specifically for car tracks. The ground is saturated, but we might get lucky."

Kirby left the room, and Malcolm took the seat next to Lucy. He picked up the note, read the message, then looked right at her.

"Looks like you've upset someone. You must be getting close."

She linked her hands together and placed them around her knees. The wide, frightened look hadn't left her eyes since he'd walked in.

"Seems so." She spoke in a whisper.

"Would you like to explain what this means?" He held up the note.

"It's a threat," she said.

"It is." He released a deep sigh. "I warned you—told you to stop probing."

She lifted her chin and boldly met his gaze. "For your information, I don't want to be a private investigator. I want to teach high school. But no one else around here has found my father's killer. If I don't do it, who will? *You*?"

Choosing to ignore her outburst, he met her challenge with steady resolve, and resumed questioning her. "Whoever did this obviously knows about your mother."

The mention of her mother seemed to douse that insolent gleam, bringing her back to the problem at hand. She pressed her fingers to her mouth. Her shoulders drooped.

"Oak Haven. Where is that?" he asked.

"Little Rock." She straightened up and turned toward him. "A few years ago, my mother had a car accident and suffered a brain injury. She's been there for the last three years while I finished my undergraduate and graduate degrees."

"Who in this town knows about your mom?"

She shrugged. "Uncle Bob and his wife."

Uncle Bob? He sat back, momentarily dumbfounded. "Who else might know?"

"Not long ago, I mentioned it to Jan in one of our conversations. She or the others could have told anyone, I guess."

"Do you know of someone in Little Rock with a connection to anyone here who may have said something?"

She shook her head, causing wisps of brown hair to bounce around her shoulders.

"What about the other night at The Club? Did you mention it in a conversation with anyone?"

"No." She pressed the palms of her hands to each side of her head. "I guess that leaves only three who *do* know. One of them must have told someone else."

"Officer Kirby said you saw the man?"

"Briefly. He was wearing a mask. It frightened me. When I screamed, he ran away."

"Can you describe the mask? Was it at all like the one worn by the man who followed you?"

"Yes—exactly like that. It's similar to the ones worn at the Policeman's Ball—but larger—it covered his entire face, just like the one worn by the stalker. Dark—purple, I think —and it glistened with sequins and something like small, sparkly stones."

"That's some kind of detail."

"Lightening appeared overhead as he stood there. It was clear as day."

"Good." He continued to write.

"Do you think someone from the ball did this?" Her glistening, green eyes grew large with dismay. "Like a police officer?"

"I shouldn't think so. I don't recall anyone at the Officer's Ball wearing a full mask."

"Me neither," she said.

He glanced at Kirby's notes. "You say this happened around eight this evening?"

She nodded. "I left the living room and was about half-way down the hallway went I heard the glass break. When I came back, it was like this." She nodded toward the broken shards. "I froze for a second, saw him in the window, then ran to the door. I opened it, but he was gone."

"You opened the door?"

"I know—stupid move on my part. Fear and anger propelled me. When I realized what I'd done, I slammed the door and locked it. Then I picked up the brick. I realize now I should have called you before I touched it and the note."

"That's okay." He jotted something down on his notepad, then looked at her. "The main thing is that you weren't hurt."

She was on edge, and he decided not to press her any further. "I'll have this checked for fingerprints." He slipped the note into a plastic bag. "Hopefully, we'll find someone's other than yours, mine, and Kirby's."

Kirby entered the room. "I found a partial tire track at the front of the property. I'll have forensics get right on it, and I'll have the window boarded up for the night."

"And have this checked for fingerprints." Malcolm handed him the note.

"Yes, sir." Kirby took the note and left.

Malcolm stood and gazed down at Lucy. "You okay?"

She rubbed her hands along her thighs, then stood. "Just a bit shaken." She wrapped her arms around herself, hugging them to her chest. "What about my mom? What if—?" Her wide, green eyes gazed up at him in mute appeal.

"I'll have the police in Little Rock assign round-the-clock protection." He studied the room. "And we need to talk about what it is you know." He turned his gaze back to her. "But first, let me help you clean this up. Get the supplies while I make the call to Little Rock."

She didn't argue, but left the room and returned a few

minutes later with a broom, dustpan, and a black, plastic trash bag.

He took the dustpan. "Everything's all set. LRPD is on it."

"Thank you."

Her eyes filled with misty tears, and he had the sudden urge to take her in his arms. Instead, he smiled. "You sweep," he said, "and I'll hold the pan."

They worked in silence, careful not to cut themselves. Every minute or so, Malcolm glanced at her somber face. She had every reason to be worried. He'd warned her to be careful—to leave the investigating to him. And he didn't like the fact that she lived alone and on the outskirts of town, with the closest neighbor a mile away.

"Tomorrow, I'm having deadbolts installed on all of your doors and as well as a wireless, camera system."

"Now, just a second. I can't afford that."

"No one's asking you to." He stopped working and gave her his no-nonsense stare. "It's either that, or I'll have you moved into town, bodily if I have to. And if you still refuse, I'll arrest you and put you in jail. Heaven knows, I have more than one reason to do so." He stood—glaring—towering over her. "If you don't take your safety seriously, then I will." He paused for a breath. "Is that clear?"

Her chest heaved, and she folded her arms. "Your Scottish accent gets quite brogue-ish when you're angry."

"I'll take that as a *yes*."

They had just finished with a final vacuum of the area when two men from the department showed up with tools to cover the window until a carpenter could be hired. The noise of sawing wood and hammers lasted about thirty minutes before it finally stopped.

Once everyone had left, Malcolm walked to the side table along the wall and studied the suspect board. He'd had his eye on it throughout the evening. He reached up and unpinned the photo of himself. She'd obviously taken it while he had been looking at the sedan.

Considering he'd had the benefit of having read the report, her investigation had the signs of someone who knew more than she'd let on. He turned toward her as she approached him.

He held up his photo. "Am I a suspect?"

"Of sorts," she said.

He scoffed a laugh. "What does that mean?"

"I think you're connected to all of this. I just don't know how yet." She slipped the picture from his fingers and pinned it back on the board. "Aside from that, what do you think?"

He shrugged, not about to give too much away. "It's impressive. Where did you get your information?" He focused on her face, trying to read any change in her expression.

She gave no response.

"I see you've pinned up the article mentioning Alex Crandall and the black sedan, but what about this other stuff?" He pointed to the printout of the yellow-green Mustang. "That's an unusual color. Why choose that when there're hundreds of Mustang photos online." *I knew the color, but how did she? From her mother?*

"Because that's the color of the Mustang my mother saw driving by before the shot was fired."

So, she *did* get it from her mom. What else had her mom told her? Maybe he should talk to the woman.

"That's the color you were hoping to find at Curbside Classics, isn't it?"

With her eyes on the photograph, she tugged slightly on her right ear. "Yes." She lifted her gaze and pinned him with her big, honey-green stare. "I take it, you also came away from them empty-handed."

He smiled and nodded. "I did, indeed."

"In your position, you could check with the DMV. Or, does the police report tell you who owned the car?"

He gave her a slight smile. "Are you asking if I've read the report?"

"After our break-in at Crandall's, I figured you already had by now. And that, my dear detective, was confirmed after running into you at Curbside. I knew the car and color had to be in the report."

She stuffed her hands into her pockets, gazed at the floor, and then back up at him. "I think you're the only person I can trust."

He blinked. "Now that's a loaded statement." He gnawed the inside of his lip. "What about your *Uncle* Bob?" Malcolm was curious to see if she'd reveal her recent conversation with Holland. "I take it you've known him most of your life. Why not ask him?"

She rolled her eyes. "I did. He assured me it had all been thoroughly looked into. There was no reason to open up old wounds...yada-yada." Raw disappointment filled her eyes as the words fell from her lips.

In that moment, Malcolm came close to laying his cards on the table by sharing his recent conversation with Holland regarding this very subject. But the time just wasn't right for him to reveal his connection to her father and that his interest ran much deeper than mere curiosity.

He watched her for a second, hoping she'd tell him more. She didn't, so he turned his attention back to the board.

"What about those shoes? What's their significance?" He thought about the shoe size. Should he reveal that little tidbit? *No.* Until he knew where she came by that information, he'd keep that to himself.

She hesitated and ran her finger along the side of her mouth. "I'd rather not say at this time."

"I see." He folded his arms and stared down at her. "And the picture from the wall at The Club? I see you managed to sneak a copy, after all. You got anything to say about that?"

"I snapped a photo of it when your back was turned." She glanced between him and the photo. "I know it seems odd, but I like it." She gazed at him and clamped her lower lip with her teeth. "It's that simple. My young father is in this picture. Something about it moves me." She lifted her hands. "It's like the calm before the storm. You know? Everything in his life was good and right...until it wasn't."

Her words moved him. He figured she hardly remembered the man, yet she grieved for him.

"Don't you have plenty of photos of him?"

"Not in his uniform."

He hadn't realized that. "Maybe your mom has some tucked away somewhere."

"Maybe." She lifted a shoulder. "I'll have to ask her."

He continued to study the board. "And this photo of a cassette tape? Is that private, too?"

She stared at the picture. "Right now it is."

"And the microchipping article?"

She sucked in a breath. "Still private."

He chewed the inside of his lip and focused on her until she had no course but to raise her gaze to his.

"I can't help you unless you come clean with me about all of this," he said.

"It's too soon. I'm not even sure what half of it means."

"And yet, you got it all from somewhere." He shrugged. "But, I understand. Building trust in someone takes time. So when you're ready to tell me more, I just might be able to shed light on some of this."

Her green eyes widened, and her expression morphed from one of doubt to hope. "You *have* read the police report. You must have. After all, you do have access to it."

He didn't say word. The woman had the tenacity of a pit bull.

"Which means you also know something that you could share with me," she said.

"I'm sorry." He shook his head. "I have nothing to share with you. Trust runs both ways."

"I have to trust you first, is that it?"

Without taking his eyes off her face, he nodded, slowly and deliberately.

She dropped her head and ran the toe of her sneaker across the floor.

"While you think on that... You got anything in that freezer?" he asked.

She lifted her head. "A frozen pizza."

"That'll do just fine."

CHAPTER 15

Malcolm and Lucy chose to eat in the living room, and they settled on the sofa. Lucy took a bite of pizza and glanced at Malcolm's profile. He'd just finished one slice and had reached for another. Malcolm Knox. He was quite something. Earlier, she'd told him that she trusted him, but then withheld pertinent facts. How was that trust?

But *he'd* also withheld information. Obviously there were *still* trust issues with him, too. As for her trusting him first before he would trust her...well, how was that fair?

"You know, I feel like I've heard your name somewhere before." She licked sauce off the tip of her finger. "Can you think of a reason why that might be the case?"

He swallowed, then took a swig of soda. "I don't know. I can't imagine where you could've heard it."

"It's probably nothing." She bit down on the cheesy point of a new slice. "When we met, you told me you were here on some sort of exchange program."

"That's right." He set his plate aside and sat back." Diamond Creek's police department is a hosting agency in the program."

"Sounds suspicious if you ask me." She raised a brow.

"What do you mean?"

"Come on. Of all the places you could've chosen—Los Angeles, Miami, or Las Vegas, and you pick the backside of nowhere?"

"Hey, I like it here," he defensively said.

"I do, too. It just doesn't seem to fit you, that's all. I can't imagine a town the size of Diamond Creek would offer you very much." She shrugged and took another bite of pizza. "I think there's more to your being here than you've let on."

"Still playing detective, I see."

She dabbed red sauce off her mouth. "So tell me, what are some of the differences between where you were in Scotland and here?"

"I was in Edinburgh. It's a much larger city and really no comparison to the rural town of Diamond Creek. The crimes are much fewer in number here, and I find as a rural officer, I must resolve the issue by myself—or with limited support."

"Is that a challenge for you?" She licked a finger, then took another bite.

"Sure, but in a good way." He reached for another slice. "With so few in number, I'm allowed to take charge and handle the dispute the way I see fit."

"I've never been to Scotland. Actually…" She scrunched up her face. "I've never been anywhere." She tipped her head toward his phone. "Show me a picture of your home?"

He lowered the slice to his plate, then grabbed his phone. After scrolling a bit, he stopped and pointed at the screen. "Here's the house where I grew up. My dad still lives there."

"A stone cottage. How lovely." She couldn't help but sigh. "That wall at the entrance is beautiful."

"Thanks, the mason who did the work is a real artist." He slid right with his thumb. "Here's one of the out-buildings. I love the English ivy and how it covers that entire side."

"And your parents? I'd love to see them."

"My mom died years ago, but here's one of my dad." He scrolled to a photo of a lean, dark-haired man somewhere in his late fifties.

She smiled. "He has a strong, honest face. I like him."

"Let me see if I can find more of him." Malcolm began sliding through photos again and paused at one of a pretty blonde with him standing beside her.

"What a beautiful girl," Lucy said. "Who is she?"

"Becca Sinclair." He stared at the photo.

"She has a sophisticated, almost regal, look about her," Lucy said, hoping to hear more.

"That she does," he said. "She was worldly and experienced, a beautiful woman."

Lucy studied his profile. A slight frown creased his features. "Is she the one you left behind?"

He tore his gaze from the photo and faced Lucy. "No. Not for a long time." He blew out a breath. "We had a serious relationship once, but that was years ago."

Lucy bowed her head and ran her finger along the sofa edge. "So, there's no one back home anxiously waiting for your return?" She held her breath and waited.

He tipped her chin upward and searched her face. Heat crept up into her cheeks.

"No. No one."

She squared her chin. "If you don't mind telling me, what happened between you two?"

"I'll have to save that for another day."

"I'm sorry." To her horror, the heat deepened. "I didn't mean to pry."

"No, please." He lifted a hand. "Believe me, it's not you."

"Too soon, huh?"

He eyed her and shook his head. "You're not going to drop it are you?"

She scrunched up her nose and shrugged.

"Let's just say, Becca wasn't nearly as committed to our relationship as I was."

"That must have been difficult."

"Somewhat." He clicked out of photos and reached for another slice of pizza.

Maybe Malcolm wasn't quite over this Becca person. To lighten the mood, Lucy shifted to the side, brought one leg underneath her on the sofa, and hugged her glass to her chest. "Tell me a secret."

A slow smile lifted the corners of his well-shaped mouth. Seemed he was also happy with the change in conversation.

An engaging twinkle lit his blue eyes. Fascinated, she watched his face. From the minute changes crossing his features, she knew he had plenty to share.

With that twinkle-eyed smile still in place, he shook his head, then popped the last bite of pizza into his mouth. When he finished, he swiped his mouth with a napkin, then tossed it on his plate. "I don't think we've known each other long enough for me to share my secrets."

"Come on," she said. "Surely you can tell me some little, itty-bitty secret."

"I skipped school once."

"That's not a secret. Everybody's done that."

"As the son of a police detective, that's secret enough." He shifted toward her. "What about you?"

"What about me?"

His smile broadened. "I've known you for two weeks, and trust me...you have a secret, all right. Something to get off your chest, maybe?"

Like before, heat rose in her cheeks. Problem was, she had tons of secrets she'd like to share. Burdens, really.

"Even now, the color in your face tells me so."

"You already know my secret. I'm James Ross's daughter."

"You, my dear hen, are knee-deep in secrets."

"Hen?" She reared back. "Are you calling me a chicken?"

He laughed. "Don't take affront and don't confuse it with a feathery creature. It means female or young lady. It's a Scottish word of endearment—like sweetheart. It does have another meaning, which I'll share with you another time."

Had he just called her sweetheart? She chewed her bottom lip, deep in thought.

"Come on, hen. You have another secret. I can see it in your eyes."

"I was shot once," she blurted out.

* * *

Malcolm sobered. "What?"

"It's true." She set her glass aside and leaned toward him. "See?"

He inched closer and lifted his hand to brush her hair from the spot she'd noted. A thin, pink scar started right at her hairline, ran about two inches long, disappearing into her dark, wavy hair. He sat back and gazed at her upturned face.

"Admit it," she said, "my secret is much more intriguing than yours." Her green eyes danced.

"I'll say."

"Don't look so serious. It happened a long time ago."

"Don't joke," he reprimanded with a stern voice. "When did this happen?"

"Oh, that would count as another secret, so I can't tell you that." She sipped her drink. "Unless *you* have another one to share."

"I'm afraid I'm all out." Jaw clinched, he glanced at his watch. "It's late. I should be going." He stood and strode to the door.

She scrambled to her feet. "Malcolm, wait."

He stopped and turned toward her.

She stepped over to the corkboard and pointed her finger at the black sedan. "Twenty years ago, a man jumped from this car and shot me and my father."

So, she'd been shot at the same time. *That wasn't in the report.*

She swallowed convulsively. "The bullet grazed my hairline two inches above my right temple before it hit him."

That explained the amount of blood on the side of her face in the photo. It was *hers*.

"From the moment I got this scar, I've had very little memory of my early childhood. I remember my mom but little else. When my memory didn't fully return, my mom put me in therapy for a while. When I was thirteen, I tried counseling again, but with no luck.

"Today, I do have an occasional appointment with my mom's therapist, but so far...nothing." She lifted a shoulder. "Since it happened so long ago, I didn't worry too much about it. It wasn't as if I'd lost my memory as a teenager or young adult. I guess if you have to lose a memory, the best time would be in your early childhood years."

She lifted her hands in mute appeal. "My goal wasn't to joke about something so serious. But I learned a long time ago humor lessens the pain."

He crossed the room and took her in his arms. "I'm sorry, too. I overreacted."

She tilted her face and gazed into his eyes. "Does this count for trusting you *first*?"

For an answer, he released one hand, cupped the nape of her neck, and lowered his mouth to hers. When he lifted his head, a captivating tilt caught at the corners of her sweet, full lips.

She breathed a contented sigh. "Does that mean, yes?"

"That and much more." He ran the back of his finger along her left cheek. "I've posted an officer outside for the night. Will you be okay in the house by yourself?"

She hesitated. By the look in her glistening eyes and glowing face, she wanted him to stay and not just for protection.

"Yes, I'll be okay." She shook her head. "I'm a big girl, and there's an officer outside."

She didn't sound at all convincing. "I could take the couch," he said. "It wouldn't be the first time."

He released her, and she stepped out of his arms.

"I am a bit tired," she said.

They stood, staring at each other.

"But... Would you mind staying until I fall asleep?" She pulled on her ear—the action reminding him of a young child.

"Of course. I'll be here if you need me."

"Okay. Thanks for tonight and for helping me clean up and you know...for everything."

"And thanks for the pizza."

As she turned away, she stopped and looked back at him. "I want that note back for my board."

"No can do. It's evidence."

"A photocopy then?"

"All right. Get some sleep."

Lucy left the room, and Malcolm stood, savoring the feel of her mouth against his. He hadn't meant to kiss her and had fought the urge for days. But her glistening green eyes, her upturned face, and her soft, parted lips, had given him no choice but to comply with the longing he'd seen in her eyes.

The fact that he'd be gone in nine months had held him back from pursuing her, and frankly, still concerned him. Tonight, he'd take this as a first step and see where it led. He'd worry about how much time he had left, later.

The memory lingered as he stepped over to the suspect board. He studied her creative collage of facts. She was good. Some of it was right on. Except for his picture. He shook his head. That shouldn't be there, and he had a mind to take it off.

He slipped his phone from his back pocket, leveled it on the board, and snapped a couple of photos. He found the wingtip shoes a curious addition, as well as both the cassette tape and the article on microchipping. Neither one fit with what he knew at that point. Looked like he, too, needed to do more digging.

He rubbed his bearded chin. Where did she get this stuff? From her search of those old boxes, or the cassette tape? That might explain the shoes, but not the article on human microchipping.

From his own research into the police report, he knew it

was missing some key things. Maybe she had privy to them from her mom or someone else.

She'd confessed another secret and knew the ball was now in his court. Not ready to divulge all, he'd have to give her something. A promise was a promise, and she'd hold him to it.

Malcolm glanced as his watch. 2:30 a.m. He walked down the hall to the last bedroom on the right to check on Lucy. Careful not to wake her, he turned the handle and cracked the door before fully opening it. Sound asleep and with her hair splayed across the pillow, she was lovely. He lingered his gaze a second longer, then gently closed the door behind him.

When he reached the living room, he paused and walked over to the board. He picked up a three-by-five card from the table, made a quick note, and pinned it next to the yellow-green Mustang, then left.

Back at home, Malcolm printed out one of the photos he took of Lucy's suspect board. He taped it to his refrigerator door and stood back. He'd pretty much exhausted his search from the clues in the case file. Now, he had something else to look into, even though they were a bit weird.

CHAPTER 16

Lucy woke the following morning with the memory of the previous day's events fresh on her mind. In spite of that, she'd slept well. Falling asleep with Malcolm still in the house brought a strange and wonderful sort of comfort.

She got out of bed, stuffed her arms into her robe, and cinched it around her waist. Her heart hammered foolishly as she ambled down the hall to the kitchen. Thoughts about that sweet, unexpected, kiss lingered. And what had he meant when he'd said, *that and much more*? That sounded promising. When he placed his lips on hers, a ripple of excitement had surged within her. It had been way too short, making her long for much more. Maybe that's what he'd meant.

She sighed. Or. Maybe his kiss had merely been one of comfort. Malcolm was a man of the world and as such had probably handed out many kisses like that—short and sweet, but with little meaning for the one giving them. If that were the case, she'd take whatever she could get. On that depressing thought, she turned on the tap and filled the coffee canister.

While the coffee brewed, she walked to the living room and peeked out the window. The blue-and-white squad car was still there. Maybe she should fix the officer some coffee.

She quickly slipped on jeans and a white sleeveless blouse and went back to the kitchen. After she filled two mugs, she added cream and sugar to both and carried them outside. She stepped carefully across the yard, avoiding the mud and puddles of rainwater.

Officer Kirby smiled as she approached the vehicle. "Good morning," he said. "I hope you had a good night's sleep."

"I did, and it was all because you were out here making me feel safe. I fixed you some coffee." She held up the mug. "It's sweet with cream."

"Thank you. Just the way I like it."

She handed him the mug through the window, then turned at the sound of a car coming up the driveway. It was Malcolm.

"I believe that's my relief for the day." Kirby stepped out of the car just as Malcolm pulled up beside them.

"Good morning, Officer Kirby, Lucy... How was your night? You sleep okay?"

"I did, thank you. I just fixed Officer Kirby a cup of coffee. Would you like one?"

"I'd love a cup." He rested his hand on the hood of the police car. "Thanks, Kirby. Go get some shut-eye."

Malcolm and Lucy watched Kirby leave, then turned and walked toward the house.

"Benny's Lock and Key will be here this afternoon to install the locks," Malcolm said. "I'm still working on who to use for the cameras."

"The locks are fine." She mounted the porch step. "But I think the camera system is overkill."

"Leave it to me, will you?"

"Okay."

In the kitchen, Malcolm took a seat at the table while Lucy fixed his coffee. She set it before him and sat down on the chair opposite.

He took a sip and eyed her. "Well," he said. "Don't you have anything to say?"

She narrowed her eyes. "About what?"

"About what I left on your suspect board last night."

She gaped at him and sat perfectly still, then jumped up and rushed to the living room, sloshing coffee along the way. Malcolm followed, catching up with her in a matter of seconds. She perused the board, stopping at the photo of the yellow-green Mustang. She spun toward him and grinned. "You left me a clue?"

He chuckled. "I did."

She read... *According to the police report, this fact has not been followed up.*

"What does this mean?"

"It means exactly what it says."

"No. I mean... are you going to help me find out who owns it?"

He folded his arms and looked right at her. "It means... I'm giving you one clue for you to work on."

"Oh, I see. Give the dog a bone to keep him occupied. Me being the dog, of course."

"That's not it at all."

One corner of his well-shaped mouth lifted, bringing last night's kiss to the forefront of her mind.

"I'm trying to keep you safe," he said. "And if I know what you're working on, then I can keep tabs on you."

His attempt to control her actions didn't bother her one

bit. Growing up without a father, she saw his attempt to keep a protective eye on her rather sweet. She turned her attention back to the board and the Mustang.

"Maybe they—the driver—saw something," she said.

"After twenty years, it's unlikely we'll find out anything. They could have just been visiting or driving through. This is a state road and it leads to other towns."

He selected another index card and drew a mask." You need this up there, too."

She dutifully pinned it and stood back.

"But this other stuff," he lifted his hand toward the board, "means nothing to me. I've read the report, and frankly, I don't know how the microchipping fits in, or the cassette tape, for that matter."

She ran a finger along the rim of her coffee and stared up at him.

"Honestly, I was hoping you might fill me in on those details." He lowered himself to the sofa. "Tell me what you found that makes you put this stuff up as clues."

"That's three clues." She lifted a brow and sat next to him. "You've only given me one."

"So, it's still tit-for-tat, is it?"

She shrugged and sipped her coffee, never taking her eyes from his face. "Do you have the report?"

"I've read it." He lifted the mug to his mouth and drank. "The original is back at the station."

"You made a copy?"

"Sorry, I'm not at liberty to confirm that." He pressed his lips together and shook his head. "I've incriminated myself enough."

She set her mug down and plucked up a stone from the small dish on the center of the coffee table.

"That's pretty," he said.

"I found it behind my house the other day. There're several more but not as pretty as this one, or the other one I found after I first arrived. I took that one to a jeweler in Little Rock. He's going to make a pendant out of it."

"This is amazing." He took the stone from her fingers. "It's really beautiful. Just like the ones you dropped off at Hamilton Jewelers."

She stared at him. "You've been following me?"

"Simply following my leads as I get them, or *see* them." He sipped his coffee and eyed her. "I saw you go in, and my curiosity was aroused—"

"And you flashed your badge, is that it?"

"Don't look so shocked. You've got me on your suspect board."

"*Touché*, Detective Knox." She tipped her head, then picked up her mug and took a swallow.

"Would you like some breakfast?" She stood and moved toward the kitchen. "I have eggs and bacon if you're interested."

"I can't." He shook his head and followed her. "I just came by to check on you—see how you felt after last night's scare."

She held out her hand for his mug, then placed both in the sink. "Thanks, but you didn't have to, not with Officer Kirby in attendance."

"He's a good man."

"I know." She pulled a face. "Even though he arrested me."

Malcolm laughed. "No more than you deserved."

She smiled and stuffed her hands in her robe pockets. "Come on, I'll walk you out."

Benny's Lock and Key arrived around noon and added new locks. Lucy opted to keep the old ones in place, as they were original to the house. While they worked, Lucy decided to tackle the third bedroom. In the process of dragging out a large box from the bottom of the closet, her phone dinged with a text.

It was the jeweler from Little Rock. The stone turned out to be a two-carat diamond, champagne brown, worth twelve hundred dollars. He enclosed a photo of the type of pendant he thought would look nice with the stone, and if approved, he'd have it ready the following week.

The layout was a simple, fourteen-karat, open design with a single twist holding the stone in place. She loved it, and more importantly, her mom would, too.

After she *okayed* the design, she moved to unpack one of the heavier boxes. But first, she had to deal with a narrow, hook rug that lay at the base of the bed. Worn and tattered, she'd wanted to replace it since she'd moved in. It took only minutes to roll it up and drag it out of the way, making it a lot easier to shove the large box to the light of the window.

She unsealed the box with the blade of a small kitchen knife and found layers of unfinished quilt pieces inside, some of them quite exquisite. Maybe one of the local churches had a sewing group who might want them.

One of the boards moved under her left foot as she stepped across the floor. She stopped and stepped on it again. It was definitely loose.

She grabbed the kitchen knife and pried up one end, then using her fingers, lifted it off. A narrow, metal box sat wedged underneath. Her heart surged with excitement. She lifted the box out and set in on the floor. Heart pounding, she opened the lid. The contents were few.

What did you expect? Another tape explaining everything from all those years ago? A message exonerating your father, revealing the real culprit?

Disappointed, she sat cross-legged on the floor and lifted out the meager items inside. Two photos. The first was exactly like the one she'd taken a picture of at The Club, picturing her dad, Holland, and the third man whose identity was still unknown. *How odd. Why hide this particular picture here?* "I wonder who he is—where he is?" She stared at the unfamiliar face. "I bet you could tell me about my dad." She flipped the photo over, but nothing was written on the back.

More than likely, someone at the precinct could identify the man in the middle, but it was too soon for her to start asking questions. Malcolm might be a better source in that department.

The other photo, pictured her with her mom and dad. She looked to be the same age as in the video. Lucy's heart squeezed as she gazed at the three happy people. She gently touched her father's face. "I so wish I'd known you."

She flipped it over and sucked in a breath. A small envelope had stuck to the underside of the picture with the single word, Cara, written across the front.

Lucy stared at the envelope, knowing something of significance had to be inside. She believed whatever the note contained would change her life. Using the knife, she slit open the top and pulled out a single sheet of paper. She unfolded it and read the bold script...

My dearest Cara,

If you're reading this that means I'm gone. I know you had questions that I couldn't answer at the time. There's criminal activity in our police department that runs deeply into our community. Do not trust anyone. The answers are with our darling Lucy. She holds the key to all of this. You must keep her safe.

I love you both,
James

CHAPTER 17

*Lucy is the key...don't trust anyone...*ran over and over in Lucy's mind. Malcolm—surely she could trust him? She clutched the note to her chest. He was new to the precinct and lacked history there. If she could share this with anyone, it would be him, but the fact that he still kept information from her made her cautious.

She lifted her fingers to her right shoulder. *Lucy is the key*. Had she been microchipped? *Is that where the answers lie?*

She called Dr. Saylor's private number again and left another message. She'd barely hung up when her caller ID showed him calling back.

"Is this really Lucy Ross?" he asked.

"Yes, I'm Lucy. Do you remember me?"

"I do. That night was one of the strangest experiences of my life. I knew your father, and although I wasn't privy to his investigations, I was aware he'd been looking into something serious."

"What can you tell me about that night?"

"James showed up with you in his arms right at closing and asked me to put a message on a chip and insert it into your shoulder. I had never done such a thing to a human before, but he said his life depended on it. That the message was for your mother in case something happened to him."

"But my mother was there. Why wouldn't he just tell her?"

"I asked him the same thing. I remember they gave each other a particular *look*. One that said, she trusted him."

"So there's actually a message on the microchip?"

"Yes."

"I need to read it." Her heart ratcheted up a notch. "I need to know what it says."

"You're welcome to come here and have me do that for you, but today you can buy a decent reader online for about thirty bucks. That way you can keep the information private."

"I hadn't thought of that. That's a great idea. Umm, one more thing."

"Yes?"

"I understand, I cried a lot. Is that procedure painful?"

"Not at all. You were fine until James placed you on the cold, metal exam table. It was the room and everything in it that frightened you. When James picked you up, you settled down, but he had to hold your arm still as I inserted the chip."

For a moment, Lucy clung to the image of herself safe in her dad's arms. "Thank you so much." Lucy paused. "Is there anything else you can tell me about that night?"

"Nothing more than what I've already told you, I'm afraid. The three of you were literally in and out within minutes."

"Thank you, and thank you for calling me back."

"Of course, and good luck."

Everything was happening quickly. Maybe she was close to getting some answers. She snatched up her phone and searched *microchip reader* online.

Yes! There were several priced from twenty-one dollars to three hundred and seventy. After reading the pros and cons, she ordered one for thirty-five dollars. Hopefully, it would read whatever she had implanted in her shoulder.

She read the letter again. From her father's words, it sounded like he'd told her mom where to look if anything happened to him. But if that were the case, then why leave the box under the floorboard? The letter was sealed, so she couldn't have read it. Had he been killed before he could tell her where he'd hidden it?

Lucy needed to get outside—needed to think. She folded the note and slid it into her shorts' pocket. Benny had just finished with the locks when she entered the living room.

"Here are your new keys, miss."

"Thanks. How much do I owe you?"

"It's all been taken care of, miss." Benny handed her his business card. "Let us know if you need anything else."

Lucy got on an old bicycle that had been left with the house and peddled down the road. The breeze was much cooler underneath the large oaks with their massive limbs covering the street like a canopy—a relief from the summer heat. She'd gone about a mile when she spotted Malcolm unloading a van. He was carrying a box.

He turned at her approach and smiled.

"So, this is how you get to my place so quickly." She stopped and straddled the bike. "Are you moving in here?"

"I am. I've been renting a room above the hardware store

since I arrived. Three-and-a-half months too long if you ask me. This place became available last week, and I've been slowly moving in when I had the time."

"Need any help?"

"Sure. Grab something from the van."

She got off the bike, put down the kickstand, then picked up a basket of folded towels and followed him inside. It was a charming little cottage, quite adorable really, and somehow didn't fit with his tall, masculine persona. He set his box down near the fireplace, then took the basket she was holding and set it on top.

She stood, looking around. "This place looks as unruly as mine."

"I know." He headed toward the door. "Let's bring in one more load and take a break. Come on."

They walked back outside to the van.

"Any luck on the Mustang and who owned it?" he asked.

"I called the DMV, but no one there would give me that information." She pulled a small box from the van and hugged it to her stomach. "I even tried to pull the, *I'm a private investigator card*, but they wanted credentials." She pulled a face. "A fact I'm certain you knew would happen."

He laughed. "Lucky for me, I wear a badge." He slid out a large box and heaved it to his chest. "Unfortunately, their offices suffered a fire some years ago, and the records from that time were destroyed."

"That is unfortunate." She followed him inside and set her box on the floor.

"Would you like something cold to drink?"

"Yes, please." Maybe during the break would be a good time to show him the note.

He left the room, and she stood, looking around the cluttered space. A small desk under the window faced the front yard. She stepped over and lightly fingered some of the documents on the desktop. Her intention hadn't been to snoop really...it was more curiosity than anything else. She'd been so used to looking through similar items at home that her fingers just began rifling through stuff. At least, that's the lie she told herself as she glanced over her shoulder toward Malcolm's kitchen.

As she flipped through the papers, she noticed an unmarked file folder. After another quick glance over her shoulder, she lifted one edge—just for a peek. *James Ross* jumped off the page. It couldn't be? But it was. Malcolm *had* made a copy and it was sitting right there. She took one more quick glance behind her.

She'd just started to read the first page when she heard footsteps. She snapped the folder shut, spun around, and held the file behind her back.

Malcolm entered the living room, and she nonchalantly pushed the folder into the back of her pants.

He stopped, and his eyes narrowed. "What do you think you're doing?"

She locked her gaze with his and swallowed. He set the drinks on the nearest side table and turned his attention fully on her.

Heart pounding, she stared wordlessly across at him—an unwelcome blush crept into her cheeks.

"Hand it over." His clear, observant eyes didn't miss much.

She licked her lips. "What?"

He snaked out his arm and spun her around so fast she fell forward over the desktop. With his left hand pressed to her back, he yanked the file from the top of her shorts with his other, then stood her upright.

His response had been so quick that all she could do was blink and stare at him. She gulped air, leaned back, and pressed her palms against the desk to steady her legs and her nerves.

"Are you serious?" He stared at her in utter disbelief. "Do you actually think I'm that stupid? I could see your reflection in the window."

Voiceless and humiliated, she rubbed her flesh where he'd gripped her. "I'm sorry... Please let me read it?" Tears gathered in her eyes. "What would be the harm?"

"One—it's police property, and two—I've been ordered not to show it to you."

"James Ross was my father." Her temper flared. "That gives me the right."

"Your rights stop with the police department." His deep-blue eyes turned to flint. "And in case you haven't figure it out, I don't work with liars and thieves."

Lucy felt the blood drain from her face. All she could do was stare. Was that what he thought of her?

"You need to go," he bit out.

His anger had barely subsided as he took her by her arm and marched her to the front door. She blinked back tears. No way could she reveal the note now. She got back on her bike and peddled away like a dog with her tail between her legs.

* * *

Malcolm had stopped her just in time. He'd panicked when he realized what she had behind her back, then anger got the better of him.

He ran his hand across the back of his neck. With her, it

was one step forward and two steps back. He thought they'd entered a different level in their relationship after that kiss. And just when he started to trust her, she pulled this juvenile stunt.

If he hadn't returned from the kitchen when he had, she may have seen the pictures. No daughter should see such crime-scene photos like those of her father, especially the one with her as a toddler, covered in his blood.

He brushed his hand through the top of his hair. Now she *knew* for certain he had the report. So what next? Should he burn it? But knew, as he thought it, he wouldn't. He trusted his father and even more, his investigative instincts. If Stuart Knox believed something was wrong, then it was.

After Malcolm caught her trying to steal, he had come down on her hard. He understood her need to see it, but that didn't excuse her behavior. Aside from being ordered not to show it to her, mostly he'd withheld it for her protection. It would go a long way if she'd simply trust him, instead of trying to steal from him.

Maybe at some point in the future, he'd reveal the contents. Only when the time was right, and when she learned trust went both ways. But having just thrown her out, only heaven knew when that would be.

In the meantime, he'd keep the file and continue with his own investigation. He'd planned to help Lucy when and where he could—help with her own leads even though hers still made no sense to him. But her recent action put a wedge in that for the time being.

Malcolm dropped into the nearest chair and rested his head in his hands. *Infuriating woman*. One minute he wanted to kiss her—the next—arm-wrestle her.

He hated leaving things the way they were. He'd been

drawn to her from the moment he'd set eyes on her at the ball. When she left after his *scolding*, tears had glistened in her beautiful, green eyes, and he'd been the cause of it. He understood her motives—her desire to get to the truth. If he were in her shoes, he'd feel the same way.

He stood, moved to the bedroom, and started hanging up his clothes. He'd taken the day off to finish moving in. Later, he'd head over to Lucy's and talk with her when he had a cooler head.

According to her suspect board, she obviously knew something about her father's death that wasn't in the initial report—something that could get her killed. She was in danger, and if he wasn't watching her, then he'd see to it someone else would be.

CHAPTER 18

Lucy stood in front of the board and studied the photo of the three officers. She'd been looking at it when the brick came through the window, reminding her that she'd forgotten to look for more photos that might help her identify the third man.

A minute later, she kneeled beside the box with the letters and photos and began going through them. She pushed back a wayward strand of hair, picked up the envelopes, and started reading the return addresses. She had gone through about half when she spotted a familiar name. *Stuart Knox*. Her jaw dropped. The stamp date showed 2004. She quickly opened the letter.

Dear Cara,

I've just heard the news of James's passing. I'm shocked and heartbroken that I didn't know before now. You know I would have been there for you and little Lucy had I known. Even though I'm on the other side of the world, I'll do my best from here to keep up with the case. Please know you and Lucy are in our prayers.

Stuart

Malcolm's father knew her parents and apparently, her, too. And from the tone of his note, he'd cared for them. She folded the letter and slid it back into the envelope. Malcolm had kept this from her? But why?

In the letter, Stuart mentioned the case, and from her talks with Malcolm, she knew his dad was a detective in Scotland. So how and where did Stuart know her father?

If she hadn't had that embarrassing confrontation with him earlier, she'd drive to the precinct now and demand some answers. This situation had certainly taken on a whole new level and given her a lot to think about. In the meantime, she would soldier on.

That afternoon, Lucy pushed through the door to one of the boutiques in her search for the elusive mask. She strolled through the shop, perusing the shelves, but didn't see the one she was looking for.

A woman appeared from the back. "May I help you?" she asked.

"Yes." Lucy smiled. "I was here a couple of weeks ago and bought a mask for the Policeman's Ball. Recently, I saw a man wearing a very unusual one similar to the ones worn that night by some of the officers. I was really hoping to buy one like it. It's quite extraordinary."

"Can you describe it?" she asked.

Lucy did, and when she'd finished, the lady nodded. "I do remember that one...very unusual. But that was from last year's stock. Due to the shape of the mask, I wasn't sure if they would sell, so I only bought two."

Lucy placed her hands on the counter. "So. You didn't sell that style this year?"

"Sorry, no. I tried to order more for this year's event, but the company quit making them. I'm not surprised. Most people don't want to cover their entire face."

Lucy tried another tactic. "I would really love to have one. Would you have a record of who bought those?"

"Probably."

"Would you mind telling me who they are?"

"I'm sorry. I can't give out customer's names."

"I understand. Would you be more comfortable sharing that information with Detective Knox?"

"Malcolm? Are you a friend of his?"

"I am."

"I would tell him, of course. He can either call me or stop by, and I'll be happy to give him those names."

"Thank you. I'll let him know." *When hell freezes over.*

Lucy left, disappointed, but understood the woman's position. No way would she ever ask Malcolm now. Besides, more than likely, he was already on it and would have the names by suppertime.

After his recent treatment of her, she had very little interest in ever seeing him again, much less asking for his help. Then there was the matter of the condolence letter from Stuart Knox. They were linked together through their fathers, but Malcolm chose to withhold that information. He'd proven he had no real interest in helping her. If he had, he'd have let her see the file and told her of his family's connection to hers. Instead, it was a crumb here and a crumb there.

She left the shop and stopped at the grocery to pick up a few things for dinner. It was still early yet, so Lucy drove home through the center of town. It was a bit longer that way, but she enjoyed the downtown area and its early twentieth-century charm.

As she drove, she continued to smart over her embarrassing incident at Malcolm's, when he'd spun her around and bent her over the desk for the report. Finding herself in that totally, humiliating position, she felt like a naughty child who needed discipline. And had a moment of horror that the brawny Scot was just the type to deliver some, too. Considering his size, she'd have been hard-pressed to fight him off. Her relief when he jerked her back to her feet was palpable. Her face burned at the thought.

It was twilight when she left the store. The evening mist morphed into fog, filling the streets on her drive home. Not surprising considering the amount of rain they'd had lately. The fog gave the streetlights an eerie glow, and in the distance, Main Street seemed to disappear in the darkening mist.

When she got home, all she could think about was de-stressing in a nice, warm bath. She put her groceries away, stripped down, and wrapped her fuzzy, pink chenille robe around her.

Minutes later, she sat on the edge of the tub and turned on both the hot and cold. No water—nothing. "You've got to be kidding me." She slumped. This could not be happening.

She turned the knobs in the opposite direction and stood. After grabbing the soap and a towel, she stepped into her slippers and headed out the back door. The last few days, the rain had filled the old water trough to the brim. Today had been unusually hot, and hopefully, the water was still warm enough to bathe in.

She stopped at the edge of the trough and dipped her fingers into the water. It was barely warm, but it would have to do. She tossed the towel over the fence, slipped out of the robe, threw it beside the towel, and stepped carefully inside the tank.

She lowered herself into the water and sighed as the semi warm bath covered her shoulders. She delighted in the feel of rustic luxury as she watched the water dance in the misty moonlight. Admittedly, something about this experience was rather enjoyable. Although a nice, unique experience, it left her feeling rather vulnerable and exposed.

She took her time soaping up, certain she would never bathe in a watering trough again. She lifted one leg and ran the bar along her calf and thigh, lowered it, then did the same to the other. She soaped her arms and chest, then went down into the water, fully submerging herself into the trough. When she came up, the moon had disappeared in the mist, adding an eerie, unnerving sensation to the night. Crickets and frogs and other unfamiliar sounds of the night pricked her ears and seemed menacing in the darkness.

A sudden crunching sound came from the left. *That wasn't a frog.*

A Raccoon?

Footsteps?

Her body tensed—she sucked in air and waited. A long shadow fell across the tub, blocking the light from the house. She yelped and snatched the towel from the fence, trying frantically to cover herself.

Malcolm stuck his hands into his pockets and stood looming over her and the trough. "Now this is something I never thought I'd see in this century."

"I don't have any water. Not that it's any concern of yours," she spat, maneuvering the towel up to her chin.

"None of the houses in the area have water. There's a break in the water main. Should be fixed shortly."

"And you came here to tell me that?"

"No."

"Then what the heck are you doing lurking in the shadows?"

"I wasn't lurking. I spotted you as soon as I came around the corner of the house."

"Then you should have said something." She seethed at having found herself in another humiliating position.

"But I was enjoying the view."

She could hear the smile in his voice as he said it. She so wanted to hit him with something.

She squeezed her eyes tightly together and shrank deeper into the water. "Well, as you can see, this is not a good time for me. So if—"

"I'll wait. I don't like the way we left things this afternoon." He turned and made his way to her house. "And take your time!" he hollered without looking back. "I have all evening."

Lucy removed the towel, which was now soaking wet, and lowered her body one more time, fully rinsing off any lingering, soapy residue.

She glanced toward the house. When she was certain he had left the yard, she stood and slung one leg over the edge of the trough. Using her left foot, she tapped the earth until she found one of her slippers, then did the same with her right.

She quickly put on her robe, cinching it together at the waist. When she reached the back door, she entered the kitchen to the smell of coffee. "I take it the water's back on."

"It is." He poured the hot, black liquid into a floral mug. "I hope you don't mind. It's been a long day, and I need the caffeine."

"Unpacking difficult for you, is it?" She smirked.

The corners of his mouth lifted. "I wasn't referring to the unpacking." He spooned sugar into his mug and stirred.

"I'm not leaving here without some answers." He settled back in the chair and stretched out his legs, crossing his feet at the ankles. "So, if you'd like to make yourself a little *less* comfortable..." He ran his gaze over her robe and fluffy slippers. "Up to you, of course."

"I'm sorry." She folded her arms. "Did I say you could stay?"

The right side of his mouth hitched into a lazy smile. "I see you're still sporting that malevolent gleam from earlier." He leaned toward her. "Like I said, I'm not leaving here without some answers. I can either bring you down to the station and question you there, or we can chat here." He blew across the top of his coffee, continuing to eye her.

She rolled her eyes and huffed out a breath. "Fine," she said and marched off. She quickly dressed in slim-fitting jeans and a blue-checked shirt, spotted the Knox letter, and stuffed it in the front of her waistband.

Leaving her feet bare, she ran her fingers through her damp hair and made her way back to the kitchen. She stopped in front of him, placing her hands on her hips. He slowly studied her.

"Your buttons are off."

She glanced down and quickly took the chair opposite him, doing her best to keep *that malevolent gleam,* going.

His eyes held a gleam, too. One that said, *I'm the detective, and you're not.*

"While you were changing, I did a quick study of your suspect board."

"And..."

"What's your interest in that photo of the three officers? I see you now have the actual photo. You steal that, too?"

She clamped her teeth over her bottom lip. "To answer the first part of your question... I'd rather not say."

"And the second?"

"The answer is no. I did not steal it."

"Look at you." He shook his head and scoffed. "You're just a child playing games—dangerous ones at that."

"Good heavens." She lifted her chin. "How old are you?"

"A lot older than you."

"I thought you said you were here because you didn't like how things were left today," she argued.

"That's right. But if you thought that meant I brought you the file, you can think again."

She reached into the top of her jeans, pulled out Knox's letter, and slapped it on the table in front of him. "Seems you're withholding a lot more from me than my father's report."

He swallowed, his dark eyebrows slanted in a frown. He picked up the letter, opened it, and silently read it. Seconds later, he folded it and tucked it back inside the envelope. "I had every intention of telling you. I—"

"Is the third man in that photo your father?"

He nodded. "I've just been waiting for the right time to tell you."

"How about now?" Her chest heaved. "Is now the right time?"

He leveled her with his blue-eyed gaze. "Actually, it's not."

How dare he act so cool—so collected? She shot from her chair. "I need to see that report. I've waited years for this, and one way or the other, I intend to find out what's in it. No one is going to stop me, and that includes *you*." Her voice broke.

"If you're so hell-bent on it, why didn't you look it up online when you had the chance?"

She lowered her gaze and fiddled with the edge of her blouse. "I didn't know I could."

"Your *detective-in-training* manual not tell you that?"

"Truthfully," she winced, "I haven't read all of it."

"Just the parts that taught you to how to break in and steal?"

She sucked in air and jerked her head up. "If you're not here to help me, then you can just go."

He eyed her for a second, stood, and then tossed the dregs of his coffee in the sink.

She marched to the front door, yanked it open, and waited for him. As he crossed the space between them, his deep-blue gaze bore into hers.

He stopped in front of her and didn't seem in any hurry to go. She licked her lips and yanked the door open even wider. If that wasn't an invitation to leave, she didn't know what was.

Without a word, he stepped through the door to the outside.

"Looks like you're leaving here without answers, after all," she said, with every intention of having the last word.

"Looks like it."

"Well. I want answers, too. If you'd just let me see the file, maybe I—"

"Not. Going. To. Happen." He gripped the doorknob and pulled it closed behind him.

She stood, staring at the door—now shut—and thought about the other note in her pocket. She'd so wanted to show it to him, but now realized she'd made the right decision not to.

"Hardhearted, infuriating man." Her father's case had been closed for twenty years. What would have been the harm in letting her see it?

She shuffled over to the sofa and slumped back against the cushions. The suspect board seemed to mock her from its position along the wall. She'd reached a standstill. How could she move forward without more information?

She leaned further back, resting her head along the top of the couch. At least she had her dad's note and the strong possibility her shoulder had been microchipped. She'd wait for the chip reader to arrive and go from there. She certainly didn't need Detective Malcolm Knox for that.

CHAPTER 19

Saturday morning, Lucy popped a slice of bread into the toaster, then filled a mug with hot coffee. After the previous night's tangle with Malcolm, she hadn't slept well, so she made her coffee strong and black. With one hand cradling the mug and the other pressed to her left temple, she shuffled to the kitchen table and sat down.

Heat crept up her cheeks at the memory of Malcolm having found her bathing in a horse trough. She retrieved her toast and set her mug aside to slather an ample amount of marmalade on top.

Two hours later, she'd managed to declutter the last of the boxes and a chest of drawers in the smaller bedroom. Finally, she had finished.

Within hours, Grace Works arrived to pick up the donations, followed shortly by Nick's Trash Pickup Service for the rest of the clutter. The house seemed to breathe a contented sigh with the last of the donations and bags of trash gone.

She glanced around at her handiwork and took stock of

the living room with its dingy walls and frayed rugs. It was now time shop and to paint—and not necessarily in that order.

She fixed a second cup of joe, added cream and sugar, then headed to the patio. Dreams of color schemes for the house filled her mind as she settled onto the settee. She thought of the pretty stones she'd found with their soft hues of green, gold, and yellow. As she mixed and matched color combinations in her head, she gazed out over the small acreage. *What in the world?* She blinked and stared.

The mid-morning sun caught and reflected hundreds of shiny objects on top of the ground. She stood, set her coffee on the seat, and walked forward.

Marveling at the sight of jewels, she bent down and picked up one of the stones. Where had they all come from? Did the past few days of rain bring them to the surface? Dumfounded, she gaped at the scene before her. Her coffee forgotten, she ran back inside, grabbed a mixing bowl from the upper cupboard, then hurried back outside.

She fell to her haunches and, one by one, gathered every stone she could find. Half an hour later, she had a bowlful. This was incredible. Her mind raced over what to do next. *Crater of Diamonds in Murfreesboro.* She'd call them. Someone there should be able to help her.

She carried the stones to the living room and looked up Crater's number. Since they weren't opened yet, she bookmarked it to call later.

While she waited, she photocopied the note from the floorboard. After putting the original back in the metal box for safekeeping, she went back to the living room and pinned the copy at the far end of the clue board.

She stepped back and perched herself on the edge of the

coffee table. With her fingers pressed to her temples, she contemplated the clues. At this point, the note added absolutely nothing, and until she got the chip reader, she was still unable to go forward with that angle.

Her phone dinged. It was from Amazon. *Your package will arrive tomorrow between 10:00 and 2:00 p.m.*

Her phone dinged again. This time, a message from Jan.

I finally have information about the facility for your mom. I'm heading over to Baillie's Italian for lunch in about an hour. If you're available, why don't you join me and we can go over what I found out.

Since Dr. Edwards had convinced Lucy not to move her mom, it was a moot point. She wouldn't dare tell Jan and may as well get the information...just in case something changed.

That's wonderful, Jan. Isn't that on Main Street?

Yes, next to Dart Drugs. See you at noon.

Lucy placed a 'thumb's up' on Jan's final comment. She glanced at her wristwatch—almost ten thirty. Now might be a good time to call Crater of Diamonds.

A pleasant voice answered on the third ring.

"Hello, may I speak with your gemologist?" Lucy fingered one of the stones in the bowl.

"Of course. I'll connect you."

"Hello, this is Blake."

"Blake, my name is Lucy Ross and I need your advice about some stones I've found on my property."

"Sure."

"This morning, hundreds of stones appeared on the surface of my property. I've gathered up an entire bowlful."

"That's incredible. Where are you?"

"Diamond Creek."

"That's not too far from here. I'd love to bring my equipment and see what you've got. I'm leaving for vacation in a few hours. Unfortunately, it'll be a couple of weeks before I can get there."

"That'll be fine," she said.

They agreed on a date and time, and Lucy gave him her address. She hung up, wondering if her mom knew about the stones. Most likely not, or she would have told Lucy.

Lucy sat perfectly still and focused on the stones in the bowl. Griffin Gate was turning out to be more than just the Ross family homestead. How could three generations of Rosses live on this twenty-seven-acre plot of land and not know about the value underneath their feet?

After her shower, Lucy dressed in a simple, tailored, brown-and-white polka-dot dress, slipped on a pair of strappy sandals, then headed out.

She found a parking space a few doors down from the restaurant, got out, and locked the Subaru. As she did so, she spotted a police car across the street. Over the past couple of days, she noticed the same type cruiser seemed to be somewhere in her vicinity. That wasn't unusual as this was a small town, but still.

She gnawed her bottom lip and walked over to the vehicle. As she got closer, she saw it was Officer Kirby. With a fist on her left hip, she lifted her right hand and tapped on the glass.

Kirby glanced up and rolled down the window.

Lucy lowered her head. "License and registration, please."

Kirby gave her a sheepish grin. "Hey, Lucy."

She rested her forearms along the doorframe. "Are you following me?"

"Orders from Detective Knox," he said. "Simms and I have been taking shifts. We just want to make sure you're safe."

She removed her sunglasses and squinted at him. "Or, keeping me from getting into trouble."

"That too, ma'am."

She straightened, rested her hand on the window ledge, then slipped back into her shades. "Thanks, Kirby. I'm having lunch with Jan Kelly, so, if you want to grab a bite while I'm in there, feel free."

"Thank you, but I'm fine right where I am."

"Don't want to get yelled at, do you?"

"That's correct."

Lucy shook her head and made her way to the front door of the restaurant.

Jan waved to Lucy as she entered. They both ordered the day's soup-and-salad special—Caprese salad and Italian wedding soup. In minutes, the waitress delivered their lunch. "Enjoy, ladies."

Lucy wondered if she should tell Jan about her extraordinary find that morning, but decided to keep mum until she learned more.

"What a pretty blouse," Lucy said.

"Thank you." Jan flicked the red-and-white-checkered napkin onto her lap. "I just love linen. Way too hot around these parts for anything else."

"And such a pretty color, too."

"It matches my car," Jan said.

"But you drive a white Volvo." Lucy spooned soup into her mouth.

"I do, but today I'm driving my mom's vintage Mustang." Lucy almost choked.

"You okay?" Jan asked.

Lucy nodded and took a swig of her tea. She mustered a smile. "Wow, a Mustang. I'd love to see it."

"Absolutely," Jan said. "I'm just parked a few doors down from here."

It took a measure of self-control not to march right outside and take a look at that car. "What do you have for me?" she calmly asked, heart tattooing against her ribs.

"Sorry this took so long. I'll spare you the details." She lifted her napkin and dabbed her mouth. "After talking with my friends, here are the two places they recommend." Jan handed Lucy a printout.

She glanced over the information. "These look great, Jan. Thanks so much for following through with this."

"My pleasure."

Lucy slipped the paper into her handbag. "I'll read it over later, and then call my mom."

"So." Jan forked her salad. "What's happening between you and Detective Gorgeous?"

"If you're referring to Detective, *I want no nonsense from you,* Knox, then the answer is, not a thing."

Jan lifted a brow. "Sounds like he's gotten under your skin. What'd he do?"

"He's just one of those annoying by-the-book types." Fork in the air, Lucy leaned across the table "He's actually put a tail on me." She snapped up a crouton, popped it between her lips, and bit down. "According to Officer Kirby, it's to keep me safe and out of trouble."

"Sounds quite romantic if you ask me," Jan said. "I've heard he's been at your place several times lately. You had a break-in, right?"

"Yes. So you can see his visits are purely professional.

Trust me, there's nothing there. The man is an arrogant, condescending, bully." She jabbed her salad with such force the lettuce went flying.

"Oh, dear," Jan chuckled. "As bad as that?"

"As bad as that, and then some."

"Well," Jan said. "So much for his *earthy, brogue-to-die-for* accent."

"Exactly."

Lucy still smarted from being thrown out of his cute little cottage. Things had been going so well, too. She felt they'd taken a turn in their relationship—had actually been happy to see him—but now they were worse than worse.

And whose fault is that?

She dabbed her mouth with her napkin, ignoring the obvious answer to that question.

They ate and chatted for the next fifteen minutes. Lucy was anxious to finish and see that car.

Jan glanced at her watch. "I hate to cut our time short, but I have a showing in thirty minutes."

They walked a few doors down to where Jan had parked the Mustang. "It's a 1970 Ford Mustang Coupe. Nice, huh?"

"I'll say, and what an interesting color." Lucy ran her hand along the hood. "Do you mind if I take a picture?"

"Of course not."

"Does you mother still drive it?" Lucy held her breath. *Please still be alive.*

"Are you kidding? I was lucky she let me have it today. Believe me, it's rare."

Lucy waved goodbye to Jan with one thought in her head—how to wrangle an invite to meet her mother. If she'd been on speaking terms with Detective Knox, she'd rush over to the precinct now and tell him of her find, but since she wasn't, then that was that.

Diamond Creek was small, and twenty years ago, even smaller. She'd bet anything Jan's mom had known hers. That was reason enough for Lucy to meet her.

While in town, Lucy spent the next hour visiting shops and boutiques that may have sold that particular full-faced mask. She'd try one more store, then quit if she wasn't successful.

The sales clerk at the previous shop happened to be familiar with that particular mask. "There's only one in town that carries it," he said.

Lucy discovered the only shop that sold that particular mask had been the one she'd visited a few days prior where the owner wouldn't release the information. The girl behind the counter today was not the same woman Lucy had talked with earlier in the week. This girl was young—a high school student, maybe.

"Good afternoon," Lucy said. "I was here the other day and spoke to an older lady about some information I needed. Is she here?"

"She's not, I'm sorry."

Perfect.

"Is there something I can help you with?" the girl said.

"Yes. That would be great, thank you." Lucy quickly told her what she needed. While Lucy waited, she shuffled from one foot to the other. When the girl came back to the front, she held a sheet of paper in her hand.

"Sorry for the wait. The printer acted up again. Here you go. Those are the two buyers for that particular mask last year." She handed the info to Lucy, just as Malcolm walked in.

Lucy groaned and wanted to stomp her foot, but knew it would only come across as totally childish, giving him more ammunition against her.

* * *

Malcolm entered the shop and spotted Lucy at the counter taking a printout from a young saleslady. He'd bet anything it contained information about who bought the masks. His eyes swept over her defiant features as he approached.

"Is that what I think it is?"

Lucy, in the act of folding the paper in half, smugly pinched her lips together.

"I'll take that." He lifted the single sheet from her fingers, then gave it a quick perusal. "This is sales for last year, what about this year?" he addressed the girl behind the counter.

The young woman gaped between him and Lucy, a bit perplexed. To put her at ease, he held up his badge. "Police business," he said.

"Oh, okay. Well, we didn't carry that mask this year, because the company went out of business."

"I see."

He glanced back at Lucy, who stood, arms folded tightly across her chest, eyeing him with acute dislike.

"Thank you," he said to the girl and strode back to the entrance. He stopped and held the door for Lucy. He lifted a brow, giving her the same *look* he used for his subordinates at the precinct.

No way on earth would he leave her there to meddle further. In his opinion, her actions had done nothing but draw unnecessary attention to the case, hampering his investigation.

As Malcolm waited, he thought she'd refuse to join him, but instead, she tossed her head, marched forward, then through the door.

"I see that malevolent gleam is back in your eye."

She stopped on the sidewalk. "Can you blame me?" Her eyes suddenly lost that nasty gaze and turned to one of appeal. "Won't you at least show them to me?"

"I told you to leave this alone."

"That girl gave *me* those names, and if you hadn't walked in, I'd still have them." She jabbed a finger to her chest. "I went to three other places without success, before I found the right store." She took a deep breath and angled her head purposefully at Kirby who was still parked across the street. "Is that how you knew where I was?"

"It is."

"Doesn't he have anything better to do than to keep tabs on me?"

"Yes, and if I could trust you to behave and leave the investigating to the police, then he could. You're in too deep as it is, Lucy. You're dealing with dangerous people. What part of that don't you understand?" He folded the paper and slid it into his breast pocket. "Good day, Miss Ross." Malcolm left her standing on the sidewalk in front of the shop.

* * *

If Lucy thought she'd get away with it, she'd go right back in there and get the information for herself. But the fact that Malcolm had displayed his badge and told the girl it was police business—Lucy knew she'd have no chance of getting it now.

She decided to call her mom and tell her about the options to get her closer until the house was ready. Even though Dr. Edwards had given a reason not to move her mother, Lucy felt she should at least talk to her mom and see how she felt about it.

As she stood on the sidewalk, she spotted the charming little pastry shop across the street with a pretty, pink-and-green-striped awning over the entrance. She'd noticed it soon after she moved back and had wanted an excuse to try it.

While she waited for a break in traffic, she couldn't resist waving to Officer Kirby. When the light changed, she darted across the road.

The interior of *Short Cakes* was also decorated in soft pink-and-green shades. She took a bistro table by the window and ordered a layered donut with caramel icing and coffee. While her order was being filled, she dialed her mother's apartment.

"Hello," her mom answered on the third ring.

"Hey, Mom."

"Darling. How are you?"

"I'm good." Lucy paused at the sound of a masculine voice. "Who's that in the background?"

"It's all right." A muffled sound... "It's my daughter."

"Mom, who is that? Put him on the phone, right now."

"She wants to talk to you," her mom said.

"Hello, Officer Lewis here."

"Who?"

"Is this Lucy Ross?"

"Yes, it is. What are you doing there? Is my mother okay?"

"She's fine. We're just playing cards. I'm sorry if my presence concerned you. Your mother has had round-the-clock protection for several days now. I was told you knew about the protection detail. Detective Knox set this up with my department."

"Oh, yes—that's right." All tension left her body. "Of course, I remember. I'd just forgotten." So Malcolm had made sure her mother was protected and would stay that way until they figured out who had come after Lucy.

A twinge of guilt dinged her heart. She'd defied Malcolm more than once since she'd met him. Maybe he'd just been trying to protect her, too.

"Would you put my mother back on the phone, please?"

"Of course. Miss Cara, your daughter wants to speak to you."

"We're playing cards, dear. Everything's fine. Are you coming to see me soon?"

"I hope so. Things are crazy here. But I wanted to talk to you about a facility that would get you closer to Diamond Creek. It would only be a thirty-minute drive—"

"To the house?"

"No darling, to the new facility. I was just trying to get you closer to me. I could visit you more often."

"I think I'd like to stay here until the house is ready."

"Of course. I understand. Enjoy your card game. I'll see you Sunday."

Lucy signed off just as her coffee and donut arrived. Somewhat disappointed, she sunk her teeth into the sweet confection. It was probably for the best. Dr. Edwards had been correct when he said moving her mom might be too difficult for her.

Later that evening, Lucy drove over to see Malcolm. She

wanted to thank him for seeing to her mom's protection. In the short time she'd known him, she had learned one thing for certain about Malcolm Knox—he was trustworthy. And she believed she could trust him with the contents of her father's note.

She pulled her car into the gravel driveway and stopped. Unless he'd parked his car in the back, he wasn't home. She got out, walked to the front door and knocked, then knocked again. She stepped left to the window, cupped her hands to her face, and peered through the glass. About to turn away, she spotted the folder, open and lying on the sofa.

She gnawed her upper lip and looked back over her shoulder. Her lock-picking kit was in her purse. It wouldn't take much to open the door, go in, and look at that report. She'd given him more chances than she could count to let her see it and without success.

She pressed her forehead against the windowpane. *Is this how you treat the man you've now deemed trustworthy? Who has secured protection not only for Mom, but also for me?* She groaned and lifted her head from the glass.

But this may be the only chance I have to read it.

She ran back to her car, pulled the lock-picking kit from her purse, and hurried back to the front door.

She got down on her haunches and slipped the metal pick into the lock. After maneuvering it several times, she heard the click. Heart thudding, she stood, turned the handle, glanced over her shoulder one more time, then went inside.

She hurried across the room, quickly gathering up the papers. After making certain they were the Ross files, she stuffed them back into the folder. She stood for a second, contemplating if she should try to read the report there or take it home. If she stayed there, he'd never have to know. But if he showed up and caught her...

Be brave Lucy. If he finds out, he'll explode, but that's never stopped you before.

She decided to remove the report from the folder. That done, she grabbed a few papers from his desk and replaced them for the real one. With luck, she could take the report, make a copy, then return it before he ever found out.

She left the house with the file in her hands. On the porch, she made sure the door was locked, and then bolted down the steps and across the lawn to her car.

Chapter 20

Malcolm hung up his phone just as Officer Chase walked by his doorway.

"Chase!"

Chase stopped and focused on Malcolm. "Yes, sir?"

"Come in and take a seat."

Chase took the black, vinyl chair across from Malcolm's desk. "What's up, boss?"

"I tracked down the two masks fitting Lucy's description, and the two men who bought them. Apparently, one was sold to you."

"That's right. I wore it last year at the ball, and then donated it the next day to Calvary Methodist Church over on Warren Avenue for their spring bazaar. As I recall, Jan Kelly bid on it and won. She's a friend of mine. I can give her a call and see if she still has it."

Malcolm leaned back in his chair. "Do that and let me know as soon as you find out."

"What about the other mask, sir? You said there were two."

"That's been cleared up. It was purchased by Officer Kyle Blankenship. He moved to Texas shortly afterward. Kirby talked with him yesterday, and he still has the mask. He emailed Kirby a photo of it, then Kirby sent it to me."

Chase stood and headed for the door. "I'll give Jan a call right now."

Chase tapped on Malcolm's door about ten minutes later. "Just talked with Jan. Six months ago, she sent the mask to one of her friends who'd recently moved to New Orleans, so she could wear it during Mardi Gras. Jan said her friend still has it."

"Thanks, good work."

Malcolm sat forward, elbows on his desk. With fingers pressed to his temples, he blew out a breath. Another dead end. Either a third mask had been sold, or one of these two were lying.

Malcolm got home in time to fix a quick meal before he went over to see Lucy. He opened a can of tomato soup, and while that simmered, fixed a grilled cheese sandwich.

As he brought both on a tray into the living room, he thought about that short list of buyers for the mask. Malcolm had come to know Chase well and was relieved he'd been cleared.

At least he could now share this information with Lucy. He knew enough to know that she'd hound him until he did.

A few minutes later, he shoved the last morsel of cheesy crust into his mouth and reached for the Ross file. He swiped crumbs from his lap and opened the folder.

His jaw dropped. "What in blazes?" The original contents of the file were gone. He checked the folder. It clearly showed *James Ross* in black ink on the outer tag, but the document inside was from another report.

He closed the file and stared ahead, scowling at nothing in particular.

Bloody hell!

Only one person could've taken it—only one *cheeky* enough to brazenly pick the lock on *his* front door.

Jaw clenched, he stood and tossed the file against the coffee table. He could not believe it.

The audacity.

The impudence.

He sucked in a breath, grabbed his keys, and slammed his way out the door and to his car. This was one action *Miss Ross* would regret.

Malcolm arrived at Lucy's in mere minutes, and it took only seconds for him to burst through her front door. Lucy, perched on the sofa, swung around at his entrance.

He stopped and lifted up the folder. "How dare you break into my house? Steal a classified document? Then try to cover it by putting another report in its place? Do you actually think you can break the law for your own convenience and get away with it?"

He strode across the room and snatched up her, *detective-in-training* manual.

Lucy shot to her feet, stiff and wide-eyed, without speaking.

"You think you can use *this* as an excuse for what you're doing?" He slammed the book onto the coffee table.

She visibly jumped and clutched something large and white to her chest. She opened her mouth to speak, but nothing came out.

"Have you forgotten someone followed you, broke into

this house, and threatened you and your mother?" he raved. "Don't you realize you're dealing with dangerous people? I've been doing this for ten years and you've been doing this for what...two weeks—?"

A glazed look of despair spread over her features. A piece of white paper slipped from her hand to the floor. Lucy's face crumbled, and she pressed her fingers to the scar at her temple.

It wasn't until that moment that he realized what she'd been holding. With her fingers still pressed to her hairline, he focused on the floor. It was the photograph, the one of her, as a distraught four-year-old, reaching desperately for her dead father as he lay lifeless and bleeding on the ground.

Malcolm's anger abated and compassion filled him. And for the first time, he *really* looked at Lucy since he'd stormed in. Deathly white, her pupils dilated, she stood trembling, clearly in shock, the evidence of tears marking her cheeks.

He took one step, picked up the photograph, and laid it facedown on the table. Then he gathered Lucy into his arms and pulled her down beside him on the sofa.

"Lucy—"

"I remember." Her voice cracked in a broken whisper as the words fell from her lips. Her eyes darkened to a deep jade. Wide and desperate, she stared at him. "I remember that very moment." She eyed the photo, now face down. "I remember *him*."

Seeing the photograph had obviously unleashed the memory she'd locked away all those years ago. After hours of therapy, it took seeing that picture to unlock it.

Her breath came in deep gulps, and she clutched her hands to her chest. His gut churned with a one-two punch. About to take her back in his arms, she leaned toward him, slowly and deliberately. He thought she was going to kiss him, but as her face neared his chin she closed her eyes, turned her head sideways, and gently laid her cheek against his right shoulder. Resting against him, she lifted her left hand and curled it underneath her chin.

He slipped his arms around her—the rhythm of her heart, beating in sync with his, as he held her snug against his chest. As he leaned back with her in his arms, she lifted her feet and knees and curled up beside him.

Malcolm, stiff from holding her in that position, shifted his body upright, causing Lucy to slide from his shoulder to his lap. As he gazed down at her, he noticed her creamy complexion had returned, replacing that gray tinge, from earlier.

He gently ran his fingers up her cheek, along her forehead, to the pink scar at her hairline. He simply couldn't keep his eyes off her.

Malcolm had no idea how much time had passed, but as he grew tired, he rested his head along the back of the sofa and slept.

When he woke, the orange glow of the sun poured through the front window.

Careful not to wake her, he eased right, then stood. During the night, she'd curled up on her side. For a moment, he took joy in simply watching her sleep. He rubbed his hand over his bearded chin, then glanced at the mysteries pinned to her suspect board. Maybe it was time they shared what they knew. He grabbed a small, floral quilt from the side chair and gently covered her.

He made his way to the kitchen. While the coffee brewed, he grabbed a quick shower. Ten minutes later, he carried two mugs into the living room. When he walked in, Lucy was sitting up with her knees drawn to her chest. Hair tousled and with raccoon eyes, she reminded him of a beautiful, but lost, waif. She glanced up when he entered and ran a hand through her hair.

"I must look a sight," she said.

She *did* look a sight. A sight he wouldn't mind waking up to every morning. He smiled and handed her a mug. "Made you coffee."

"Thank you." She lowered her head and placed her lips along the rim.

"I took a shower in your hall bath. Hope you don't mind?"

"Of course not."

"Do you feel like eating something?" he asked.

"Not right now. I'll finish this and take my shower."

* * *

After Lucy showered, she called her mom to tell her she wouldn't be coming for her Sunday visit. She was totally fine with that, as Lucy knew she would be. After promising to come later in the week, she rang off.

Lucy dressed in white shorts and a blue sleeveless blouse, slipped on her sneakers, and then came down the hall. Malcolm had been nothing but kindness last night. He hadn't deserved her deception. She sucked in a breath and blew it out. No time like the present to eat crow.

She entered the living room, and he glanced up when he saw her. There was a smile in his eyes as he looked at her, one she felt she didn't deserve.

"Malcolm, you've been nothing but fair, patient, and trustworthy, and I've been..." She paused, searching for the right word.

"A wee scunner," he said.

"A what?"

One side of his mouth quirked upward. "It means... You're a little nuisance."

"Now you're just being generous. I've behaved *much* worse than that."

"True, but I forgive you. Come." He patted the seat next to him. "I made pancakes while you got ready. They're a mite cold but still good."

"And he cooks, too." She sat next to him, picked up the plate, and forked an ample portion into her mouth. "Mmm, even cold these are delicious."

She finished eating, then set the plate aside and turned toward him. Her heart ached with remorse. "I'm sorry."

His lips formed a slight smile. "I take it you've read the report?"

She shook her head. "I got about halfway through before I decided to look at the pictures. It was awful seeing my father like that... And the one with me..." She stared into his serious face.

"Last night you said you remember. You remember that moment and him. Is that correct?"

"Yes. As painful as it was, as shocking, and as horrifying... It unlocked something deep inside my brain. I now remember that moment—nothing before or after. Seeing the photograph helped me. And more importantly, it's helped me to remember *him*."

"That's a good thing."

She nodded. "I think I told you that I'd been in therapy twice in my life trying to unlock any memory of that time but without success."

"Yes, you did."

"Dr. Edwards told me the shock I'd experienced had suppressed that memory to someplace deep inside my mind. And that something would eventually trigger it to come forth. As difficult as it was seeing that photograph, it helped me to remember. And I'm thankful for that."

"I was so angry at you when I came in last night. I said a lot of things..." he hesitated.

"All of it true," she said.

"Maybe so, but I regret having said them while you were in a state of shock."

"Truthfully, I think I missed half of it. I registered your anger and a few *choice* words..." She smiled. "But that's about it."

"Good. I feel better now." He took her hand in his. "It's important you know that I tried to protect you from that photo."

"I know."

"In hindsight, I wish I'd told you about it, and then we could've looked at it together. I hate that you saw it by yourself." The sincerity in his eyes squeezed her heart.

"Thank you for trying to protect me. And on that subject, the reason I went to your house yesterday was to thank you for putting the police detail on my mother. Believe it or not, I'd forgotten all about that."

"They're taking good care of her. I insisted on a daily report from them."

"I called her yesterday and found out that an officer was there with her. So thank you." She lowered her gaze and laced her fingers together. "Then I saw the report through the window, and the rest as they say...is history. I thought I could take it home, make a photo copy, and return it without you knowing."

She glanced up and caught the slight smile that had formed on his face. The intensity in his gaze reminded her of the night she'd met him. His blue eyes held that same keen interest now as they had then. Instinct told her he was about to say something. She held her breath and waited.

"I guess this is as good a time as any to ask."

"Ask me what?"

"Hold on."

His smile did strange and wonderful things to her insides.

"The Hollands are having their annual summer party," he said. "Would you like to go as my *plus one*?"

She gaped at him and licked her lips.

"A simple yes or no will suffice."

Heat rose in her cheeks. "I'd love to go."

"Good. I understand it's rather informal. I'll find out the exact dress code and let you know."

"Sounds like fun."

CHAPTER 21

Malcolm loved it when Lucy blushed. Her cheeks filled with the prettiest pink, like a primrose along the moors in spring.

The past twenty-four hours had not gone as he'd planned. The day before, he'd marched in there, ready to strangle her. But she'd ended up sleeping in his arms, and that morning he'd asked her to a party.

The woman was fast getting under his skin, and the fact that his time there was short loomed before him. And then there was Becca—a constant reminder of what happened when you fell for a much younger girl. There'd been an age gap there, too, and look how that turned out. He ran his hand over the back of his neck. Maybe he had a type?

After Becca, he swore he'd never date a woman so much younger than him again, and there he was, falling for one even younger than the last. But honestly, it was more than the age difference. He only had eight more months there before he was to move back to Scotland.

Was it selfish to pursue Lucy, knowing that? He liked the aggravating lass—a lot. He could tell she liked him—*more* than liked him. What would be the harm in seeing if it went anywhere? But she was young, like Becca. And like Becca, would Lucy come to realize she had a lot of living to do before settling down?

And so went the constant tug of war when it came to his feelings for her.

Wait...what was she saying?

"You know how when you look at a photo from when you were little and you say, oh, I remember that. And you recall many little details of that moment? Well, every time I watched the video, I didn't recall a thing. But now I do."

"Wait." Intrigued, Malcolm eyed her. "What video?"

Lucy got up and walked to the pine dresser along the entry wall and pulled out an old video camera. She sat back down and opened the viewer screen.

"I'm about to show you something I discovered a few months ago. It was in my mother's things, hidden in the back of her closet at our house. Ever since she went to live at Oak Haven, I've occasionally made an effort to clean things out. That's when I found this. She doesn't know I have it, and frankly, I'm not even sure she'd remember it."

"Okay."

"I'm pretty certain what you're about to see has never been seen by anyone else—certainly not the police or this tape would've been taken away years ago as evidence."

She held the camera between them and pressed play.

Malcolm watched a young Detective Ross hold his four-year-old daughter in his arms. The joy in this young father touched him—and the happy scene made Malcolm smile. After a few seconds of filming, the person holding the camera turned it toward herself and made a silly face.

"That's my mom, Cara."

Then Cara turned the camera back to Ross and Lucy. Moments later, Ross's smile disappeared, turning to anger, then he ran his hand across his throat—motioning for Cara to stop filming.

As she turned the camera, she caught the front and then left side of the sedan as it pulled to a stop. The camera lowered, and she caught part of the man's legs and feet as he got out of the car. The last few seconds on the screen was of the grass before it went blank.

Malcolm sat, stunned. "This has been in your mother's possession all these years?"

"Yes. I knew he'd been shot sometime after the camera went dark." She gazed up at Malcolm with a sad, but hopeful, expression in her eyes.

He raised one hand to the side of her face, lifting it to the scar at her hairline. "And the day you got this?"

"Yes, and the day my father was murdered."

He nodded and took her hands in his, giving them a gentle shake. "And we're going to solve his murder... together."

Her sweet lips lifted and broke into a smile.

After a moment, he tore his gaze from hers. "I take it, this is where you discovered the make of the car and the shoes on the shooter."

"My first clues. Then later I found the article confirming the car and its owner."

"Let's watch it again," he said.

Lucy rewound the tape, then pressed play. They sat in silence, watching the short video. When it ended, Lucy pressed stop and turned off the camera. "What do think?"

He looked at her. "I think we have a lot to talk about. It's important you don't show this to anyone else. Is that clear?"

"I'm glad you feel that way. I was afraid you'd take it from me."

"I guess it's okay to tell you this now. I tracked down the men who bought the masks fitting your description. Both men are officers, and they've checked out."

"Good. It's a relief to know it wasn't one of them."

"I agree. By the way..." He lifted out his phone from his pocket. "I actually have a photo if you'd like to see it. Kirby tracked this one down."

She took the phone from his hands and enlarged it with her thumb and index finger. "That's not the mask." She handed the phone back. "That's not what I saw."

"Are you sure?"

"Yes."

"Then where the heck is it?" he said.

Lucy's eyes darkened, and her brow furrowed. "We're not getting very far, are we?"

"It certainly seems that way. This is a very old case, remember? It's going to take time."

She pursed her pretty lips and nodded.

"Are you up to watching this one more time?" he asked.

"I've already watched it a hundred times. Believe me, one more won't make any difference..." She looked right at him. "Actually, now that you're here, maybe it will."

"Good girl. I'd like to have you pause it at certain spots while I make notes."

* * *

Lucy paused the tape when Malcolm asked her to and watched him make notes in his tablet before telling her to continue. The process took a bit longer than she thought it would, but obviously, Malcolm was seeing things she had missed—and most probably due to the fact that he had fully read the report.

His expression serious, his dark eyebrows knit together in concentration as he viewed the tape. She bit her nail and studied him, realizing she was witnessing a real detective at work—his thoroughness unmatched. Confident and professional as his strong, capable hands scribbled notes across the pad. Detective Malcolm Knox knew what he was doing, and he was good at it.

This Scottish, bearded, god was extraordinary. Rocking her world like no one else had ever done before. Just sitting there, he stirred something deep within her. She searched for one word to describe this magic—this pull, and there was none.

It had been days since that heart-stopping kiss, yet the feelings it evoked hadn't left her. Tender, yet persuasive, and with an urgency that took her breath away.

The tape finally came to the end, and she turned the camera off and set it on the coffee table.

He glanced up at her suspect board. "Okay, we know about the sedan and who owns it. Initially, I'd planned to talk with Crandall, but he'd alert Holland, who'd put an end to my investigation, messing up everything I've done so far."

"Isn't there any way to get information without spooking him?"

"I don't think so. And believe me, I've racked my brains for a way."

"If I'd found him that first day, I'd have asked him plenty," she said.

Malcolm gave her one of his *looks*. "From the video," he continued, "we have the black-and-white wingtip shoes. Not sure how that's going to help us. But the killer was wearing them and that's *not* in the report. But I did discover the shoe size when I looked at the physical evidence. It's a ten."

"That could have been a real clue twenty years ago." She ran her index finger along the side of the chrome camera.

"It may still be." He wrote size ten on the card and pinned it next to the shoes. "So. Where did you find the actual picture of Holland and the other two men?" He lifted a brow.

"I found it in one of the boxes here."

"Have you gone through everything, even the drawers?"

"Pretty much."

"That leaves the microchip article for you to explain. There's nothing in this videotape that points to such a thing, so…" He fixed Lucy with a stare, which she chose to ignore.

"I'll get to that later," she said. "What about the mask?"

"Fine, have it your way for now. I'll follow up on the mask, but frankly, if it's not like the one I showed you, I'm not hopeful that piece will ever be solved, unless and until we find another way to locate the stalker."

"And the note that was on the brick? Did you make me a copy?"

"I did." He reached into his pocket, grabbed a pin, and attached it. He started to turn away, then it seemed the note she had intended to show him, caught his eye.

Lucy held her breath. He didn't make a sound, just stood there reading it.

He turned toward her. "I take it this is the second thing you'd planned to tell me."

"It is. I found it underneath a floorboard a couple of days ago." She clasped her hands in her lap. "The day I came over to your house, I'd planned to show it to you."

"But then I caught you trying to steal the report, and you decided not to tell me."

"That's correct."

"I hope you know by now that you can trust me."

"I do." She nodded. "I do."

He removed the letter from the board, sat back down next to her, and re-read it. Then he leveled her with one of his intense stares. "What do you think he means by, *Lucy holds the key*?"

She took a deep breath and exhaled. "You might find this next thing rather strange, but I think I've been micro-chipped."

CHAPTER 22

Malcolm stared at Lucy. "Microchipped? That's ridiculous."

"Please stop looking at me as if I had two heads. I'm serious."

He shook his head. "No one mircochips people."

"The Swedes do."

"Not twenty years ago." He shifted toward her. "Where did you get such an insane idea?"

"My mother."

"She told you, you'd been microchipped?"

"Not in so many words." She tucked a stray lock of hair behind her ear. "It's a long story."

Malcolm chewed his inner lip. "Maybe it's time I had a talk with her."

"You are aware she has memory issues, right?"

"Yes, you mentioned it."

"Maybe it wouldn't hurt for us to pay her a visit." She shrugged. "But she can get quite agitated when I bring up the past. I think it's better for me to tell you what she said, and then we can look into it. Or better yet, you could use the chip reader on my shoulder and see if anything's there."

"You have a chip reader? Please tell me you did not steal that from our local veterinarian."

She rolled her eyes. "You still think so badly of me, don't you?"

He smiled and shrugged. "When I've been burned more than once, I become extra cautious."

"To answer your question, no. I did *not* steal it. I bought it online." She folded her arms. "But to your credit, I did think about it."

"Where is it?"

"It arrives today."

"That's good. In the meantime, what did your mother say, exactly?"

"When I was little, I noticed that I had this scar on my shoulder. Mom told me I'd gotten it in a fall. Then on one of my visits, she asked me how my shoulder felt. I had no clue what she was talking about. I'd forgotten all about the scar on my shoulder. It's barely noticeable."

"May I?" He reached for her shoulder.

She angled left, and he ran his finger along the tiny scar.

"Then," Lucy continued, "as my mom sometimes does, she stared off into space and got all cryptic and said that I'd cried and cried and that he'd hurt me. When I asked who, she said, the vet. When I asked her why Dad would take me to a vet, she didn't answer, just kept saying that he hurt me and I cried. As you can imagine, I decided to investigate."

"How have you done that?"

"I first called all the veterinarians in the area, and when that was unsuccessful, I started calling the ones in nearby towns."

"Did you find out anything?"

"I got a lead, yes."

The muffled sound of a car engine came from the front. "I bet that's the scanner." Lucy jumped up and opened the door. She returned to Malcolm, carrying a package.

Malcolm got to his feet. "Is that it?"

"I think so." She ripped open the padded envelope and pulled out the contents.

"You ready?" Malcolm stood over Lucy who now sat in the wingback chair to the right of the fireplace.

Her sparkling, green eyes held a bit of hesitancy as she gazed up at him. "What do you think we'll find?"

He gave her a measured smile in the hope she'd relax. "I don't know. Are you afraid?"

"A little."

Malcolm ran the back of his hand along her cheek. "What are you afraid of?"

"Of what I might find." Her voice wavered. "That it might prove that my dad *was* a dirty cop." She hung her head. "I'm not sure I could handle that."

She pushed a strand of dark hair behind her ear. "I've gone through my whole life looking for my father. Four years with him was not nearly long enough. It's as if I never had a father and barely the memory of one.

"Uncle Bob came close to filling that void, but no more than that. I'm now at a point in my life that I either have to find out what happened, or put it all behind me and move on. Those are my choices, and the latter is unacceptable. Even if I find out the worst about my dad, I have to know. I have to have closure. Otherwise, it will always be at the back of my mind. I'll always wonder."

"Do you think he'd actually put something on this chip that would incriminate him?" Malcolm placed his finger underneath her chin and lifted. "Your father adored you. I saw that in the video. He imbedded a message underneath your skin to protect something of great importance. It's as if he'd entrusted *you* with it. In the hope that if something happened to him, the truth would come out through you."

She sat in the chair, her fingers gripped tightly in her lap.

"We can find out now, or we can let it go, stop the investigation, and go have a nice dinner at Baillie's Italian."

"Go ahead." She swallowed. "Let's find out what's there."

* * *

Lucy held her breath and watched Malcolm's face. A slight frown marked his features as they waited for the result of the scan.

"What does it say?" she asked.

"A name, and..." He held the reader for her to see.

"Miles Grayson, and that looks like—"

"Longitude and latitude," he said.

"Who is Miles Grayson?"

"I have no idea." Malcolm pulled his phone from his back pocket and clicked on the maps icon. "But right now, Miles can wait." He typed in the GPS coordinates as Lucy stood next to him, her eyes on the screen.

"It's here," she said. "It's on this property."

They stared at each other.

"This way," he said.

Lucy walked beside him, through the living room, down the hall, and past the kitchen to the back patio. She hurried forward to open the door, held it, then followed him outside.

With his eye on the screen, he stepped forward, then left, with Lucy at his side. About fifty feet from the house, he stopped.

"This is it," he said. "These are the coordinates."

"I've got shovels," Lucy said.

"And gloves, if you have them." Malcolm followed her to the small, detached garage.

"We're going to need some drinking water." Malcolm grabbed the gloves and shovels. "Why don't you take care of that, while I start digging?"

A few minutes later, Lucy placed an ice bucket and several bottles of chilled water on the seat of a small chair she carried out to the dig site. After tugging the leather gloves over her hands, she grabbed the second shovel and joined Malcolm.

They'd gone about eighteen inches deep before Lucy's shovel came against something hard.

"That sounds like metal," Malcolm said.

They stared at each other, then continued to dig. Minutes later, Lucy stopped for a breather. She wiped the sweat from her forehead, jabbed the blade into the dirt, and leaned on the handle.

Beads of sweat glistened on Malcolm's upper lip and forehead, as well. He lifted the back of his hand to his hairline and swiped right.

They continued to dig until Lucy dropped to her haunches and began moving the dirt with her hands. Malcolm tossed his shovel aside to help her.

"You'd think with all the rain we've had this would be a lot easier," she said.

"After twenty years in the ground, it's packed in, all right," he said.

She kept digging. "Who do you think Miles Grayson is?"

"The fact that his name is on your chip, I'd say someone extremely important."

With a combination of prying the box edges and loosening the soil, it took about fifteen minutes longer before they were able to lift it out.

It was twice the size of the metal box she'd found under the floorboards.

They both took an end, gripping the handles at each side.

"Ready?" he asked.

She nodded.

"One, two, three." They lifted up, then out to the side, lowering it to the ground.

"I suggest we take it up to the house and open it there," he said.

"I thought it would be much heavier."

"You expecting gold bars?"

"Wouldn't that be nice?" Lucy picked up both shovels while he lifted the box. At the back door, she propped the shovels against the wall while Malcolm carried the box inside to the kitchen table.

* * *

Lucy and Malcolm removed their gloves and quickly washed their hands.

"I think you should do the honors," he said.

Lucy raised an anxious gaze to his face, licked her lips, and nodded. She placed her hand on the latch, flipped up the end, and lifted. The box opened, and they peered inside. A large manila envelope, sealed at one end, covered the bottom of the box with an eight-by-ten spiral notebook wedged underneath.

Malcolm pulled both items out, then emptied the contents of the envelope onto the table. It held a thick, gray folder. He picked up the notebook first and opened it.

"Are those his notes?" she asked.

"It's a logbook. Look. He's recorded the time along with the action." He set the book aside and opened the folder. It held a stack of photographs and some loose notes.

"Look at this." He pointed to initials at the bottom of one of the loose notes. *M.G.*

Eyes wide, Lucy gazed up at him. "Miles Grayson."

Malcolm flipped through each sheet of paper. "Looks like he signed each note with his initials."

"But who is he?" she asked.

"If I were to guess, I'd say he was your father's informant."

Malcolm spread the photographs out on the table. "These were all shot from a distance. Your father must have taken them during his investigation. This had to have taken him months." He stared at her. "No way was James Ross a dirty cop."

"And he buried all of this for safekeeping until he could prove it." Lucy picked up one of the photos and tapped her finger on the face of one man. "This is Uncle Bob. I wonder who the other man is?"

"Your guess is as good as mine. Twenty years is a long time, and people change. This could be Crandall or anyone."

She flipped the picture over to see if her father had written a name on the back, but it was blank. Together, they checked the backs of each photo. Some had names and numbers, but not all of them.

"It looks like Ross only recorded the names he knew,"

Malcolm said. "He must not have had the chance to find out who some of these men were before he was killed."

He picked up the notebook. "Reading through this could help to identify who's pictured in the rest of these photos. It looks like James was well organized."

He handed her the logbook. "I've got to go to work. Keep all of this in a safe place while I'm gone, then we can both read through the rest of his notes later."

Lucy flipped back a few pages. "Look at this." Heads together, they bent over the page and read. Lucy lifted her eyes from the paper to Malcolm's face. "Is he saying what I think he's saying?"

Malcolm nodded. "According to this, Ross discovered Holland had been taking bribes for years and most from Alex Crandall."

She closed the book, her eyes filled with anxiety. "So, Holland looks away while Crandall does what, exactly?"

"Any number of things, and all of it illegal," he said. "Crandall must have spent years building up his corrupt consortium. No telling how many people in this town were involved with his illegal dealings—Holland, as well as others, and how many of them in *way* too deep?"

"That's gold to someone like Crandall," she said.

"Even now, these people are most likely still on his payroll. He hadn't built this syndicate overnight, and it would be impossible to duplicate again at this stage in life. I'll certainly be investigating Crandall further."

"Have you found out anything about him yet?"

"I have, but I don't have time to go into it now."

"After work then," she said.

"I'll pick up something from Dottie's and come right over." He slipped the photos back into the envelope and stood. "My guess is Crandall and Holland are still working together and trying to run you off in the meantime. So, please be careful."

"But Alex isn't even in town."

"A man like him doesn't get his hands dirty if he can help it. He hires it out. I found out he lives part of the time in Hot Springs. But I'll fill you in later, with the rest."

She followed him to the door. "After we sort all of this out, what do we do with it? Who do we take it to?"

"No one here, that's for sure." He stopped near the door and turned toward her.

"What if this isn't enough?" she said.

He brushed his fingers down her cheek. "Before you go down that road, we need to put this new piece of the puzzle together and see where it leads. This could be enough to clear your dad's name and bring the others to justice. Normally, I'd say twenty-year-old notes written by a dead man might not be enough, but notes, along with incriminating photographs, say plenty."

"How dare he?" She began to pace. "How dare he!" She stopped and spun toward Malcolm. "You should've heard the things Holland said to me. He told me not to bring up the past, that my father had disgraced his badge and dishonored his oath. It was *Holland* who did those things."

Angry tears welled up in Lucy's eyes. "How could Uncle Bob let my dad take the blame for his crimes? What kind of man does that? He was Dad's friend—his partner. When I think of all the times he came over to this very house while I was growing up here..."

She lifted a devastated gaze to his face. "He took me to my first father-daughter dance. That two-faced monster—all these years—acting like he cared." She covered her face with her hands and sobbed.

Malcolm pulled her into his arms. "I'm so sorry, Lucy. I know you feel betrayed. But it's very important you act normal at their party."

She sniffed and pulled back. "You expect me to go— now?"

He took her hands in his. "I don't expect anything. I'd like you to go because it's a chance to further our investigation."

"Our?"

"Yes. *Our*. There could be something in that house. Think of it as being undercover. Holland just won't know it."

Lucy's phone dinged with a message. "It's Rick. He needs my help tonight at The Club." She raised her gaze to his. "I guess we'll have to forget Dottie's."

"Then, I'll see you tonight at The Club."

CHAPTER 23

During Lucy's first thirty minutes at work, she couldn't help but notice how the vibe at The Club had changed from her last visit. Instead of the welcome she'd received before, an air of secrecy met her. The officers were rigidly polite, and her ready smiles were met with a lack of eye contact and indifference. Since she hadn't done anything to receive such treatment, maybe she was imagining all of it.

Lucy stopped at table three to fill their water glasses.

"You remember Detective Ross."

The low voice came from the table behind her, and she listened as she poured.

"The one that took bribes?" another man said just as low.

"Yeah. That's his daughter."

"You're kidding."

Horrified, Lucy quickly moved away. Heat burned the back of her eyelids as she hurried over to another table. *Just breathe*. Refusing to let a couple of gossipers get the better of her, she made an effort to regroup while clearing the next table.

She'd been working for about an hour when she noticed two of the older male guests had cornered Rick on the far side of the restaurant. They seemed to be in a heated discussion. Rick lifted his gaze and looked right at her. This couldn't be good. She turned her attention back to the job and continued taking an order from the foursome at table seven.

She moved to take drink orders from her next table, and Rick motioned for her to come to the bar. After handing the orders to the bartender, she joined Rick at the end of the counter.

"Lucy I don't know how to say this, but several of the older officers don't want you here."

Her heart plummeted. "Why?"

"Because you're James Ross's daughter."

A quick glance over her shoulder revealed the two men in question. They eyed her with what she could only call, distaste. She briefly hung her head, then peered at Rick. "What do you say?"

"If it were up to me, I'd tell them to go jump in the lake."

She couldn't help but smile.

"But I don't own this place. I just work here."

"It's okay. I know it's not your fault." She untied her apron and handed it to him. "I guess it had to come out sometime."

"So you *are* Ross's daughter."

"I am."

"Just so you know, I don't hold that against you. We can't help who are our parents are. That said, I liked him." He shrugged. "Like I told you before, I didn't really know him, but the man I knew briefly, I liked."

"Thank you, Rick." Lucy grasped his left hand and squeezed.

"Why don't you slip out the back," he said. "That way you can avoid the ogling eyes."

Lucy's tears fell to her cheeks as she unlocked her car. No one could see her, so it didn't matter. On her way home, she passed the town cemetery, slowed to a stop, and got out. She hadn't visited her father's grave since the day she and her mom left town. After locking the door, she walked through the iron gates at the entrance.

She strolled along the main path, trusting her instincts to find her way to his grave. About ten minutes later, she spotted his headstone underneath an oak tree. She kneeled before the granite monument and ran her right hand lovingly across each letter of his name.

James Edward Ross.
Beloved Husband and Father

"I remember you." She smiled through her tears. "There's so much I wish to say, but I'm suddenly weary. I've been working some at The Club. Tonight, I was asked to leave because of you. Maybe I *should* go and let Malcolm take over. What do you think? Should I leave?"

Silence filled the black void as she waited. A sob broke from her lips. "We found your documents. I know the truth, Dad." Tears flowed down her cheeks. "I just thought you should know." She swiped her wet cheeks and stood, then made her way back to her car.

* * *

Malcolm arrived at The Club, dateless for a change. His heart had turned completely toward a *wee scunner*. He'd planned to have his meal at the bar, hoping for some one-on-one time with Lucy. If they could sneak in a word or two about the case, then all the better.

He sat down and picked up the menu, periodically glancing around for her. Rick approached him with a smile. "What can I get you, Detective?"

"I thought Lucy was working tonight."

Rick's smile faded, and he shook his head. "She was—for about an hour."

Malcolm could tell from Rick's expression that something was wrong.

"What happened?"

"Officers Jenkins and Peterson told me she had to leave."

"What?"

"They found out she was James Ross's daughter, and they didn't want—and I quote—*the likes of her here.* Said they were speaking for all the other officers."

Malcolm stood. "Somehow I doubt that." Rancor sharpened his voice. "Thanks Rick, but I won't be staying."

"I understand." Rick picked up the menu. "Believe me, if I didn't have to work here, I'd leave, too. That girl is the sweetest thing, and there's no call for her to treated like this."

Malcolm was in his car in record time and placed a to-go order at Dottie's for pick-up on his way to Lucy's. As soon as he arrived, he ran up the steps to Lucy's front door and knocked. Since the lights were on, he assumed she'd gotten back home.

Seconds later, he heard the rustling of the chain on the latch. Lucy cracked the door and peeked through the opening, then stepped back.

She stared up at him—a pint of rocky road ice cream in

one hand and a large spoon in the other—her raccoon-rimmed eyes evidence she'd been crying.

Without saying a word, she turned, walked over to the sofa, and plopped down. Shoulders hunched, she jabbed the spoon into the carton.

He shut the door behind him and joined her on the couch. She wouldn't look at him...just sat licking the sweet cream from the spoon. Unsure what he should say, he set the to-go sacks on the coffee table and waited.

"I went to the cemetery tonight to see my dad." She drew her tongue over the stainless-steel spoon. "I hadn't been back there since Mom and I left years ago. I told him I remembered him, and that I now know the truth."

Brow furrowed, she licked the spoon, then dipped it deep within the sweet cream. "It's important that he know that." A tear rolled down her cheek, then another, and another. "I asked him if I should leave."

"You're not giving up now, are you?"

Head lowered, she lifted a shoulder.

He took the ice cream and the spoon from her hands, set them on the coffee table, and pulled her into his arms. Sobs broke from her lips as he hugged her against his chest. Her muffled cries broke his heart, tempting him to go back to that club and plant a fist in each man's face.

She sniffed and turned her head to the side, keeping snug against him. A short while later, she pulled away and swiped angrily at her tears. "I guess you're here because of what happened."

"They're a bunch of old pricks, Lucy." He rubbed his hand up and down her arm. "You don't deserve that kind of treatment. Rick told me it was only two of them."

"Except it wasn't just them. Everyone there knew. I even

overheard a couple talking about my dad and how he took bribes." She shuddered. "I was horrified."

"I wish you wouldn't let it bother you."

"If you say so." She reached for a tissue to blow her nose, and he picked up her ice cream.

"May I?"

She bubbled a laugh as he'd hoped she would.

"Of course," she said. "It's practically melted. I have French vanilla if you'd rather have that?"

"No, this is fine." He spooned an ample amount and shoved it in his mouth. "This *is* good. I can see why you tried to drown your sorrows in it."

She nodded. "There *are* worse things one could use. Good thing I don't like alcohol."

He licked the spoon and watched her.

She slid her palms between her knees. "Do you know those men?"

"Jenkins and Peterson?"

She nodded.

"I've met them on occasion. They're both retired from the force."

"Maybe we should include them as suspects." She sniffed and continued to gaze at him. "I wonder how they found out?"

"Who knows?" He angled his body toward her. "In a town this small, it was bound to happen."

"Holland knows, maybe he said something. It wasn't like I told him not to." She pulled her palms from her knees and ran her fingers along the hem of her blouse.

"He's also working with Crandall, don't forget. Someone in this town has been trying to run you off since you arrived."

She lifted her gaze to his. "You think tonight's episode is related to the break-in and the stalker?"

"Think about it—makes perfect sense. Besides me and Holland—and possibly Crandall—is there anyone else who knows your real name?"

"The other officers at the precinct. They have to know."

"But not initially."

"I used my mother's maiden name with Jan. No one knew during that first week or so. I think you were the first one to find out. And I didn't visit Bob Holland until the second week after I'd arrived."

She fingered the delicate gold necklace at her throat. "I can see Holland spreading the word that James Ross's daughter was back, but he couldn't have done the other stuff." She rolled her eyes. "Not that he isn't capable, he just didn't know I was here then, so it couldn't have been him."

"He would've told Brenda after he found out," Malcolm said, "but that doesn't help us with who knew in the beginning."

"Someone did, though." Lucy frowned, her eyes filled with concern. "You were going to tell me what you found out about Crandall."

"Only that he hounded your father for this property. He's a developer, so that in itself isn't unusual."

"I guess." Shoulders slumped, she clasped her slender hands together.

He set the carton and spoon down and gazed at her furrowed brow, her red nose, and splotchy cheeks. "That's enough worrying for now. Go wash your face. I have something to tell you."

Malcolm was standing at the suspect board when Lucy got back. He unpinned the photo of the three officers and pulled her down beside him. He threw his arm over her shoulder and drew her close to his side.

He held up the photo. "As you already know, the man in the middle is my father. Not long after I became a police officer, I asked him if there was ever a case that really bothered him... you know, one that had never been resolved.

"He told me about an unsolved murder that happed years ago. It was the first time I heard the name, James Ross."

Lucy's eyes widened. He focused on her sweet, upturned face, with that inquisitive expression, and questioning gaze —so dear to him.

"Even though my dad was in Scotland, he'd kept up with the case. He felt it had been rushed, and then closed way too quickly, bringing with it more questions than answers."

He clasped Lucy's left hand and held it. "You asked me once why I chose this town for the exchange program when I could've picked from other, far more exciting places, to spend my year. I came here to solve your father's murder."

Lucy inhaled sharply, and her lips parted.

"My father knew your father. They were rookies together in this very town."

"So, he's an American?"

"Yes. Lucy...they were best friends, pals. Because of their relationship, I came here at his request. And he's the one who told me who you were."

Tears filled her eyes, and she turned in his arms, wrapping hers around his waist. "You've been on my side all this time?"

He hugged her close. "I certainly have."

She pulled back. "Why didn't you tell me sooner?"

"First of all, I didn't know who you were until the night we broke into Crandall's garage. I was cautious after that. I didn't know who your friends were and who you might be confiding in.

"My father had told me not to trust anyone, so I couldn't take the chance that you would tell someone who I was and why I was really here. I couldn't run the risk of alerting the department, or of anyone knowing I was inquiring into the Ross case. That could've been detrimental to any discovery I may have found.

"You showing up and getting involved disrupted my plan to secretly look into your father's murder."

"By bringing unwanted attention to it," she said.

"Yes, and the reason I tried to get you to pull back. I didn't want you *mucking up the works*. That and your secretive actions made me hyper-cautious where you were concerned."

Lucy brushed her bangs aside and stayed focused on his face.

"Mostly..." He touched her cheek in a wistful gesture. "I didn't want to raise your hopes and unearth more pain if my investigation didn't go anywhere, or worse, didn't clear his name.

"As you recall, you came back to this town suspicious of everyone, including me. I didn't want you to think something nefarious about me or think I was a part of this."

"Oh, Malcolm. Just knowing I'm no longer alone means the world to me." She jumped up, unpinned his photo, then swung back around. "The mystery surrounding Detective Malcolm Knox has finally been solved."

CHAPTER 24

Lucy handed Malcolm his photo with a flourish.

"Well, that's a relief," he teased. "The people we need to add are Chief of Police Holland and his missus."

He stood, stepped over to the board, and picked up a three-by-five card and a pen as Lucy perched on the edge of the coffee table. With his body angled, he could see her out of the corner of his eye.

As Malcolm wrote Holland and Mrs. Holland's names on separate cards, he peeped at her over his shoulder.

Lucy gazed up at him with her whole heart in her eyes openly displayed for him to see. There was no shame in her adoration. She held nothing back as sweet longing flowed from every pore in her body.

He smiled. "It's a good thing I'm a gentleman. That kind of look could get you in trouble."

"Promises, promises," she said.

He pinned the cards to the board and turned fully toward her. "You do know that it's the man who likes to do the pursuing, don't you?"

"And that belief, my dear sir, is from the Dark Ages." She stood, took one step forward and, lifting her arms to his shoulders, laced her hands behind his neck. "In case you haven't noticed, I'm crazy about you, Detective Knox."

His heart thudded. He breathed in deeply, fixing his eyes on her upturned face, her rosy cheeks, and her soft, parted lips.

"Lucy," he groaned. "What am I going to do with you?"

"Kiss me." The words flowed from her mouth with such urgency, the twinkle in her eyes turning serious. "Just kiss me."

Never one to deny the request of a beautiful woman, he lowered his mouth to hers and did just that.

Moments later, he lifted his head and gazed into her dreamy eyes. He'd been bamboozled by a pretty hen once before and had seen a similar expression in that lassie's eyes. He searched Lucy's flushed and rosy cheeks, looking for what—confirmation that this girl—this time—was the real deal? He ran the back of his hand along her cheek. "Our hamburgers are getting cold," he said.

Lucy blinked and nodded. "Right." She stepped out of his arms. "The hamburgers."

"Let's eat while we go through James's notebook. Let's see what your father left us."

They started with the loose notes from Miles Grayson. Malcolm split the papers up between them. They ate quietly while reading their respective pages. Every few minutes, Lucy glanced at him until he finally felt he had to say something.

"Lucy?"

She looked up—guileless and innocent.

"I like you...a lot. Don't think that I don't. It's just—"

"You have to leave in a few months. It's okay. I-I know.

But just so you *know*... I'm not like her." Lucy's lips parted in a sweet, broken smile and then focused back on the notes.

Malcolm felt terrible. She'd opened her heart to him, and he didn't respond as she thought he would. If he broached the subject again it would only make things worse for her.

He lowered his gaze to the notes in his hand and got back to work. Malcolm finished his set first, opened up the notebook, and continued to read. "This is amazing work."

Lucy stopped reading, giving him her full attention.

"On each page, James has listed the crime, its details, and the people involved, with links to specific photos for clarification."

"Oh, my gosh," Lucy said. "Here's one mentioning Officers Jenkins and Peterson. No wonder they want me gone. I'm a reminder of their criminal deeds."

"Lucy, there's enough here to arrest everyone on this list —and clear your father's name."

"And his murder?"

"I don't know yet," he said. "But we're certainly moving in the right direction."

They stared silently at each other.

"I'll need a day or so to go through all of this in more detail," he added, "then I'll take it to Little Rock."

"Why not someplace closer, like Hot Springs or Pine Bluff?"

"This criminal activity goes back years. Who knows how far and wide the reach?"

After he compiled the loose notes with the coordinating photograph, he checked the envelope for anything he may have missed.

"Wait, there's something else." He took out a folded document and opened it. "Lucy..."

"What? What is it?"

Malcolm handed it to her. "It's an appraisal of this property. According to the date, it was done over twenty years ago. Look at the value."

"Seven hundred and fifty thousand dollars!"

"No telling how much it's worth now," he said.

"I didn't pay near that amount. How is this possible?" She sucked in air. "Unless…"

"What?"

"It's the stones." She stared at him. "The jewels, the diamonds. It has to be."

"Believe it or not, that thought has already crossed my mind. This just confirms my suspicions. As a developer, Crandall knew the value of this property. Having grown up in Diamond Creek, he'd know about the diamond mine in Murfreesboro. As a successful developer, Crandall must have discovered its value, tried to buy it, and your dad refused."

Did that get Ross killed? He dared not voice that thought out loud. Not until he knew for certain.

* * *

Lucy and Malcolm met for lunch the next day at Baillie's Italian. They had just started looking over the menu when Jan and her mom walked in.

Lucy waved the two ladies over.

"Lucy, this is my mom, Rachael Kelly," Jan said. "Mom —Lucy. And Mom, you probably remember meeting Detective Knox at Dottie's last month. I introduced you when we were there for dinner."

"Of course, I remember. It's nice to see you again, Detective, and nice meeting you, Lucy."

"Won't you two join us?" Lucy said. "We just sat down and haven't ordered yet."

"We'd love to." Jan and her mom took the two vacant chairs.

"Jan, I think it's time I clarify something." Lucy gazed at Malcolm, and he nodded. "You know the detective that was murdered at my house twenty years ago, well, in case you haven't already heard, I'm his daughter. I'm Lucy Ross."

Jan's eyes widened, and Mrs. Kelly's face blanched.

"So, your name isn't Carmichael?" Jan asked.

"That's my middle name. So technically I didn't lie to you, but I did deceive you. It was for my protection. I didn't know who I could trust."

"That's extraordinary." Jan said.

"Oh, my," Mrs. Kelly said. "I knew both your parents, Lucy. So, so terrible about your father—even after all these years. How is your mother?"

Lucy briefly explained about her mom's accident and her recovery. "I plan to move her back here with me once I get everything at the house settled."

"I'll look forward to seeing her again, then."

"If you have any memories about my father, I'd love to hear them sometime. I was little when he was killed, and I don't recall much about him."

"Of course. I'd be happy to share any memories with you."

"Mrs. Kelly." Lucy shot a furtive glance at Malcolm. "Jan tells me you drive a 1970 vintage Mustang. I understand it's an unusual color. A yellow-green." From the corner of her eye, Lucy caught a glimpse of Malcolm's raised brow and stunned expression.

"My baby." Mrs. Kelly smiled. "The color is Light Ivy Yellow or New Lime."

"My mom saw a car matching yours about the time my father was shot."

Mrs. Kelly's smile faded, and she sat perfectly still.

"Do you recall driving by that day, and if so, did you see anything?"

Mrs. Kelly glanced between her and Malcolm. She clasped her hands together and rested them on top of the table, then looked at Jan.

"It's okay, Mom, tell them what you know. You can trust Malcolm."

She licked her lips and swallowed. "I did see something, but I didn't realize it until much later. I'm not sure it'll help."

"Go on," Malcolm said. "Any little thing could turn out to be important."

"I saw Crandall's black sedan, and saw him get out of the car. As I drove by, I thought it odd he wore a mask. I didn't see his face—only the back of his head. And it wasn't until much later that I remembered seeing blond hair." She swallowed. "It happened so fast, and it was all a blur."

"I understand." Malcolm nodded. "Go on."

"My husband bought the car for my fortieth birthday. That afternoon was the first time I'd driven it." She cleared her throat. "I'm afraid I was going a bit too fast, trying it out and all."

"But not so fast that you couldn't see the black sedan."

"Correct."

"And yet, you could see the mask and the shooter's hair color?"

"That's right. When I realized I was speeding by the detective's house, I slowed down."

"I see." Malcolm smiled.

"We left for vacation the next day, and I didn't learn what had happened to the detective until we'd returned. I ran into Bob Holland about two weeks afterward. He was on Main Street admiring my new car."

Malcolm and Lucy exchanged glances.

"I told him what I'd just told you, except for the hair color."

"Did he actually write down what you said?"

"Yes. He thanked me and said he'd get back to me if he had any further questions. Frankly, I was relieved when he didn't. I just didn't want anything to do with..." Mrs. Kelly frowned.

"Go on, Mom," Jan said. "Tell him."

Mrs. Kelly lifted a worried gaze to Malcolm's face. "I don't want any dealings with Alex Crandall."

"Explain."

"My late husband, Carson, was also a developer. Over the years, he'd made bids on certain properties, but Alex always won, even when Carson's bid was the lowest. Carson and I always felt Alex used unethical methods in his business."

"Like what?"

"Without sounding petty, we believed our personal business losses were due to Alex's unscrupulous practices, but it could never be proved. Carson believed someone in this town had to be taking bribes and kickbacks."

"Any thoughts on who?"

"A city councilman—a police officer. Your guess is as good as mine." She turned to Lucy. "I'm so sorry, honey. I realize now I should have said something sooner about the hair."

"It's okay, Mrs. Kelly. You've told us *now* what you know."

"I agree," Malcolm said. "What you've shared has been very helpful."

"It's important you both know that I did give Bob a statement that was true and accurate at the time."

"What was it that made you recall seeing the blond hair?" Malcolm asked.

"It was when Alex didn't get arrested. I was stunned. I thought for sure it had been him—everything I saw pointed to him. But when I went over the details again in my mind's eye, I realized the back of the head I saw was blond. The image was as clear as day. The man I saw had blond hair. Alex's hair is dark."

* * *

Lucy sat in her living room, perusing the written part of her father's file. "Maybe the Mustang hadn't been followed up on because Holland had discovered the owner."

"He should have still written that up in the report," Malcolm said. "Speaking of...when did you find out about the Mustang?"

Lucy sniffed and paused in her reading. "I discovered it by accident. It came out one day in a conversation with Jan—two days after you threw me out of your house."

"I see." He couldn't help but smile. "And when were you going to tell me about it?"

"I wasn't. I was going to keep that little morsel to myself. Show you that I could solve this without your help."

"I noticed."

She tossed down the report. "Nothing about blond hair in there."

"Don't change the subject."

She glanced at him with a wide-eyed innocence that was

merely a smoke screen. "Well, you know now." She grinned. "That's what counts."

Malcolm wrote *blond hair* on a note card and pinned it on the board by the car.

Both Malcolm and Lucy, arms folded, stood together in front of the variety of clues and pondered what it all meant.

"Do you think it would have made any difference in solving the case if Mrs. Kelly had come forward sooner?"

"I doubt it."

"Really?" She turned slightly with a questioning glance.

"Think about it. If someone in the department *was* dirty, that person would have had access to everything. He could've manipulated the facts, removed evidence, and even planted it."

"That seriously makes my blood boil," Lucy said.

"There's an answer here—has to be," Malcolm said.

"I know."

There had to be a way to flush Holland out. He'd tail him—do his own reconnaissance—take his own photographs—and he'd include Lucy in the hunt. He'd wanted an excuse to spend more time with her. He longed to see where this *thing* with her would lead and what better time and place than a few hours alone in a car?

Lucy's face held a pensive expression.

"In the meantime," he said, "how would you like to go on stakeout?"

They took Lucy's car to be less conspicuous. Malcolm parked the Subaru down the street from Crandall's but close enough so they could keep watch. They ate Chinese food and chatted and took turns looking through the binoculars.

"This is boring," she said. "Do you have to do this sort of thing often?"

"No, not often." He glanced sideways. "This is part of being a detective. I thought seeing another side of things would be good for you. It's not all breaking and entering, you know."

"You're never going to let me live that down, are you?" She chuckled and inched toward him.

"Hey, none of that now. Keep to your side," he teased. "This is serious work."

"Are you trying to teach me a lesson, Detective?" She drew her legs underneath her, turned toward him, and rested her left elbow on the seat back. "Is it your way of saying I should leave the investigating to the *real* detectives?"

"Unfortunately, I believe that ship has sailed." He popped a salt-and-vinegar chip into his mouth.

Lucy ran her finger around the top of her soda can.

"What are you thinking?" he asked.

"That I miss having you call me, Just Lucy."

He smiled. "Why?"

She stared out the windshield. A wistful expression settled on her features. "There was this wonderful mystery in our relationship, then."

"Oh, don't worry, there's still *plenty* of mystery. You can be certain of that."

She turned to him. "Like what for instance?"

"Just because I know your real name doesn't mean I know everything about you." He searched her lovely face. It would take a lifetime and she would still hold a special mystery for him. She had *layers* of mystery, and he longed to peel each one back and discover more about her. But he simply said, "You're rich with mystery." He cupped her face with his hand. "For now, let's leave it at that."

Sometime later, Malcolm glanced right and caught Lucy stifling another yawn. "We could be here most of the night." He scrunched up an empty potato chip bag and tossed it to the back with the empty soda cans. "It's okay if you need to take a nap."

She leveled him with a wide-eyed stare. "Some partner I'd turn out to be. I'd never dream of doing such a thing."

Another thirty minutes passed, and Lucy's head lolled against his shoulder, making him smile. He gazed down at the top of her head and caught a whiff of coconut from her nut-brown hair. He inhaled deeply, savoring the sweet fragrance. A couple of times in the past, he'd caught the tropical scent but hadn't been close enough to identify it.

As he breathed in, movement from across the street caught his eye. Crandall was in the act of driving his Mercedes off his property.

"Lucy, wake up." Malcolm gently shook her. "Crandall just left."

Lucy jerked awake and blinked as she fumbled for her seatbelt. They followed Crandall from his house, through the neighborhood, and across town. Malcolm kept the appropriate distance as he tailed the car.

"I can't believe I fell asleep. You should have awakened me."

"Lucy, it's okay, really." Malcolm turned right on Sydney Lane a few car lengths behind the Mercedes.

"Crandall is actually going to Holland's house," she said.

Malcolm slowed, pulled over, and parked on the left side of the street, several houses down from the Holland's.

"Stay here." Malcolm grabbed his camera and left. He crossed the street and made his way toward the back of the property where Crandall had just disappeared. He spotted the two men, stopped, and crouched behind a tree.

He lifted the camera and began taking pictures. They spoke in low tones, making it impossible for Malcolm to understand what they were saying. At one point, Holland raised his voice. Crandall grabbed Holland's upper arm and yanked Holland closer. Holland wrenched his arm free as another figure ran out of the house. It was Mrs. Holland. She threw her hand in between the two men.

Somebody wasn't happy, and it was obvious Brenda's words did the trick as the men stepped away from each other. Malcolm clicked several more photos and lowered his camera when both Hollands walked back inside their house. For a millisecond, Crandall didn't move, then he turned and walked toward Malcolm.

Malcolm slid further behind the tree and waited for Crandall to pass. He counted to ten, then followed after him. Crandall's car pulled away from the curb just as Malcolm reached the street. Malcolm ran to his car and got in.

"Which way did he go?"

"Straight ahead," Lucy said.

Malcolm started the car and drove forward. "Looks like he's going back to his house." He relaxed. "We're done for the night."

They got back to Lucy's at 2:00 a.m.

She stifled a yawn. "Can I see the pictures?"

"Yeah."

They sat side by side at the kitchen table. Lucy propped her elbow on the table edge and rested her chin in her hand.

"Here's what I got." Malcolm clicked through each frame showing the two men in conversation.

"Could you hear what they were saying?"

"No, but Holland raised his voice at one point and Crandall grabbed his arm, shutting Holland up." He clicked through a few more pictures. "Right there, see?" He paused the photo.

He clicked through a few more. "Here's where Mrs. Holland joined them."

"She's in on this?"

"Looks like it. Seconds later, they split up."

"Nothing was exchanged, not an envelope or anything?"

"Nothing."

She collapsed back in her seat. "So, tonight was a wash."

"Not really. At least now we know Mrs. Holland is somehow involved."

"That's something, I guess."

He gazed at her profile and could see she was having trouble staying awake. "Most stakeouts produce very little," he said.

Lucy's eyes fluttered closed.

"It's late," he said, pushing the chair back. "Get some rest before you fall asleep on your feet. Tomorrow is another day."

She stood and stuffed her hands in her jeans pockets. "I have an extra bedroom if you want it." Glistening, emerald eyes lifted to his face—displaying that sweet yearning from earlier—a clear invitation for him to stay. It would've been so easy to get lost in the way she looked at him.

His undeniable attraction to Lucy was growing by the hour. Since the moment he spotted her at the Policeman's Ball, he thought of little else until he could see her again.

Then he'd have to remind himself that he'd be gone in eight months, certainly long enough for her to fall for him and for him to break her heart when he left. At twenty-four, he'd swear she hadn't yet had her heart broken, and he had no intention to be her first.

"Thanks for the offer," he said, "but I'm just a mile down the road. I should go home."

She leaned slightly into him, tilting her face toward his.

His breath hitched. "Is that an invitation?" He smiled into her adoring, sleepy-eyed gaze.

"What do you think?" She lightly ran a finger up and down his forearm. "We've been alone for hours and you haven't even *tried* to kiss me."

He focused on her upturned face, lowered his head, and gave her one single peck on her lips. "You taste like sweet-and-sour pork."

"Gee, thanks." She rolled her eyes.

He laughed. "But I like sweet-and-sour pork."

"Well, in that case..." She lifted to her toes and returned his kiss. She swayed, gripping his arms for support. This time, her lips lingered against his, moving over them with innocent seduction. Did she have any idea what she was doing to him?

A moment later, he lifted his head, breaking contact. Her eyes stayed closed, and she rested her head on his shoulder.

"Are you asleep?"

"Hum?"

He glanced down at Just Lucy, fully relaxed against him —eyes closed—her long lashes resting like tiny fans along her cheeks. He couldn't get enough of her. His gaze followed the line of her perfect nose, to her full slightly parted lips, and along her slender neck. His stomach dropped, and an unfamiliar flutter tugged somewhere deep within his chest.

He swung her into his arms and carried her to her bed. Gently, and ever so lovingly, he laid her down. Her head lolled onto the pillow as he did so, and she turned onto her side to- ward him. He slipped off her sneakers and tucked her in.

Dropping to his haunches, he rested his arms along the edge of the mattress and watched her.

She'd fallen for him, and heaven help him, he'd fallen for her, too. Ten years her senior—he recognized all the signs— all the symptoms. He'd been torn as to what he should do and how he should handle it, when the inevitable happened.

It would be impossible for her to join him overseas. No way could she leave her mother, and he'd never ask her to. And if they tried to make a long-distance relationship work, the miles between them would make it all but impossible.

He lifted his left hand and ran the back of his fingers along her soft cheek, his thumb over her sweet full lips, de- vouring every crease and nuance of her beautiful face.

"*Mo chridhe, my heart.*" He stood, leaned forward, and kissed the scar on her forehead.

Good night, Just Lucy.

CHAPTER 25

Thursday afternoon hadn't come soon enough. Lucy had shopped for days looking for something special to wear on her date with Malcolm and found it on a sale rack in a quaint little boutique in town.

A ripple of excitement ran through her as she chose the pink, green, and white floral sundress for the Holland's summer party. Since the night of the ball, Malcolm had rarely seen her in anything other than jeans and shorts. So, she took extra care in her appearance.

The simple design of the champagne-brown pendant hung from her neck, completing her outfit. She'd recently picked it up from Rose Hill Jewelers, and at the last minute, decided to wear it once before giving it to her mother.

She slipped on her strappy heels and had just added a touch of pink to her lips when she heard the knock on her front door.

Malcolm.

With one final glance in the mirror, she grabbed her pearl clutch and left the bedroom. With her purse at her waist, she opened the door. Malcolm greeted her with his dangerously gorgeous smile, and her heart squeezed.

"Wow— hen." He eyed her from head to toe. "You look lovely. And speaking of lovely, that must be the necklace you had made for your mom."

"It is. I'm planning to give it to her when she moves here."

"Well, it looks great with your dress."

"Thanks." Yes, speaking of lovely, his smile wasn't her only weakness. His alluring accent did all manner of delightful sensations to her insides. Dressed in a navy sport coat, and a crisp white shirt and slacks, he was all masculine and completely gorgeous.

"And you're *braw* looking, this evening."

"What?"

"It means, fine—good-looking," she said.

"I know what it means." His blue eyes twinkled. "It's just funny hearing you say it."

"Did I not say it correctly?"

"You said it just fine. You just need a little help with the accent." He winked. "Shall we go?"

When he settled Lucy in the passenger seat, he stepped around the hood, then slid behind the steering wheel.

Lucy pulled on her ear and turned toward him. "There's something I've wanted to ask you all day."

"Sure."

"What happened last night?"

"A lot happened last night." He put the car in reverse and backed out. "What are you referring to?"

"This morning, I woke up in my jeans and blouse."

"Oh, that. You fell asleep while we were kissing."

"I did not," she huffed, emphatically.

He laughed. "You most certainly did."

She gaped at him. "Gosh, that's terrible—I'm so sorry. That's just rude on every level."

"No need to apologize. I'm happy to give you another chance to redeem yourself."

"If I fell asleep, then how did I get to bed?"

"I carried you, *and* I even tucked you in."

Wide-eyed, she stared at him. "You carried me?"

"Uh-huh." He signaled and turned left.

"I slept through that, too?"

"Yup."

Sheesh, when did she become so lame?

The Holland's home was every bit the Southern estate. Corinthian columns graced the wide front porch, with an assortment of white-wicker seating and lush, hanging ferns positioned along both sides of the front door.

They pulled into the circular drive off Sydney Lane and stopped at the main entrance. The Hollands had provided valet parking for the evening. While one young man took Malcolm's keys, another opened the door for Lucy.

Malcolm took Lucy's hand as they mounted the stone steps. "How does Holland afford this on police pay?" Malcolm asked.

"I believe Brenda comes from money. This was her family home."

Chief of Police Holland greeted them in the foyer. "Detective, Lucy, so glad you could both join us this evening."

"Hello, Uncle Bob." Lucy practically choked over the endearment.

He hugged her and shook Malcolm's hand, then led them into the living room.

"Sorry we're a bit late, Chief."

"You didn't miss much, just the tour of my library. It houses several rare books and some fine collections. Be sure to take a peek in there before you leave."

"I'd love to," Malcolm said.

Holland turned to Lucy. "Brenda is giving a few of the ladies a tour of the house. We've made quite a few changes to the place since you were last here. Why don't you join them while I take Malcolm to the patio for a cigar? They should be in the dining room," he said, as he motioned for Malcolm to follow. "Brenda loves showing off her grandmother's silver."

The house had certainly been updated. The color pallet had been changed to warm creams and browns with a touch of blue, which blended well with the family antiques perfectly placed throughout the grand house.

Growing up, Lucy had visited their house often and always with great anticipation. Today was a different story. She'd become a spy on the hunt for proof that Bob Holland was behind her father's murder.

A short, stocky man came toward her as she crossed the living room. When she stepped right to let him pass, he stopped her.

"Hello, Lucy."

"I'm sorry." She paused, studying his face. "Do I know you?"

"No. We haven't met. I'm Alex Crandall. I knew your father."

So, this is Alex Crandall. "I had no idea you and the Hollands were friends," she lied. Normally, upon meeting someone new, she'd smile. But for him, she couldn't even force it.

"We go way back." He reached up and lifted the stone from around her neck.

Lucy sucked in air, and her heart thrummed.

"Lovely piece of jewelry." He twirled the nugget between his fingers.

Having him this close with his stubby fingers at her neck repelled her. She did *not* like this man, but she was so tempted to mention just how much she did like his black sedan.

"I take it, you found this on your property."

"Yes, I did." She stepped back, and he let loose of the stone.

Crandall eyed her with an air of superiority. "Enjoy the rest of your evening."

What a creepy individual. Your days as a free man are numbered. She watched him amble away.

She passed by the entrance to the kitchen as she made her way to the dining room. From the shiny, stainless-steel appliances, to the gleaming white cabinets, it too, had been updated.

As she watched the activity of the servers, she spotted a hand-written grocery list on the work desk stationed just inside the doorway. On impulse, Lucy tore off the sheet, quickly folded it, and put it in her purse.

By the time Lucy found the small group, Brenda was in the midst of her tour. Lucy stood quietly at the entrance and listened.

"The Victorian silver serving pieces are some of my favorite in Grandmother's collection. As you can see from the more modern pieces, I've added to it over the years." Brenda replaced an ornate goblet to the sideboard and glanced up. "Nice to see you, Lucy. Please come in, we're just getting started."

The tour ended in what Brenda called her music room. A Steinway piano sat angled in the left corner, allowing ample space for a small, but comfortable, seating area. The entire space was truly lovely and overlooked a well-manicured yard and flowerbeds in full, colorful bloom. Lucy thought about her own attempts at gardening and wished she knew Brenda's secret.

Brenda took a seat at the piano and played a few cords for everyone. Lucy listened but also glanced at an array of family photos—all beautifully framed—on a narrow table along the back wall. One in particular caught her attention.

She stepped closer and picked up the burl-wood-framed photograph. It was a group photo, and she could tell it was from some years back. Mr. and Mrs. Holland stood in the middle of the group, arm-in-arm, smiling. Uncle Bob's hair was a light, sandy color. She'd forgotten his hair used to be blond. Brenda's hair was short and blond, and she wore a pair of wingtip shoes, just like the ones in the video.

Heart pounding overtime, her breathing shallow, Lucy stood perfectly still and stared.

"Nice, isn't it?"

Lucy jumped and spun toward Brenda. She hadn't realized Mrs. Holland had stopped playing.

"That picture was taken about twenty years ago." Brenda gently removed the photo from Lucy's fingers. "Bob and I were so young here. Back then, I was still a natural blonde." She smiled and looked at Lucy. "Avoid coloring your hair for as long as you can. Believe me, once you start, there's no going back."

Lucy forced a smile. "Sounds like good advice." She swallowed. "Great shoes, by the way," Lucy added, eyeing the photo.

"Wingtip." Brenda nodded. "Sadly, only the men seem to wear them these days. Bob must have half-a-dozen pairs in his closet." Smiling, she replaced the photo on the table as the ladies filed out of the room.

* * *

Malcolm was seated on the patio, having a drink with Kirby and his date, when Lucy crossed the stone pavers to join them. She approached him quickly and latched onto his arm. Her face had lost its color, and the intensity in her gaze spoke volumes.

"How was the grand tour?" He kept his eyes on her anxious face.

"Enlightening."

Her smile to the other two was forced. Something had clearly upset her.

He furrowed his brow. "How so?"

"Tell you later," she whispered. "And Alex Crandall is here. I just met him."

"He's here?"

"Yes. Such a creepy man."

Dinner was delicious, consisting of barbecued ribs, creamed corn, field peas, and hot rolls. Followed by an assortment of Southern pies, from lemon chess, and chocolate meringue, to pecan. As good as it was, Lucy picked at her food and nervously looked around her throughout the meal.

"If I don't gain twenty pounds by the time my year is up, it'll be a miracle," Malcolm said.

"I know what you mean." Kirby laughed and forked an ample piece of pie. "Try living here full time with food like this always at the ready."

Malcolm kept his eye on Lucy for the remainder of the

evening—evident she had seen or heard something and was eager to tell him about it.

Kirby and his date moved to the opposite end of the patio to visit another couple, and Malcolm took the opportunity to turn his full attention to Lucy.

"Are you okay?" he asked.

She grabbed his forearm. "I saw something in the music room," she whispered. "I think Brenda shot my dad."

Malcolm stared at her. "Okay, listen. We need to finish out this evening, and you can tell me all about it later."

The party began to break up around ten. As they made their way to the front of the house, Malcolm wanted to see the library before they left. He'd meant to check it out earlier, but the evening had gotten away from him.

"Chief, before we go, I'd love to show Lucy the library."

"Of course, take the hallway to your right as you leave. Follow along until you come to a set of French doors on the left. You can't miss it—"

Malcolm gave the chief a nod, then led Lucy away.

"Do you think we'll find something more in the library?" Lucy asked as they made their way down the hall.

"You heard him earlier. It's where he keeps his treasures. I've been here over four months now, and I've never been invited to this house." Malcolm placed his hand to Lucy's back and led her forward. "This may be the only chance we get to check it out."

They found the library on the left, just as Holland had said. They entered the walnut-paneled room and stopped. The Oriental rug covered most of the oak flooring. A leather sofa and taupe-colored wingback chairs formed a seating area in the center with books and artifacts covering three of the four walls.

"How masculine and old world," she said. "I imagine a place like this makes you homesick for Scotland."

He gazed at her upturned face. Her eyes sparkled with a question. "It would have the first few months, but not any longer." *Not since I met you.*

Lucy's lips parted in a soft smile. He smiled back, then turned his attention to the books.

"This is quite a collection." He stepped right to get a closer look at one in particular, while Lucy went left.

"Malcolm," Lucy squeaked.

He spun around. Lucy stood on the opposite side of the room, staring into a glass case filled with ancient masks. Stunned, he stepped over to her side.

"This is incredible," he said.

Lucy's face had gone white. She lifted a finger and pointed. "That's it. That's the mask."

"Are you sure?"

"Yes," she choked, continuing to stare at it.

There were five masks hanging in a custom-built shadow box designed specifically to showcase each piece. The masks were locked behind a glass door. The box housed a single, low light bulb at the top, enhancing the stones embedded in each mask. All five were ornate and exquisitely made. Four of the festive masks sparkled with colorful stones and silk threading. The fifth was the only *full* mask in the case. A background of dark, silky-black fabric, embedded with deep purple stones, and stitched together with lavender sequins and clear, tiny beaded jewels. It was magnificent—a work of art.

He removed his cell phone from inside his coat pocket and snapped two pictures. As he slipped it back, he took Lucy's arm. "Let's go." He led her into the hallway and toward the foyer. "Deep breaths, Lucy. And put a smile on your face."

In the foyer, both Hollands were saying goodbye and shaking hands. Malcolm glanced at Lucy as they approached the couple. She smiled brightly and thanked them for a lovely evening. She even kept the smile in place while they waited for the valet to bring the car around.

Once seated and on their way, she closed her eyes and rested her head against the leather.

"I know this evening was difficult for you." He glanced at her profile. "But you did great tonight."

She pulled a note from her purse and handed it to him. "I took this off Brenda's kitchen desk. I thought it might be worth comparing her handwriting with that from the note on the brick."

He nodded. "Good idea, except we don't know for sure who wrote this list. But if it matches the one from the brick —that'll be huge."

"We have them, right? With this, the mask, the shoes— and Dad's notes and the photos—that's got to be enough proof."

"Yes...we've got them. But we don't have enough to prove murder. The wingtip shoes in the video and those on Mrs. Holland's photo strongly suggest she's the shooter but doesn't prove it. It's not enough by itself. We need other evidence we can add to this."

"We need a confession." Lucy clenched her fists. "I knew I should have taken that photograph."

"And then what...have her come after you?"

"Yes. That woman killed my father."

"And do you want to be next?" He ran his hands through his hair. "Besides, we don't know that for sure. The mask points to both her *and* the chief."

"I'm not afraid of her...or him either."

"I know you're not, but that's no reason to set yourself up as bait."

"I'd only do that if you were waiting in the wings—listening to their confession."

"You've been watching way too many crime shows."

CHAPTER 26

The notes from the brick and the Holland's home lay side by side on the kitchen table. Lucy sat next to Malcolm while he meticulously compared the handwriting between the two.

"I'm no expert, but the handwriting from these two notes are very similar, and I'd say were written by the same person. See how she rounds the *a* in both, and the slant of the *t* in each note looks the same? Tomorrow, I'm taking these to a handwriting analyst in Little Rock. He's part of LRPD's forensic science department. After he examines the notes, he'll know for certain if they've been written by the same person."

"Of course, we don't know for sure who wrote the note," Lucy said. "I feel certain it's Mrs. Holland's, as she's the woman of the house."

"I think that's safe to assume, at least as a starting point," Malcolm said. "To be certain, I'll have them pull up her driver's license and check her signature against the two notes."

Lucy stood and walked Malcolm to the door. "I'm glad to have the Holland's party behind me."

He placed his hands on her arms. "I know you dreaded going," he said. "But tonight, we moved the investigation forward, and that's a plus in my book."

"I know."

"Chase will be keeping an eye on you while I'm gone."

She nodded. "Good."

"I have business to attend to in the morning, so I won't leave for Little Rock until tomorrow afternoon. I'll have to stay the night, because my meeting with the department isn't until the following morning."

"Okay."

"I should be back by five. I'll come straight here."

"Sounds good," she said. "I'll fix some chili and cornbread for dinner."

Malcolm pulled her close and placed a soft kiss to her lips. "See you soon." He tapped her nose and left.

* * *

Lucy locked up behind Malcolm, then leaned back against the door. *One of these days, I hope to get more than a mere peck on the lips.* She'd been open about her feelings for him, even actually saying it in so many words. How many clues did a body need?

She'd sensed his reserve and wondered if it had anything to do with the fact he'd be gone in less than a year. Time was short all right. She'd learned that the hard way. After losing everything she'd lost, she'd learned to hold nothing back, especially when it was important.

She pushed herself away from the door and flounced the

skirt of her sundress. For the first time since she'd arrived, she was at a loss as to what to do next. The house was finally clean and pretty much in order.

Malcolm had told her to wait and be careful. Unfortunately, waiting was not one of her strong points. She locked the door and checked the windows, the latter having become a habit since the break-in.

Thirty minutes later, she was in bed, staring at the ceiling. That night's discoveries had made her bit anxious. Why would the Hollands, with their wealth and position, jeopardize their standing in the community? She could almost expect it from Brenda, having grown up with wealth, but Uncle Bob?

Lucy had always known him to be a kind and generous man—a friend of her father's and of her and her mom. How could she and her mom have been so naive? He'd fooled them both, but unlike her sweet mother, Lucy had her faculties. She was young and strong and determined to bring justice to the memory of James Ross.

She and Malcolm were close to doing just that. And in two days, he'd be back with proof.

CHAPTER 27

The following afternoon, Malcolm texted Lucy that he was on his way to Little Rock and would keep her posted on any and all developments in the case.

So now, what to do? She'd been meaning to paint and decided to go to the local paint store to look at some color options. She planned to start in the living room and hallway. She chose a soft-yellow on the paint chart called, Corn Silk, then paired it with a creamy-white trim.

She paid for her purchases, then stopped by the local burger joint and picked up dinner.

After popping the last French fry into her mouth, she connected her phone to a small wireless speaker, scrolled down to one of her upbeat playlists, and got to work.

Trimming was the most tedious part and took most of the evening. That done, she moved to the walls. She dipped the roller into the yellow and started on the wall behind the suspect board.

At several stages in the process, she stepped back to view her work. Her mother would love this color. Lucy had always heard yellow stimulated conversation—perfect for the living room. Because of the nature of the floor plan, continuing the color down the hallway would tie that entire area together.

The following afternoon, Lucy stood in the middle of the living room to admire her work. "Not bad," she said. After she cleaned the brushes and stored the leftover paint, it took about an hour to push the furniture back in place and rehang all the paintings.

She marveled at how a fresh color could change the mood of a room. It had a completely different vibe from the previous dingy, off-white.

Her phone dinged with a text from Malcolm.

Good news! The lead detective here is going through your dad's files. What he's found so far is enough to confront Holland. And the handwriting definitely belongs to Brenda. Stay put and trust me. I'll tell you the details at five.

Lucy's heart squeezed with relief, and she responded with a red heart. Finally, they were near the end. She checked her wristwatch. Malcolm would return in three hours.

Lucy had worked on Griffin Gate for almost three weeks now, and it was time to think seriously about getting her mother there. She fluffed a floral pillow at the sofa corner and stood back. Maybe Malcolm could help with the move. It would give her mom a bit of time with him without infringing too much on her mental state.

With a few hours to kill, she wondered if Jan would be available for coffee. She liked Jan. She was one of the few people Lucy had gotten to know since moving back there. Until she cleared her father's name, she hadn't been ready to search out any of her childhood friends.

She punched in Jan's cell and waited. Jan picked up on the second ring.

"You ready for an afternoon break?" Lucy asked. "I've a hankering for that three-layered caramel thing at Short Cakes."

"Ooh, I'd love that," Jan said. "What time?"

"How about three?"

"Perfect. That gives me an hour to finalize this offer."

"Great. See you then." Lucy hung up. That gave her plenty of time to visit with Jan, and then get back home by five to meet Malcolm.

Lucy had just slipped into her flat, strappy sandals when she heard a knock at the front door. She tucked the front of her blouse into the waistband of her white slacks and made her way down the hallway. At the door, she peeked through the peephole.

Brenda Holland!

Lucy's heart pounded. A visit from Mrs. Holland could not be a good thing. Was it possible she knew they were onto her? She stepped back from the door. "Just a minute!" She grabbed her cell phone, pressed record, then slid her phone in the back pocket of her pants.

She quickly unpinned the photo of Mrs. Holland from the board and set it on the coffee table. She then drew an arrow on one of the note cards and placed it next to the photo. If anything happened to her, then Malcolm would know Brenda was behind it.

She inhaled, blew out a breath, and opened the door. Brenda stood before her, beautifully dressed, as usual. Even now, she exemplified the perfect Southern lady. Lucy caught a whiff of perfume that she couldn't identify but assumed it was expensive.

"Mrs. Holland. This is a surprise."

"May I come in?"

Lucy had no desire to let the woman inside. "You know, I'm just heading out. It would be best for me if you came back another time."

"Well, that isn't best for me." She smiled brightly. "Besides, this will only take a moment."

Lucy wavered a few more seconds, then caved. "All right."

Lucy stepped back and caught a sound from behind her as Brenda crossed the threshold. Lucy swiveled her head. A strong hand pressed a smelly cloth firmly against her nose and mouth. His other arm grabbed her around the waist.

Heart racing, she clawed flesh and struggled against the arm banded about her. She held her breath as long as she could against the foul odor. With her lungs ready to burst, she finally inhaled. Instead of blessed air, she breathed in a nasty chemical, went limp, and passed out.

* * *

Malcolm arrived at Lucy's place at five sharp and parked next to her little Subaru. He mounted the steps and knocked. She didn't answer, so he knocked again. He stepped left and peeked in the window. The lights were on in the living room, and her purse was sitting on the coffee table.

He walked around back, found the French door from the deck open, and stepped inside.

"Lucy!"

No answer. He walked past the bedrooms, down the hall, crossed into the kitchen, and into the living room. Something was wrong. He quickly dialed her cell, and it went to voicemail. "Lucy, I'm at your place and you're not here. Please call me when you get this. I'm worried about you."

He texted her next, and when he still got no response, his stomach churned. He stood thinking, scanning the living room. He spotted Mrs. Holland's photo on the table with a red arrow pointing to it. He glanced from that to the suspect board. Lucy had left him a clue.

He sprinted from the house to his car and drove into town. He spotted Jan walking along the sidewalk and pulled up. "Jan!"

She walked over. "Hey, Detective."

"Hey. Listen, have you seen Lucy? We were supposed to meet at her place at five, but she's not there."

"Oh, no." Jan's brows drew together. "She was supposed to meet me at Short Cakes this afternoon, but she never showed up. I called and texted but got no answer."

"Okay, thanks. If you hear from her, please let me know."

"Of course."

Malcolm gripped the steering wheel. The thought that Brenda could have kidnapped Lucy was insane. But the arrow—the photo—it couldn't be anything else. It was time to put his plan into action. He sent a group text to Kirby and Chase.

We're on sooner than I'd thought, gentleman. You know what to do. Get yourselves in position.

Minutes later, Malcolm strode into Chief of Police Holland's office. Holland's head shot up when Malcolm entered.

"Detective," Holland said. "You startled me. In the future, I'd suggest you knock first."

"I'm sorry, sir, but I'm here on urgent business." Malcolm closed the office door.

Holland sat back, his lids shuttered over his eyes. "I'm waiting."

"You and I have something to discuss." Malcolm slammed

the stash of documents, photos, and Ross's notebook on Holland's desk. "There's enough there to put you and your missus away for a long time."

Holland bristled. "What on earth are you talking about?"

"Bribes, kickbacks—your shady dealings with Alex Crandall, as well as a number of other sordid characters."

Holland's face blanched.

"All of which we'll discuss at length, but right now, I need your help finding Lucy."

"I haven't seen Lucy since my summer party."

"Not the response I'd expect from someone who's known Lucy all of her life. Aren't you even a little concerned? She's the daughter of your old partner. You took her to her first father-daughter dance, for crying out loud."

"Of course, I'm concerned."

"And yet you sit there and do nothing," Malcolm said.

"Why on earth would you think I'd know where she is?"

"Because I believe Mrs. Holland has kidnapped her."

"That's nonsense. Brenda has nothing to do with my misdeeds."

"On the contrary. She's in this up to her neck."

Holland pushed back his chair and stood. "You'll never prove it. Do you think I'm going to let some fly-by-night Scot come into my precinct and undo what I've protected for the past twenty years?"

"I don't have to." He eyed the documents on the desk. "Detective James Ross has already done that."

Malcolm rested his palms on the edge of Holland's desk. "You're done. You're going to prison. I know for a fact you haven't killed anyone yet, but I have proof your wife shot and killed James Ross, and unless you want another murder on your conscience, you'll help me find Lucy." Malcolm reached across the desk and gripped Holland by the collar. "If anything happens to that girl you *will* answer to me."

"All right—all right."

"Kirby, Chase!" Malcolm yelled as he released Holland with a shove. The two men opened the door and walked in. "Did you get all of that?"

"Yes, sir," Kirby and Chase answered at the same time, the latter holding up a recording device. Malcolm reached inside his shirt and pulled out a wire and microphone, then handed it to Chase.

Malcolm focused again on Holland. "Where is she?"

"Brenda's family owns a warehouse on Pine Street. It was a distribution center during her grandfather's era. They haven't used it since his death. If she's taken her anywhere, it's probably there. Over the years, Crandall and I used it for most of our...*transactions*."

"I've tracked her phone," Kirby said. "She's there."

"Take me to her, Holland." Malcolm turned toward Officer Chase. "Secure those documents. Kirby, help me escort Chief Holland to my car."

Kirby pulled his handcuffs from his belt and stepped toward Holland.

"That's not necessary," Malcolm said. "The less attention we draw to this, the better."

CHAPTER 28

Lucy's chin hung to her chest. She could barely lift it. She moaned against the constant throbbing in her head. It took some effort, but she managed to lift her eyelids.

She blinked away most of the blur to see her sandaled feet staring back up at her from a concrete floor. From the corner of her eye, something small and gray scurried at the base of a wooden crate to her left. She sucked in air—her heart slammed against her ribs.

She lifted her head and squeezed her eyes against the harsh light—the mouse—the least of her worries. She focused on her surroundings. She was in some sort of storage facility. She blinked again and turned her head toward the voices floating from somewhere nearby.

As she came fully to her senses, she realized her hands were tied together with duct tape. She tried to stand, but her ankles were secured to the front legs of the chair.

"I see Sleeping Beauty is finally awake," Mrs. Holland said. "You were out so long, I feared Alex may have killed you."

Lucy jerked her head up and stared at Brenda in horror. The woman strolled toward her, head cocked to one side, with a gun dangling from her right hand.

"What am I to do with you?" Brenda said.

Lucy swallowed. "Untie me and let me go, for a start."

"I'm sorry, but I can't do that."

Lucy shook her head, trying to clear the cobwebs left from the drug used on her. "Mrs. Holland, why are you doing this?" she barely managed to whisper.

"Because, my dear child, you wouldn't leave." Mrs. Holland began to pace. "It's not like I didn't give you plenty of opportunity. I tried everything I could to scare you away." She stopped abruptly and looked down at her. "First, I followed you from Dottie's, hoping to frighten you, but when that didn't work, I snuck into your house and shut off the lights."

"I'd only been in town a couple of days," Lucy said. "How did you know who I was?"

"From the night of the ball, I knew I'd met you somewhere before. I admit, it took me a while—a couple of days in fact—but not even your mask could hide your identity for long. And once I discovered a Carmichael had bought Griffin Gate, I realized the girl at the ball was you."

"I see."

"When the first two scares didn't move you, I thought the brick through your window threatening your dear, sweet mother, would convince you, but even then you stayed."

"Why run me off? Is it for the stones—the diamonds?"

"Diamonds?" Her diabolical laugh chilled Lucy's blood. "My dear child, I'm swimming in diamonds." She ran a slender, manicured finger along the gun barrel. "This isn't about diamonds. You can keep your paltry stones."

Lucy shook her head, trying to make sense of a Brenda's words. "So that *was* you in the mask? I recognized it when I saw it in your library, but I never dreamed you were literally the one behind it."

"And the wingtip shoes? You were quite mesmerized by them."

Lucy eyed her. "What about the shoes?"

"Come now. I know full well you recognized my wingtips on the night of my party. But I can't figure out how, especially after all these years."

"I don't know what you mean—"

A stinging slap rang across Lucy's cheek. "Don't lie to me. Somehow you discovered I was wearing them when I shot your mettlesome father."

Lucy's eyes filled with tears. "You! Why..."

"Because he'd confronted Bob and had convinced my weak and easily manipulated husband to turn himself in. The fool had agreed to humiliate himself, but his confession would have brought disgrace to many more than to him. Generations of my family, my heritage would've been ruined. I couldn't let that happen. I pleaded with him not to do it—begged him—but he wouldn't listen."

Deep anguish filled Lucy as she gazed up at Brenda. "Uncle Bob had planned to turn himself in, and you killed my father because of that?"

"I was angry."

"You took everything from us," Lucy cried.

"I only meant to frighten him!" Brenda screeched.

"So, Alex Crandall knocked me out and carried me here?"

"Yes."

"I'm assuming he's helped you in hopes of finally getting control of my property."

Brenda's red-lipstick smile revealed even, white teeth. "I take it, you gleaned that from your detective work. Such a clever girl."

Jaw clenched, Lucy glared at her.

"But he's long gone. And I'm only telling you his involvement because you won't be leaving here. Look around you." Brenda made a sweeping motion with her gun hand. "There are so many nooks and crannies where I could hide you. I wouldn't even have to kill you, you'd simply die, slowly, over time."

She was mad—evil. Lucy searched her mind for something to say. "Detective Knox knows everything. You won't get away with this."

"You're bluffing."

"No, Brenda, she's not."

Brenda swirled toward the voice of her husband. Detective Knox and Officer Kirby stood behind him—guns drawn—pointing at her.

"You fool!" she screeched. "How could you bring them here?"

Bob Holland stepped toward his wife. "It's over, Brenda."

"Alex always said you were the weak link in our endeavors," she sneered.

Lucy watched their exchange in stunned silence. She glanced at her taped wrists. *I wonder.* She raised her arms overhead, then flung her hands down and out to her sides. The duct tape ripped apart just like the instructor had said it would. She quickly bent and unwound the tape at her ankles.

"Please, put down the gun," Holland said.

"And spend the rest of my life in prison?"

Lucy launched from the chair, sprang forward, and plowed into Brenda's back. The gun went off as Brenda went flying. Lucy tumbled to the floor. Pounding feet and raised voices surrounded her and Brenda.

Malcolm was beside Lucy in seconds, lifting her off the floor. Chase handcuffed Chief Holland, and Kirby was in the act of yanking Brenda to her feet and cuffing her.

A pair of strong, wonderful arms suddenly engulfed her as Malcolm pulled her to his chest. "Dear Lord. Are you all right? If anything had happened to you, I'd never have forgiven myself." His accent thickened and grew richer with every word he spoke.

"Malcolm, I'm fine. Really." She clung to him, savoring each second in his arms—breathing in a whiff of citrus and sea salt.

He released her and gawked at the tape hanging from her wrists. "How on earth did you do that?"

"My detective-in-training audio book. It came with the hardcopy."

He shook his head in wonder. "Of course, it did." He walked her over to Kirby and Chase who were in the process of leading the Hollands out to the wail of sirens.

"Uncle Bob!" Lucy yelled.

Chief Holland turned and stared at her.

Lucy walked up to him. "How could you—his friend—have dishonored him?" Pain squeezed her heart. "You were like a father to me. We loved you." She pressed a fist to her chest. "*He* loved you."

"You remind me of him," Holland said. "Your persistence, your determination, your efforts to not be thwarted— all the qualities that made your father a good cop." Deep regret filled Bob Holland's gaze. She got the impression he'd wanted to say more. Instead, he hung his head and didn't say another word. His tormented, pain-filled eyes had said it all.

* * *

Malcolm sat across from Holland in the interrogation room. Just one day earlier, the man had been an outstanding pillar in the community, now he sat on the opposite side of the table, beaten and out of uniform.

"It's a sad day for this department," Malcolm said. "I take no pleasure in what I have to do."

"I never thought I'd find myself on this side of the table," Holland said. "It's a relief, really."

Malcolm opened up the folder in front of him. "Because of Detective Ross's exemplary investigative work, we have enough proof of your crimes, including bribes and kickbacks, that will put you away for long time."

Malcolm leaned back and hitched his right elbow on the back of his chair. "Are you sure you don't want a lawyer?"

Holland clasped his hands tightly together on the table. "I'm sure."

"All right, then." Malcolm leaned forward, pressed record, and sat back. "Let the record show former Chief of Police Robert Holland has waived his right to council."

Malcolm placed a stack of evidence on the table and pushed it toward Holland. "This is the result of Detective Ross's investigation prior to his death. I've found his informant, and he's willing to testify in court. Knowing this new information, do you still wish to waive your right to council?"

"Yes."

"Then proceed."

"I took my first bribe when I was a rookie cop. I knew it was wrong. I rationalized it—convinced myself no one would know. I was newly married and money was tight. Brenda's father had lost most of their family fortune in bad investments. My intent was to keep her in the lifestyle she'd grown up with. So, I looked the other way, and I took the money.

"The next time it happened, it was a little easier, and by the time I made detective, it was a way of life for me. I never took a large sum of money, or anything that would have been easily traceable. It was always cash.

"Then one day I realized, I was in way too deep, and I didn't know how to get out. I'd just started working with Alex Crandall. He talked me off the ledge—made it seem easy. He knew things—the loopholes. Said he'd been doing this for years, and already had two other officers on his payroll."

"Jenkins and Peterson?"

"Yes. He told me it was going to be all right, that no one would ever know and fool that I was, I believed him."

"How were you connected to Ross?"

"I was his training officer."

"So, he looked up to you—admired you?"

"Yes. A few years later, we became partners. James had been a detective for a year when he finally confronted me. I'd feared he was onto me for some time, but never dreamed he'd challenge me with any of it."

"So, his confrontation was not a surprise?"

"No. He knew about the bribes and the kickbacks—the shady dealings with Crandall and members of the town council. He said he had evidence and could prove it. He convinced me to turn myself in, and I was going to, but I wanted to talk to Brenda first. He agreed that she should know."

Holland, his face creased, leaned forward. "I had no idea Brenda was a part of this. Two days after Ross had been pronounced dead, Brenda told me what she'd done. She was hysterical—said she'd only wanted to scare him, not kill him."

Malcolm shifted in his chair and frowned.

"Before that, I'd assumed one of the people I'd done business with had discovered James was onto us. And that one of them had him killed.

"When I found out it was Brenda, I panicked. I knew I couldn't do anything to bring James back. I realized I had to protect Brenda and her family—a third generation in this town—and I knew that turning her in would destroy them all."

"So. You framed Detective Ross for your crimes and manipulated the facts so the trail would go cold, never leading to you, Crandall, or the others involved."

Holland hung his head and nodded. "I felt much more guilty about that than anything else I'd done. James didn't have to come to me first, he didn't have to give me a chance to do the right thing and turn myself in—but he did. And that decision cost him his life."

"Sometime after that, you planted evidence in Ross's home," Malcolm said.

"Yes, during one of my visits to offer my condolences."

"So, in your mind it was okay to ruin a man's exemplary career in law enforcement, damage his standing in the community, humiliate his grieving wife and little daughter?"

"It was to save Brenda." Holland's eyes pleaded. "She hadn't meant to kill him, she'd only wanted to scare him."

"So you said."

"There was nothing I could do to bring Ross back." Holland slammed his fist on the table. "I was sick about it."

"I'm sure you were."

Holland rested his head in his hands. "After James was killed, my only thought was finding that evidence. As lead detective in the case, I searched his house—"

"For what he had against you."

"Yes."

"According to the report," Malcolm read, "*a wad of five grand was found stuffed underneath Ross's mattress.*" He fixed Holland with a stare. "Not very creative, but quite convenient...for you." He tossed the report on top of the desk.

"My plan was to find it and destroy it, then no one would've been the wiser," Holland said. "It would end up being a cold case, and James would keep his standing as a detective."

"A win-win," Malcolm scoffed. "But you didn't find it. You planted some of your own—casting doubt on Ross's good name. Blaming him for your crimes—making the town he loved and served believe he was dirty for the past twenty years." Malcolm sucked in air. "And that was all right with you?"

Holland didn't answer. He just sat—head down—completely silent.

Malcolm lifted his gaze to Kirby. "Take him away."

Officer Kirby stepped forward and led Holland from the room.

CHAPTER 29

Malcolm found Lucy sitting in his office. She expectantly searched his face as he entered and started to stand.

"No, don't get up." He crossed the room and took the seat next to her.

"How did it go?"

"Lucy, you should've heard him," Malcolm said. "He told us everything. As I listened, I watched a man get twenty years of guilt and shame off of his chest."

"And what about Mrs. Holland and Crandall?"

"Both have been questioned and both are behind bars." He fisted his hands. "We got most of what we needed from Mrs. Holland by overhearing what she said at the warehouse."

"And my phone, don't forget," she added.

He gave a slight smile. "And your phone."

"What else?" she asked.

"As you can imagine, Crandall lawyered up, so his cooperation was limited."

Malcolm took hold of Lucy's hand and studied her serious face. "What are you thinking?"

She let out a deep sigh and gazed at him. "I'm thinking about the respect my father deserved but never received at his funeral. No casket watch, no Honor Guard, or Color Guard, no dignitaries present, no Last Radio Call."

Malcolm reached forward as she spoke and lightly tucked a loose tendril of hair behind her ear.

"All the things that should've been bestowed on him at the time, now lost to us—to *him*," she said.

"I promise you, the department will do everything they can to restore what he should have received. It can't be exactly as it should've been, but it'll be special and honorable." Malcolm lifted her hand to his lips and gently kissed her palm. "What do you need?"

"I need to go get my mother."

* * *

The following day, Lucy called her mom and gave her a brief rundown of what had occurred over the past several days and told her it was time for her to come home. Malcolm insisted on going with her to get her mom, saying, "It's time I met your mother."

They'd barely gotten her mom settled in the house, when Lucy came to realize the truth of Malcolm's earlier words.

The days following the news of her exonerated father and former Chief Holland's arrest, the outpouring from the community was almost overwhelming. Lucy and her mom were the focus of much attention and condolences from the precinct officers, former officers, and many in the community.

Her mom, gracious as ever, blossomed with each visit from her old and dear friends. Being back in the town and in the house she loved seemed to have worked a miracle, transforming her mom into her old self again.

Her father's photo now hung in the hallway of the Diamond Creek Police Department beside the other officers killed in the line of duty. There had been a brief, but touching, ceremony when the mayor mounted his picture to the wall.

Practically every day, an article appeared in the local newspaper as well as papers in the surrounding counties exonerating her father, restoring his status as a detective who died in the line of duty. Many described him as having been an honorable officer, and how through his investigative skills, he discovered and tried to bring down corruption, not only in the Diamond Creek Police Department, but many of the town's officials during his short years of service.

When officers from the surrounding counties heard what had happened, they came together to form an Honor Guard of thirty. The officers also took shifts standing guard at his grave, a full week before the upcoming ceremony. This outpouring immensely touched Lucy.

The former Chief of Police, as well as other officers who served with her father, had returned to offer their respect and support.

Stuart Knox had even flown in to give the eulogy for his friend. Lucy was drawn to him from the moment they met and looked forward to him sharing his memories and stories of her father.

The day of the ceremony, Lucy and her mom dressed with care, then entered the limousine provided. Tears rushed to her eyes as hundreds of the town's people lined the streets —their faces somber, and some with hands over their hearts.

It seemed the entire town came to a standstill as they followed behind a full police escort as it wound its way to the cemetery.

"Twenty years ago, Detective James Ross had not been given the police officer funeral he deserved," Former Chief of Police Carlyle said. "When an officer is killed in the line of duty, his death merits full honors, which Detective Ross did not receive."

Lucy reached for her mom's hand and gave it a gentle squeeze.

"We are grieved and saddened that we did not give him the honor he deserved. We humbly ask forgiveness for this great tragedy and injustice to one who served our community well."

As the former Chief of Police spoke, Lucy took note of the officers in attendance. Each stood at attention, each wearing a Mourning Badge.

Finally, the service neared its end with the 21 Bells Ceremony. Her mom had chosen that instead of the Three Volley Salute, feeling the sound of shots fired might be too harsh a reminder of how her James had died.

As the bells tolled, Lucy's thoughts turned to the young, dark-haired man in the video, to his smile and his joy in his little daughter.

After the final toll, an officer stepped forward and presented her mom with a folded American flag, turned, and then saluted the headstone of James Ross.

Tears slipped silently down her mother's cheeks as the mournful sound of taps solemnly ended the ceremony.

CHAPTER 30

The ceremony behind them, Malcolm stood in Lucy's living room and stared out the front window. His dad and Cara sat talking on the wooden bench underneath the large oak tree where James had been killed. Malcolm turned away as Lucy walked in, carrying two tall glasses of iced tea.

"What are you looking at?" she said.

"My dad and your mom." Malcolm took the tea from Lucy's hand and continued watching their parents.

"Mom looks happy," Lucy said.

Cara smiled suddenly at something his dad was saying.

"What do you think they're talking about?" Lucy asked.

"Your mother's very attentive." Malcolm lifted the glass to his mouth, sipped, and swallowed. "Maybe my dad is sharing a fond memory of your father."

"I hope so."

They left the window and sat next to each other on the sofa.

"Dr. Edwards believes the reminders from being back

home and conversations with those who knew my father will be of great benefit to Mom's recovery."

"Cara is a remarkable woman," Malcolm said. "I find her sharp and completely cognitive."

"Unless you knew her before the accident, you'd think she was one hundred percent. She's progressed a lot since she's returned. So, I'm hopeful."

She took a swig of tea. "I guess you're tying up lose ends on this case. Anything else you've learned that I should know?"

"Let's see." He rubbed a finger beside his left eye. "Crandall finally admitted to wanting your property solely for the stones, which was the real reason he hounded your father to sell all those months."

"And most likely the reason for my father's reaction to seeing Crandall's black sedan drive onto our property," she said.

Malcolm nodded. "He thought it was Crandall coming to hound him again." He took a swig of his tea. "That man was driven by pure greed. He knew what the property was really worth, and unfortunately for him, so did your dad."

"Speaking of that, I have an expert coming from Crater of Diamonds to check the stones on the property, then Mom and I will know what we have here."

"Good thinking."

"I asked my mom if she knew about the stones and the appraisal of the property, and she did."

Cara and his dad walked through the front door.

"What are you two talking about?" Cara asked.

"About the appraisal we found in Dad's notes," Lucy said.

Cara nodded. "John Ross, your great-grandfather, discovered the stones about six months after he bought the property. When he realized his land could be another diamond mine like Murfreesboro, he borrowed the money for the equipment and hired a couple of men to mine the property.

"Unfortunately, it didn't pull in nearly is much as he'd hoped, but enough that he could live well. He sold most of the stones and put the money away for his son, Donald. And when Don had James, he did the same thing for him. After you were born, James put what was left in a college fund for you."

"But I found a bowlful, and some of them are quite valuable," Lucy said.

"Occasionally, you'll find one or two good ones," Cara said. "We did, too." Cara turned to his dad. "Stuart, let me show you the rest of the house." They disappeared down the hall.

"And here I thought I might be dating a wealthy woman," Malcolm teased.

A smile peppered her sweet mouth. "Are we dating?"

He gazed deeply into her eyes. "I'd like to think so."

She smiled shyly, and a pink flush peppered her cheeks.

It would've been easy for Malcolm to take her rosy complexion and sparkling eyes as affirmation. He'd found her shy agreement at his suggestion that they were dating, a positive step. But, he'd made one mistake in falling for a much-younger woman and wasn't about to do so again, just to discover she hadn't been serious. He studied her face, but after Becca, he wanted...needed, to hear Lucy say it.

"I think it's time we got to know each other better," he said. "Is that all right with you?"

"Perfectly all right," she said.

The past couple of weeks, she'd revealed her feelings for

him. But he wanted to be certain. She was young, right out of university, a likely teaching position in her future. He'd yet to discover what her plans were once she'd solved her father's murder. As much as he wanted to, he wouldn't presume anything at this point. "What about you?" he said.

She tilted her head. "What do mean?"

"Your future. Dating someone doesn't mean you don't have one. You have a master's degree, you've got your mother settled, and your father's murder solved and his reputation exonerated. So. What's next for you? What are your plans now that you've accomplished what you set out to do?" He held his breath and waited.

She searched his face, then lowered her gaze to the glass of tea in her hand. "I guess that all depends on you. I thought we'd just established you were part of my future."

Silence fell between them.

"You think I haven't lived enough, is that it?" she asked. "That I'm lacking in life experience?"

"Honestly, yes."

She ran a finger around the rim of her glass. "Look, I know you're leaving, but I don't care. I mean—I do care, but what I'm trying to say is I'm happy with here and now. If that's all I can have—"

"I'm sorry, but that's not good enough for me. You've still got the mind of a college student. You're used to short, flirtatious, relationships."

She reared back—highly affronted. "I certainly am not. And I'm certainly not like that Becca person." She slung the name like it was mud. "Why, I've hardly had time to date anyone seriously, not with school, making A's, and taking care of my mother.

"Becca Sinclair was a fool to let you go. Age difference

isn't related to what's in a person's heart. Are you really going to make that an excuse as to why we can't be together? Don't you see—it wasn't her age—it was her heart? If you can't see the difference between me and her, then that's on you." Her voice shook with a husky sweetness. "But if that's who you think I am—"

He placed a finger on her lips and parted his mouth in a slow smile. "Me thinks I've ruffled some feathers."

"And you would be correct. I love you! And if you haven't picked up the *blatant* clues I've been giving you, then you're one lousy detective." Her eyes darkened, and her chest heaved with each breath.

Malcolm hadn't realized just how much he'd allowed his experience with Becca cloud his judgment. Lucy was right. He'd been such a fool. As for leaving, well, he'd already taken care of that problem.

"Dearest hen, I can see that I was mistaken in that assumption. Please forgive me. I just wanted you to be sure." He slowly and methodically wrapped one arm around her, pulling her firmly to his chest. Then, tilting her chin with his left hand, he devoured every curve of her beautiful face. Her deep-emerald eyes glared up at him, still sparkling with a hint of anger.

He knew of only one way to remove the outrage in her eyes. He lowered his mouth to hers and kissed her with a hunger that belied his outward calm. She tasted like crisp, icy, lemony tea—fresh and sweet, just like her.

Sometime later, he lifted his head and gazed into her sparkling, dreamy eyes. Satisfied at the change, he said. "Besides, who says I'm leaving?"

Her lovely green eyes widened and latched onto his face. "What are you saying?"

He released her and took both her hands in his. "You know my dad is an American and that gives me dual citizenship."

She nodded.

"He's been wanting to move back here since my mother died but stayed in Scotland because of my career."

"Okaaay."

"The mayor has asked me to stay on longer at the precinct...on a more permanent basis. I'm to be *acting* Chief of Police until he appoints someone else."

A glimmer of anticipation filled her eyes, and her lips quirked into a soft smile.

"What do you think about that?"

"I think it's marvelous... Except..."

"What?"

"We never finished that conversation about *you know who.*"

For a second, he hesitated. "Ahh, right, Becca. You want to know what happened between us?"

"I want to know if you're over her?"

"Haven't I just established that?"

She shifted in her seat and pulled one of the decorative pillows into her lap. "I know. I'm sorry, it's just—the day you showed me her photo, you stared at it for a long time. And not with just any ole stare. Your gaze seemed to hold...I don't know...regret."

"There's some truth to that, but not in the way you think." *And here I've been wanting to be sure of you, while you're wanting to be sure of me.*

"All right. I'll give you the two-cent version. I was twenty-nine and had recently made detective. Becca was twenty-three. I was crazy about her, so our age difference didn't matter—not to me, anyway. But when it came down to making a lasting commitment, she wouldn't do it, said she wasn't ready, that she had more living to do before she settled down. My mistake was thinking she felt the same way about me, as I did for her. If I had been more understanding of her youth and inexperience, we may have parted friends."

"I'm sorry." A slight crease formed between her finely shaped brows.

"That was five years ago, and I swore to never again date anyone that many years younger than me. Then, you came along. Reckless and infuriating, challenging me with your courage and your tenacity. Wowing me with your devotion to your mother and to your father's memory. A beautiful woman wrapped up in mystery that had me spellbound from the very first night I saw you floating across the ball-room in that exquisite pink gown.

"But later, when I found out how old you were, I thought, no way was I going down that road again."

Resting her elbow on the cushion, she propped her chin in her hand and gazed at him, adoringly. "Not even for a fling?"

He tossed back his head and laughed. "Not even. Flings can lead to more serious relationships, and I wasn't about to have my heart broken again by some young miss."

She reached for his hand. "One of the things I love about you is how old-fashioned you are about certain things."

"So, you think me not wanting to rob the cradle is old-fashioned?"

"See. Expressions like, *rob the cradle*, is exactly what I'm talking about. As if ten years is all that big of a difference."

He smiled down at her. "Trust me, it is, in more ways than you know."

Tossing the pillow aside, she inched forward and encircled her arms around his neck. "Well, if that's the case, Detective, what changed your mind?"

He laced his arms around her waist. "As I got to know you, I discovered that a remarkable, courageous woman lived underneath that dusty-faced, twenty-four year old I met that following morning. And having to deal with your bouts of juvenile behavior was a small price to pay for the selfless, spirited lass that you are."

"You do say the nicest things." She grinned up at him.

"My mother used to tell me, *you don't marry someone you can live with—you marry the one you can't live without.* Then one day, in our short journey together, I realized, *Just Lucy* was the one I couldn't live without."

Lucy went fully into his arms. Malcolm held her close and placed a light kiss on the top of her head. The detective's daughter wholly and completely rocked his world. He loved her far above and beyond all else.

Friday night, Malcolm took Lucy to The Club for dinner. He wrapped his hand possessively around hers and walked her to the entrance. Lucy was met with nods and smiles from the other officers present as the table host led them to their seat.

"Quite a change from the last time," Malcolm whispered, tipping his head close to hers.

"I'll say."

As they took their seats, Lucy scanned the walls. He could see the eagerness in her search and hoped she would't be disappointed.

"Looks like all the photographs of Holland have been removed except for one," she said.

Malcolm glanced around. "Where is it?"

"Over by the bar where my dad's used to be."

"Of course, and how appropriate."

"A single, insignificant photo of him now hangs in disgrace," she announced. "Mounted as a reminder that if it could happen to him, it could happen to anyone."

"That sounds poetic."

"Rick's words. He said that's why my dad only had one, small, single photo."

Malcolm listened as the detective's daughter spoke. Repeating Rick's words, she'd somehow come full circle, setting things right in her world.

"The photo isn't prominent, but visual enough to be a reminder," he added. "Insignificant and yet somehow significant, at the same time."

"Exactly," she said.

For a moment longer, they both scrutinized the walls. Select photographs of Detective James Ross now hung throughout The Club with honor and distinction, as they should always have been.

"Guests, now and in the future, will learn of this outstanding young officer and detective, who served and protected his community," Malcolm said. "Would you like to take a closer look at his photographs?"

"I would, but let's wait until after we order." She reached over, giving his hand a quick squeeze. "I'm sure you're the reason this was handled so quickly. Thank you."

"My pleasure, hen."

She tilted her head to the side. "That reminds me, you promised to tell me the other way *hen* is used in your country."

"Aye, I did." He propped an elbow on the white tablecloth, rested his chin in his hand, and focused on her inquisitive face. "Hen also refers to a woman who is going to get married soon."

Lucy licked her full, pink lips and swallowed. "Am I getting married soon?" she asked with a soft, breathless voice.

"I think that could *absolutely* be arranged," he said. "But first, I'll have to ask permission from your mother."

A small smile of enchantment touched her lips.

Malcolm lifted his hand and fingered a loose tendril of hair near Lucy's scar, realizing just how close she came to being killed that day. The very thought of her not being there —with him—right now—was impossible to imagine. But she was there, with a radiant, glow of love in her eyes meant only for him.

Thank you for reading!

Dear Reader,

I hope you enjoyed **The Detective's Daughter – Secrets of Griffin Gate**. I had so much fun weaving Lucy and Malcolm's story within a romantic suspense.

I need to ask a favor. As you probably know, reviews can be hard to come by. And as a reader your feedback is so important. If you're so inclined, I'd love an honest review of *The Detective's Daughter*. It doesn't have to be long or fancy. One or two sentences is fine.

If you have time, here's a link to my author page on Amazon. You can check out all my books here: https://www.amazon.com/-/e/B0077AG3ZM

In gratitude,
Darcy Flynn